An Emporium of Automata

D P Watt

An Emporium of Automata
Publication Date: 01 Febuary 2013

ISBN: 978-1-908125-17-0

www.eibonvalepress.co.uk

For Peter and Rachel Watt

All attempts at organizing matter are transient and temporary, easy to reverse and to dissolve. There is no evil in reducing life to other and newer forms. Homicide is not a sin. It is sometimes a necessary violence on resistant and ossified forms of existence which have ceased to be amusing. In the interests of an important and fascinating experiment, it can even become meritorious. Here is the starting point of a new apologia for sadism.

- Bruno Schulz, *Treatise on Tailors' Dummies, or The Second Book of Genesis*

Contents:

The Imperium of Automata

An Introduction

by
Daniel Corrick

'An empty book is like an infant's soul, in which anything may be written. It is capable of all things, but containeth nothing. I have a mind to fill this with profitable wonders.'
Thomas Traherne

I know of many authors who can write effective stories and far fewer who can actually write effectively. Fortunately the author of the volume you are presently reading proves an exception to this last point in that he succeeds on both accounts. It was several years ago that I first became acquainted with Watt's work through a story in an anthology, *Cinnabar's Gnosis*, produced by the publisher who would later bring out the first edition of this collection. Upon reading it very quickly became apparent that his work would offer something, a certain harlequin tinted glamour, above and beyond the usual fare.

When some months later a copy of this collection came into my hands I was not disappointed. The volume kept to the high quality of that first story and proved a distinctive, not to say scarce, acquisition for discerning readers of contemporary strange literature. Like most of the books from that press it was beautifully produced but printed in a fairly small run and somewhat pricey, so I'm happy to hear of it being made available to a wider audience via Eibonvale.

Calling the Emporium's wares ghost or horror stories would be misleading, because though there are macabre twists aplenty, their final effect often lies in the sinister implications revealed throughout the narrative as a whole. Even this generalisation fails to do justice to the range of material herein. There is a vast thematic selection verging from grimy period tragedy to curious antiquarian mystery to unnerving interlocutory monologue about a, or possibly the, reader's potential destiny. What keeps them together and allows the book to retain its over-arching cohesion is the richly distinctive prose style and the surprising dexterity with which it is employed. At its height his style could be described as narcotic: it's burgeoning with bizarre similes and sharp-toothed metaphors; springing forth with exotic colours, textures and scents to an almost feverish intensity—the closest comparison I can give is to the tragic Polish Surrealist writer Bruno Schulz. But unlike Schulz, whose stories occasionally risked getting bogged down under the weight of their own prosody, Watt is capable of a more restrained but no less compelling descriptive rhetoric when the situation calls for it. Given his taste for visual flare it is not surprising that the intermingling between sensation and narrative plays a considerable part in some of the stories, e.g. the correspondence between the written word and the unearthly musical chords, the sound of texts, in 'The Condition'.

One will notice the book is divided into three sections. Like the works of certain mediæval Latin scholars its architectural structure represents the philosophical ascent of the outings therein: the reader encounters a rising thematic hierarchy from historical tales to ominous forays into the nature of Reality. There are of course exceptions to this order, 'rays from above' and 'shadows in high places', as the reader shall soon discover.

Earlier on I mentioned about Watt being comfortable with more traditional themes. 'Erbach's Emporium of Automata', with its fading recollections of childhood in post-war Britain, and 'Room 89', a demonstration of measured prose, are more reminiscent of Sarban than Schulz. As might have been guessed from the title puppets, dolls and clockwork models frequently make an appearance, thankfully used in a far more suitable fashion than the tired old *L'homme machine* denouncement. His characters too are rarely un-self-aware: as the stories move on they gain ground to develop their own visionary fixations (with corresponding ruthlessness of course) but they always retain a degree of intellectual and emotional realism, an unfortunately rare factor given the parodic, forced prosaicness many seem to delight in. The incisive humour, a quality which livens the intense prose, so perfectly typified by dialogue between the Inspector and his mysterious nemesis in 'Dr Dapertutto's Saturnalia' is unexpectedly sobered by genuine sadness in stories like '1 ≤ 0' and 'All His Worldly Goods'.

The contents of the second section *Genealogical Devices* are more enigmatic. They are split between the daily affairs of a young woman, Roberta Reid, who may have been the unknowing victim of an on-going conspiracy, and other seemingly disparate elements connected with this intrigue. Open denouncements and revelations are kept to a minimum but as in 'Making History' where the banality of the characters conversations verges on tragi-comedy, the accounts are really there to highlight an ultimate unease over identity and personal narrative. The composite prose is more sparingly written than elsewhere: whilst description still plays an important part the focus on dialogue and mostly static scenes make one think of Absurdist dramatic dialogues.

∞

Perhaps unsurprisingly given his profession the theatre and its environs serve as a back drop to hint at productions and performances on a far grander scale. However, unlike the works of Dennis Wheatley or H.P. Lovecraft where the protagonists' involvement with forbidden knowledge leads to visceral or corporal horror, the unwanted revelations experienced by characters of Watt's fiction are often more ontological in nature: a feature which places his work squarely in a tradition of metaphysical horrors along with that of Mark Samuels and Thomas Ligotti. Though there are certainly nods to Continental philosophy by and large these feel natural for the stories and not artificial: he is too strong an imaginative writer in his own right to require a plethora of quotes from *The Anti-Christ* or *The World as Will and Representation*: the themes are the stories' own and not falsely grafted on.

In that final section, *Ex Nihilo*, writing with full apocalyptic flourish Watt allows himself free reign to orchestrate the final operation of the Emporium, the prelude to eternity. Those glimpses of the dark workings behind the curtain, behind the folds of Reality, thrown open to his protagonists by 'these poor representatives of the eternal order of things' constitute what I—speaking both from a critical and purely personal standpoint—consider to be the very best of his short fiction so far.

To draw this preamble to a close and usher in the stories, *An Emporium of Automata* represents the first major work of one of the most promising new writers of strange fiction within the British Isles. Watt has, and we hope, will continue to craft new creations—his recent novella confirms this was no one-off—but this collection shall be the foundation stone of his reputation. Consider it a token of books as yet unwritten. Savour the prose, let the rustle of pages fade into the audience's expectant whispers, and watch the play of entropic phantasms begin.

I:
Phantasmagorical Instruments

They call her 'The Rocking Horse'. I know she is Ivy Wilkins. We used to play together. Sometimes the kids will stand beside her, there at the end of the pier, and rock back and forth, or from side to side, giggling and running away when they have had enough. She never acknowledges them. She never turns away from that long stare out to sea. But it is no horizon that she watches—as though for a long lost lover to return. And it is not stormy waves she gazes at—mourning the loss of a dear one to the depths. It is a darker place her eyes fathom—an infinite expanse inwards, into the very mechanism of her soul. The course to that strange land is plotted through memory, and most specifically the memory of Erbach's Emporium of Automata.

Ivy Wilkins was the first of us to go into Erbach's Emporium. I'm glad she did.

∞

It was located at the end of the pier, in what had been a small musical theatre. That had been sold off just after the war when everyone was too hard-up to go there. That's when Erbach moved in. I don't remember it ever opening up. One day Tommy Jenkins came and got me from the sweetshop and said I had to go and see this new place at the end of the pier. I went along, thinking it was a bit of a ruse to try and throw me in the sea. But he was right, there was an amazing new entertainment arcade. A short man with black hair and a bristly moustache was cleaning the windows from the inside. There were quite a few kids there by then, all trying to peer into the windows to see what the place was. It must have been late autumn because there weren't any foreigners there. That's what we used to call the kids, and their parents, that used to come to our town in the summer so they could swim in the sea and play on the beach: *foreigners*. We never really knew why so many of them came, and didn't like it much when our favourite places were stolen by them and their silly deckchairs and hampers. Our parents said it was good for the town, but we couldn't see how; with all the rubbish and so many kids having accidents in the sea and having to be rescued all through the summer.

This place though already seemed to be special, and because there were no foreigners around it was just for us. Tommy, who wasn't usually very brave, had managed to stand on a fish crate round the back and peer through the back window. He said that the place was full of all these large cases that had dummies and statues in and that there were all sorts of tall cabinets and things that looked like clocks. We said he was a mad liar and he said he'd bet even his catapult that we were wrong.

We were wrong, because about an hour later—the crowd having swelled considerably and now with a number of adults—the door was opened by the stocky man and he carried out a brightly painted board that read 'Erbach's Emporium of Automata. Stick a Penny in the Slot and Watch'. A thick smell of wood and polish, mixed with the dark scent of pipe tobacco, wafted after him. The crowd started muttering. He stood just inside the doorway looking at us all very carefully. Then with a swift movement he bowed and beckoned us in with a little grin which seemed to put most of us at ease.

During the first few weeks it took everyone some time to get used to the place and what you were supposed to do in there. Erbach never seemed to talk to anyone. He just sat at the back of the Emporium, on a high stool, reading books and looking up occasionally at whoever may be in there. Occasionally he'd go behind a little blue curtain and come back with a little cup of coffee or a plate of curious looking biscuits. I said to Ivy that he reminded me of that imp, Robin Goodfellow, that we'd read about at school, and she agreed.

Ivy was the first to go in, as I said, before even any of the adults. By the time I got in she was already deep into the huge theatre auditorium gazing in marvel at all the intricate machines that had been assembled. There were all sorts of things, mostly great boxed contraptions. As the sign said, you stuck a penny in and it would come to life, whatever it may be.

There were the simple ones: an old dusty clown that would gyrate and wave his hands whilst laughing loudly, his fractured wooden mouth moving awkwardly up and down; a racing game where six wooden horses would creak across a metal track—and the penny back if you picked the right one; a top-hatted mannequin that played the violin as a black cat at his feet danced to the tune. Lots of the larger machines played music and he even had a brightly painted one that blasted steam through pipes to the beat of a jolly soldier with a baton as dancing maids rang bells.

Then there were the intricate ones. These were mostly scenic: a tin diorama, layered to suggest a steeply inclined seaside town would carry a tin car, complete with family, up to the scenic viewpoint on a hill beyond (whose green paint had long since crumbled to reveal the dented metal beneath). There was a marching band of miniature stuffed monkeys who paraded round and round a circus ring to the applause and waves of a cardboard crowd beyond.

It was in Erbach's Emporium of Automata that I first thought about eternity.

A great favourite with all the children was the wind-up table. This was a huge flat table covered in green cloth. Thinking back it must have been a snooker table once. To us, then, it was the size of a field. For those too small to see onto it Erbach would provide wooden soapboxes to stand on. At exactly midday on a Saturday he would take out a small leather suitcase and bring it to the table. From it he would extract delicate wooden and metal figures and animals and with a twist of his fingers he'd set them into life, marching, rolling or flipping across the green cloth, whizzing towards us or slowly sliding away. Eventually there would be so many fantastic gadgets parading around the table that it was difficult to make one out from the other. Was that automobile being driven by a jumping frog, or was a woodcutter taking an axe to a pirouetting ballerina's knee? I don't think I ever saw the same thing twice on that table, yet it was a weekly highlight for us all, especially in winter. He must have had hundreds of the things, probably all stored out the back, beyond that frayed blue curtain. No, sorry, there was one that I did see more often, we all did. It was the cyclist. This was a fairly large figure compared to the others. It was about six inches high. It was a bowler-hatted gentleman riding a penny farthing. With most of the others you could see how they worked: a metal cog here, a pulley there, and so on. With this there was no winding key, no pulley, or discernible mode of propulsion. It was always the final toy to be brought from the suitcase. Erbach would stand with the wheels between his hands, almost clasped in prayer. His eyes would close a moment as the final flutterings of the toys on the table top would cease. He would rest the cyclist on the cloth and it would begin its journey, taking detours to avoid other toys and slowly making its way towards the other side. A few inches before the edge it would stagger to a halt and all of us would cheer and applaud. But I remember always thinking how sad it was as the last few staccato movements brought the cyclist to a standstill.

It was in Erbach's Emporium of Automata that I first thought about death.

We never knew if Erbach was his real name, or if it was his surname or Christian name.

We never called him Mr Erbach, and he never asked us to. It was just Erbach.

Someone said he was an ex-Nazi, on the run, and that he'd been responsible for unimaginable atrocities. Someone else said he had been in those death camps and had been a victim of the unimaginable atrocities. We were children. We did not know anything about what had happened way back then, over ten years before. Ten years ago, to a child, is a different world—unimaginable, atrociously distant.

We did not want to know anything about Erbach.

No, that is not right.

We wanted to know everything about Erbach—but only those things that confirmed the deeper mystery. We only wanted to create more myths about what lay behind the tattered blue curtain, rimmed with frayed gold braiding; from behind which his little kettle would splutter and sing, making him scuttle like a hungry crustacean to the little pot. He would emerge with an old can cradled between his stubby fingers and the whole place would fill with the scent of tea made from rare crushed herbs and other exotic things. These were the only things we wanted; the scent of thick European bread baking in his little oven he kept on the desk, beside the cash register, and the occasional glimpses of him spooning a thin purple soup to his lips in winter. He would catch us watching from behind a machine and laugh. And as with everything about him it was a gentle laugh, only noticeable through his body which would shiver slightly as though disturbed by a draft. Then he'd look straight at us and roll his eyes in their sockets until only the whites remained. We'd squeal like little pigs and run around the machines, scared and enthralled.

That was why I was surprised when Ivy went behind the curtain one day. She was the last one, I thought, who'd want to extinguish the magic.

I only found out she'd gone behind the curtain one weekend during summer. I didn't go there much in summer, not many of us did. We were too busy playing cricket on the beach, or going hunting for shrimp in the rock-pools. Besides you had to get to the beach early in summer to get the good places before all the foreigners arrived. And also the foreigners seemed to love the pier, and Erbach's, so we tried to stay away. But that day I'd had an argument over the new ball that Tommy had gone and forgotten to bring with him and he'd refused to go home and get it even though it was mine. So I went off and thought I'd go and see if anyone else was around on the pier because Tommy wasn't my friend anymore if he was going to be like that.

There weren't many people about. It was too hot really, all the foreigners were just frying on the beach and any normal people were in home with a cool drink. When I got to the Emporium I found it empty, which was most unusual, even for the summer. Erbach wasn't on his stool and Ivy was nowhere to be seen. I looked round the place, which seemed especially dark given the bright sunlight outside. It felt very creepy. I was stood right next to the laughing clown and there was something about the way he stared at the door that made me feel scared.

Then I heard Ivy's soft laugh. It was coming from out the back, behind the curtain. Already shaking a bit I made my way over to see if I could peep through and find out what was happening.

The back room must have been quite large, but it seemed small because of all the cluttered objects. Everything was brightly lit by small electric lights which shone up into display cases that had various ornate animals and jugglers, circus artists and racing cars, all whirring and jiggling with their automatic light. In the centre of this cranking metal menagerie there was a low table just a few feet away from me, at which were crouched Ivy and Erbach. A black felt cloth was spread across the table and on it were two very curious devices. One seemed to be a large golden apparatus which had the planets turning and spinning on their axes around the sun, which seemed to actually burn with some orange flame. The more I looked though I could not see any mechanism that held the planets in place, they did not seem to be connected to a central pedestal or any sort of wire suspension grid. They just hung there, like globes animated by some incredible magician. Erbach seemed fascinated by this object and he stared into the centre of the burning sun for what seemed like ages.

Ivy was captivated by something altogether more peculiar. It was obviously quite old and had a wooden base which seemed to have had some sort of quilted material attached to it that was cushioned in places to resemble small hills. It had been covered then with a thick green cloth which had worn away at the edges, revealing the dark wooden base. Upon this patch of 'grass' there leapt and played, hopped and danced, what I can only describe as a rabbit. It would have been no more than 3 inches high and was clearly fashioned from old cloth. It wore a striped blazer and some green dungarees. Again I tried to fathom the means by which this thing operated. But there was nothing that either connected it to the ceiling or to the cloth patch around which it danced. It even appeared to react to Ivy's laughs and glee, performing ever more intricate performances for her. I was amazed. As it finished its gambols it even took a short bow and the joyful round of applause from Ivy that followed.

Then the thing saw me.

It did nothing really, except pause a moment, looking at me (if looking is the right word for a stuffed rabbit with beads for eyes). Then it collapsed, as did the other machine that Erbach had been watching. I was already running by then and so I just heard his cry as I reached the door. It was not anger, far from it. It was a word, perhaps in his original language, but the emotion it carried was pure despair.

I stood on the beach waiting to see if Ivy came out of the Emporium. After about ten minutes she did. She looked so depressed and I felt awful. I was scared to think of what I thought I had seen in those two machines without any means of operation, but I was more scared that Ivy would hate me forever.

She walked straight up to me, her arms hanging limply by her side. I had never seen her face so emotionless, so devoid of life.

'He told me something, John,' she said dreamily. 'And I don't think I'll ever be the same again.' With that she walked off and made for the long climb up to Cliff Gardens, and I presumed to have her tea.

∞

She only told me what he said to her once, shortly after that last visit to the Emporium. He had said, 'God is always in the detail.' It sounds somewhat clichéd, I know, but she then gave me a look. I say she gave me *a* look but it was more that she looked *into* me. Her face saddened and I knew she watched every small vessel passing my blood back and forth, each tiny valve that opened and closed, each cell active and energetic and those faded and dying, and finally she looked into the churning steam-piston that powered it all: my heart. How I knew this I do not know. As a child you are ready to simply accept the facts. I *knew* and that was that. Children are so much more mature than adults when it comes to the facts. Nothing is absurd or ridiculous. Things are the truth, or not the truth. All this nonsense that speaks of the idyll of innocent childhood. Children are pure rationality, mechanisms of truth. Then we teach them lies. Ivy saw inside me that day—the truth: the total system of my operation.

She smiled kindly and we never spoke again, in fact I don't think *she* ever spoke again.

Erbach's Emporium gradually declined over the years. People weren't interested in mechanical toys anymore, and the *foreigners* only seemed to come to get drunk. They didn't want attractions like the Emporium.

We didn't see Ivy for years. Our parents always spoke about her quietly, but from what we overheard she was in what they called the 'special school' or 'funny-farm'—to me that sounded quite good fun, and I thought she'd probably like it there. And that would have been true, had the place really been the 'funny farm'; but it was not.

The year after I was married, Ivy came back to our little town. I was working for the bank then and I saw her walking towards the pier one day as I cycled to work. It's strange because, despite having grown into a woman, she looked no different really. And in seeing her I was almost a boy again.

She owns that house up in Cliff Gardens now that her parents are gone and I hear she lives very simply. Every day she goes to stand at the end of the pier, right by where Erbach's Emporium used to be. It is now an amusement arcade. Perhaps Erbach would have liked the noises these new machines make, or perhaps he would have found them rather vulgar. I don't know. Funnily enough it was only last week that I saw they had thrown out Erbach's old sign board, the same one he'd put out so many years before.

For over forty years that sign never changed: 'Erbach's Emporium of Automata. Stick a Penny in the Slot and Watch'. It yellowed and peeled, there in the sun and the sleet, immune to the dull climb of inflation. Always a penny. But I suppose that is a minor detail.

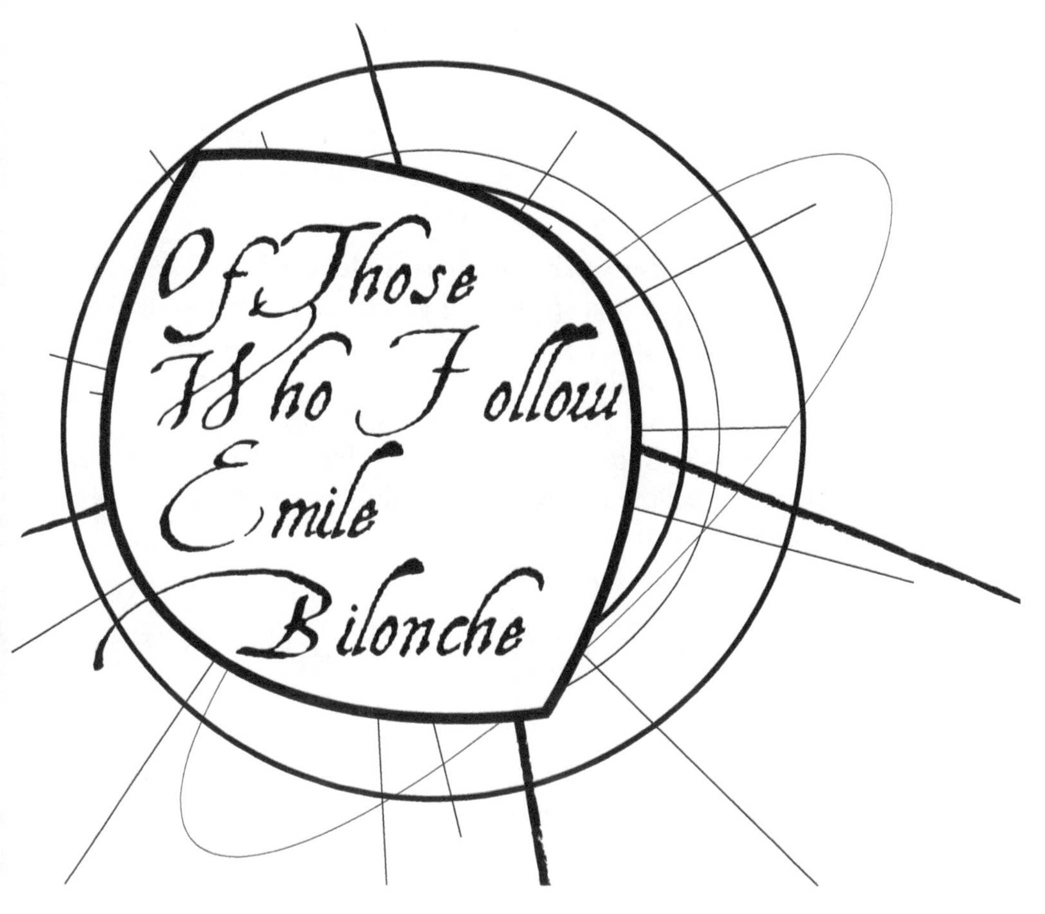

For Mario Vendredi, a troubadour, and for Rich Davies
who once whispered the rumour of Emile Bilonche to me.

Of those who follow Emile Bilonche you will have heard little. There are few of us, and those few are a scattered rabble of believers and doubters, charlatans and miscreants. Some amongst us aspire toward more refined encounters with our mentor though, to establish something like a permanent exhibition of his works, his thoughts, his clothes, his dreams; an unparalleled collection of fundamental articles and ephemera. This is *my* aspiration and it is something I feel is within my reach, achievable here in the tunnels, in my rags, beside my most precious collection.

∞

I have given my all for this work, you must understand that, all *my own* time. I found these books and spent such money as you will only dream of accumulating upon them. Yes, I was once rich. I once opened my bank statements and smirked at the growing digits spread across the page. But now, just look, here in this case: these treasures (I must keep them in the case to avoid damp—I hope you understand). How much richer I can claim to be now, with all the works of Emile Bilonche beside me and all *my* time left in which to follow him.

∞

How did I hear of him? Well, yes, that is interesting and perhaps provides us with a better place to start. I know I can become a bit of a bore when discussing his work. But you must understand, in his great oeuvre there is a liberation that no other literature, no words written or spoken has ever provided. They are the quintessence of the literary art. Sorry, I digress, I heard of him through Mario Vendredi. You know, the singer, the one who passes above us occasionally on his way to The Auditorium, or whatever they call it these days.

∞

I got my money when I was eighteen you know. You should have seen the little flies around me then. Move on, move on and see the world, that's what I thought then. But there's more of a world in Bilonche than any of this stinking gaudy globe can offer. There's a universe in Emile Bilonche.

∞

Am I grateful? What to Vendredi? I suppose I should be, without him I wouldn't have known where to begin.

It started after one of his concerts. I cornered him and bombarded him with questions. Music always makes me animated, talkative, inquisitive. It's like a drug for me I'm afraid. I must have rather surprised him, he seemed genuinely interested though, in all the connections I was making, with his work and certain authors whom I thought were relevant at the time. I do not recall them now. Then Vendredi asked if I had heard of Emile Bilonche and something about the name intrigued me. I said I hadn't and he offered to lend me one of Bilonche's books he happened to have with him, in his guitar case, a copy of his last book: *Our Divergent Paths.*

I waited by the entrance for Vendredi to return, as the crowds drifted away after his performance. I felt an odd pride, knowing that I had just spoken to Vendredi and that he would be returning with a book for me in just a moment. You see, at that time Vendredi had rather captivated this small town, he was on the rise, he would be leaving soon and didn't really need to concern himself with us provincials. I was younger then, of course, hadn't seen a penny of the money at that stage.

So I waited, even to the point where the cleaner came to the door and asked me if I might think of leaving. I said I was waiting for Mario Vendredi. He told me I'd have a long wait. Vendredi had left for London about an hour before and wouldn't be back until a gig the following weekend. He was busy, of course, but to not have taken the few moments merely to bring the book to me. To have shared the knowledge; to have brought another potential follower in, it's an opportunity I wouldn't have missed.

∞

I kept thinking about the name—Emile Bilonche. It has a certain cadence, don't you agree? Something you only find in the names of truly gifted people, I believe. I left a note, a number of them, at The Auditorium. There was no response. Finally I telephoned and a surly assistant in the box office informed me that they would no longer be booking Vendredi, his material was not the 'sort' that they wished to show in their establishment. They had no contact details for him. I was lost. It felt desperate, those few weeks of cogitating upon a name—Emile Bilonche, and a title: *Our Divergent Paths*. I got to the point where I began to pen a few lines of what the work might consist of. Then the money arrived.

∞

With all the financial planning and the excitement I quite forgot Emile Bilonche and Mario Vendredi. Oh, they were always there in some form, unconsciously tying together those brain connections that would lead me here, with you and my collection. Then I was busy enjoying the money, holidays and cars, passion and extravagance. It was a waste. I see that now. It might have been able to acquire a few more copies, or even a signed edition, who knows? No regrets though, best to have no regrets. I think it was about a year later that I settled down, after I'd weeded out the dead wood that called themselves my friends—mostly parasites, as you've probably guessed. But they would have been a considerable burden to me—to my *enterprise*. I have enjoyed a wonderful freedom to research, to study; impossible with all those meetings and evenings out, socialising and drinking away my money.

∞

I was at a party one night and overheard a disagreement about Vendredi. I didn't know why it had become so heated but a tall rakish man with bizarre black clownish hair was ranting (he had obviously drunk far too much) about Vendredi's influences, calling him a fake and a fraud, amongst a barrage of other insults which seemed entirely unwarranted. I joined the group, which appeared to be humouring the drunken buffoon—now so incensed that he had begun spraying a mist of spittle at his audience with each apoplectic outburst.

I asked if any of them knew the whereabouts of Vendredi, as I—an old acquaintance—would be interested in meeting up with him again. None of them had heard where he was and couldn't help me. The clownish fellow had stopped his diatribe and was now staring straight at me with a look of such complete contempt I was uncertain whether to apologise or run. He handed me an old business card: Vendredi's. Then with a twisted, toothy, sneer the drunkard punched me across the jaw before passing out at the feet of our perplexed crowd. They looked at me with some sympathy and were obviously used to it, before drifting away to other groups.

∞

Despite my aching jaw I was grateful for the information. Emile Bilonche had surged back into my mind and disparate fantastic ideas began to form themselves again: possible Bilonche's, incredibly erudite or pathetically abnormal, a man endowed with either the wisdom of age or the wit of education. I imagined all the myriad geniuses that this world has seen; of Plato, Aristotle, Bach and Einstein, Van Gogh, Baudelaire and Rilke, but they were all enfeebled by one fact: they were *known* to me. Bilonche existed in this shadow world that promised everything, his name was enough for now. I did not care whether he was a scientist, a philosopher, theologian or artist. All I wanted was to read his words, words that would shine like jewels and bathe me in the glory of their syncretic vision.

∞

I went to Vendredi's as soon as I could, having managed to ditch whichever leech lingered around me that evening. He had a flat over at The Regent's Court. It was certainly an improvement on the dens he was rumoured to have inhabited in the years before. London was certainly treating him well,

I thought. But on arriving at the address I found there was no answer. Someone was leaving and I decided to go in and up to the 5th floor, where his flat was located. The door was ajar so I entered. I called out in case he had not heard me ringing but there was no one at home. It was very sparse, two rooms were entirely empty and only the living room seemed in any way occupied. There I found a sleeping bag, his guitar and some notes for lyrics. The only other thing was a small brown notebook with many addresses and phone numbers. It looked like a common enough address book, but I know differently now. Having called those numbers, having met those dealers I now know that book to have been the only record of those others who follow Emile Bilonche: gifted, free minds that live the ideal of Bilonche. Something urged me to take the book and I did. Then I noticed a line on the top sheet of Vendredi's song notes. It read: 'The Curse of Emile Bilonche.'

∞

I was angry, yes, infuriated that Vendredi—who had so generously initiated me into the mysteries of this man—had turned against his teacher. There is no curse! There could be no curse of Emile Bilonche. His gift to this world is pure opportunity, freedom and revelation. Poor Vendredi, he did not read long or deep enough to know the true spirit of Bilonche's work. But *I* have.

In the days that followed I called all the numbers in Vendredi's book. I heard of their offers and interests, their own collections gathered over years of effort. Here I was, young and with a vast fortune—enough to persuade each one to part with their most treasured editions. So over those months I travelled, visiting each on the list. One by one I added those sacred copies to my collection. Every hand stitched edition, none escaped me. None resisted my bribes and pleas. I was the supreme collector, with the time to indulge my fascination. The money ran out though. I can't say when, this darkness seems to have gently eroded my memories. Then I sometimes stole to get those last few priceless works. But the final one, a bookseller in Wales, he claimed to have no idea what I wanted. He had never heard of Bilonche and had nothing of that title in his shop. It was, of course, that very work that Vendredi had first recommended to me, *Our Divergent*

Paths, the only title I was missing and the one I most desired to read. Well that old man couldn't stop me. He carried on the pretence though even when I visited him at the shop. He asked me to leave and then the rage began.

When my fists finally ceased their frenzy he was dead but I was free to search out that delicate jewel of writing. It was there, hidden in the desk beneath a pile of invoices. He probably treasured the work as much as I did, caressing its yellowing pages and repeating its wonderful words in his sleep. But he didn't share my plan, my *need*—to create the only full collection of the works of Emile Bilonche. I'm sure you understand that there are some ideals that necessitate terrible sacrifice.

∞

You're so cold now. I recommend you read Bilonche. It'll light a fire in you that will burn and burn. You won't need to concern yourself with all the petty daily minutiae. He keeps me going. A passion, that's what they say isn't it? You can't live in this world without a passion. You *need* a passion, and there's nothing better than Bilonche. That's what I've been trying to tell you.

But he's not for everyone you may say. True, true, there are those who find him a little too solemn, even sententious. But it's a misreading, as I hope you will come to appreciate. Nothing could be further from the truth. If you read between the lines—that's another of those bookish phrases isn't it, a little too clichéd now I would have thought—you can find all the other finer points. He's a metaphysician really, Emile Bilonche, that's what I've always claimed. I wrote a monograph you know, even got through to the final proofs and then I gave it all up because of a line I found in his notebooks: 'Criticism is the last refuge of a delinquent'. Isn't that perfect, it certainly took the wind out of my sails. That's what's so uncanny in Bilonche, almost as though you discover his words as they become relevant to you.

∞

He's certainly a presence in my life—a guardian angel, of sorts. He would be of immense interest to you, I have no doubt. You have that quiet reserve about you, a reader and a seeker after knowledge, that's you, I'm sure. Bilonche is just your thing, I know it. I only apologise that I can't lend you any of my collection. When the library is built you'll be able to come and do research though. You're more than welcome.

∞

You've been so quiet; I do hope I haven't bored you. You don't think I'm some kind of obsessive, do you? It may be true to some extent. I'm just interested, passionate, that's all. Emile Bilonche has consumed me; he's part of me now that's for certain. That's not obsession: that's possession. That's a joke. I'm sorry.

∞

In the early days of an obsession one is inclined to overlook the obvious. So enthralling are the new horizons and visionary aspects of a given artist or writer. As the acquaintance with the master grows, through reading, viewing, contemplation and reflection, the cracks appear—errors of the human kind, forgivable, inevitable. So I'll admit, as it's just us two here, that one day I examined my collection of the works of Emile Bilonche and there before me were a heap of tattered newspapers, bound in cardboard and twine. Inscribed on each, in a crayon scrawl, was the title of the work and its author—Emile Bilonche.

∞

I, like you, would have suggested that it was Vendredi who had made these copies, selling them to me in his various disguises, bleeding my fortune away from me. However this is not the case. It was *I* who discovered his works, from the faintest of rumours. *I* uncovered those words which still resound in my mind with utmost clarity; the words of a visionary man. *I* traced each elusive text from book fair to boot sale, marketplace to antique shop. *I* have been at auctions and the homes of dealers in outré antiquities. *I* have dined with princes and stolen from thieves: all to obtain this collection. Not even Vendredi can take my achievements from me. *I* wouldn't give them up now, no never! Not if you offered to return me to that moment before I had ever heard *his* name. *I* wouldn't want any of that old life back, oh no. *I* have followed Emile Bilonche, and others will do soon; for those who are committed, who persevere, will always uncover the words of a genius.

Stephen Sinclair was searching the records. He was a historian and that is what they do (I am told). It was a beautiful day outside and he wished he were somewhere else: walking on a hillside, watching the nesting birds rushing back and forth from the box on the side of his house, picnicking in the park. Anywhere outside really, rather than shut up here in the records office at the library. It was up to him though, he was an author and his time was his own. But his publisher had been waiting on this book for the last month and he had a few details to get right before he was content to send the manuscript in. It was a book on public hangings in Britain in the 19th and 20th centuries. Imagine that—if you can—mindful reader: hangings in this Eden of Europe! He was looking for the records of Harriet Tarver, a 21 year old woman hanged at Gloucester prison, in 1836, for the murder of her husband, Thomas.

It was probably his desire to complete the book, coupled with his urge to enjoy the bright spring day that made him unable to recall the details of Elizabeth Lloyd's case, for he had alighted on her name—there in the records—and *almost* remembered her story. The entry read: Elizabeth Lloyd, 25, hanged 5th August 1831, Gloucester, double infanticide.

∞

If you venture through the wooded dens of the Rheidol valley and are fortunate enough to stumble upon the broken remains of the hamlet of Ystumtuen you might pause a moment, surveying the scattered dwellings and their descent into oblivion. You might even stop long enough to notice the ditches and earthen banks that divided one homestead from another. Should the rain not be lashing down as so frequently it does in Wales (I am told) perhaps you, or another in your party, will pick up what looks to be a blackened stone and wonder—aloud—whether it might have been used to circle a hearth. There will be no clear answer to this question though and the rock will be discarded and another feature of interest remarked upon. This process may, or may not, go on for some time, until you are bored. No doubt you will press on, heading along some rambler's route or other; perhaps to visit Devil's Bridge or another tourist haunt. However, should you go slightly off your course, taken there by foul weather, or a misjudged map reference, you may stumble upon a strange mound located on the rising moorland. And if it is spring you will find—circling it—a ring of blue-purple grape hyacinths. This is where Elizabeth Lloyd entrusted her children to the fairies.

Ystumtuen had grown rapidly since the late-Eighteenth century when mining for lead in that forgotten valley began in earnest. Of those first brave miners was one Ioan Lloyd, who had spent some time at sea before declaring himself a 'land man' and burrowing the earth for his trade. He worked the mine at Llywernog for many years. It was later in his life that he met Elizabeth. They had been wed and she came to the village shortly before the arrival of the Williams brothers in 1825. With them the Llywernog mine went into heightened production and one unfortunate day, whilst repairing the water wheel, Ioan's leg was trapped and badly broken. He never really recovered and drink took its usual effect on his already embittered mind. He would rage at Elizabeth for being barren (she had not conceived in the two years since they had married). But after months of miserable poverty he seemed well enough to return to work and did so. Both prayed that this would be a turning point in their—so far—unhappy life together. However, fate had determined otherwise. In 1827 the price of lead ore collapsed and most miners at Llywernog, and the surrounding mines, were laid off. Within days a drunken binge had sent Ioan to his death, by suicide perhaps, in one of the many disused mine shafts.

Elizabeth believed herself to be alone, but within one month she found she was pregnant. For all his rage and spite Ioan had finally fathered a child with her. Had he lived long enough perhaps it may have brought them together to see the ore prices rise and for a living be made again. Elizabeth was troubled. How was she to care for a child with no husband and no work? The other villagers of Ystumtuen, whilst friendly and caring, had enough troubles of their own. And there seemed to be something more, she had visions of terrible things which even the vicar of their small church did not understand the meaning of: crowds of screaming people, flashes of blue and white and a creaking noise, as on the deck of a ship.

As the months went on she grew to love the very concept of life growing within her. She held the cold away with the warm cocoon of her own body. That winter was a hard one but the starving inhabitants of that remote village finally saw the buds of spring emerge and with them came Elizabeth's child. Once again though fate had a surprise for Elizabeth, for she bore twins, and named them Mary and Esther.

Elizabeth's fear did not diminish with their delicate smiles though. It was increased sevenfold and she wept for hours after they were asleep. Nothing could calm her anxiety and so she resolved to end all their wretched lives one night. She wrapped them in a blanket and, whilst they still slept, crept from the house, determined to cast them, and herself, into that very shaft where her husband had met his own fate. The weather was against this enterprise though and soon a storm had driven them far off track. With no bright moon to guide them they were swiftly lost in the wooded valley.

At some point she must have broken down and struggling with weakness, hunger and cold she had fallen asleep. On waking she found the smiling face of an old woman before her. The storm had subsided a little and now just a persistent rain fell. The old woman helped her to her feet and took the children into her arms. Elizabeth was too weak and tired to object and stumbled along in the woman's footsteps unsure of where they might be heading, or why.

A nearby clearing revealed the woman's dwelling place: a small huddle of rocks beneath the large branches of an old tree. The stones were curiously assembled, almost natural, and covered with a creep of ivy. Inside it was quite spacious, though simple, and most importantly: dry. Tea, of sorts, was quickly brewed and Elizabeth found herself disgorging her recent life in an upset babble of words and sobs as the old woman listened carefully and calmly. The children did not cry at all, but lay by a gently smoking stove, glancing up at the woman with their wide baby eyes.

After her tale was told and the sobbing had diminished the old woman waited a while, allowing the silence to calm them all. She spoke then, at length, about all manner of things; plants, roots, fruit and trees, about birdsong and the smells of summer. She spoke of the different winds for each season and the words you can hear on the breeze if you listen very long and still. She told Elizabeth of paths through the forest where nobody ever went and the streams that could be found there and the mosses that grew on their banks; blue and green and crimson. She told her of the dark spaces beneath the earth that glimmer with crystal walls lit with the faint light of strange molluscs and insects. As dawn broke she told her finally of the folk who used to live all across the land, little people, winged people, of curious sizes and shapes. She told her how they lived on rare fungi and had charms to bring the aid of animals and elemental creatures that humans cannot see. She spoke of how they still existed, in a far distant world, but visited and sometimes dwelt at the edges of the busy human world, watching and waiting for the return of their land. As the story continued it gradually became clear to Elizabeth what the old woman was saying. These people could care for her children, and Elizabeth believed her.

Who would decline the offer of the life the old woman described: feasting and merriment, mischief and abandon, a rich abundant harvest of another world? So Elizabeth was given the necessary instructions, which took a full five hours in the telling. It would not be without pain, of course, but the rewards were impossible to refuse and little else remained for Mary and Esther save a life of emptiness and hardship. The old woman gave her an oily balm in a small copper pot and a delicately embroidered cloth that seemed as thin as spiders' webs. She taught her the necessary process and the necessary words. After a little soup and a final farewell the old woman ushered them from the ancient dwelling and into an early evening bright with a low sun.

Elizabeth was glad, gladder than she had been in months now. With the sleeping babes gathered to her breast she headed out towards the moorland to find a low mound as the old woman had told her. She laid the girls to one side, as darkness descended, and used a smooth flat stone to dig a shallow grave. Elizabeth gathered the embroidered cloth together in one hand, as she had been told, and lifted Mary to her for one last embrace. Covering the child's face with the cloth she squeezed her to her own body and waited for the futile movements to cease. She paused a moment with Esther, seeing the still body of Mary before her. Then resolve returned and she finished the grim task.

As the last heave of Esther's tiny chest subsided Elizabeth's heart sank and all gladness evaporated. That warm feeling of well-being and contentment vanished. What a harsh gift, knowledge, for it is little more than doubt. For how was Elizabeth to know the truth? How was she to ever be sure her babes were really with those other people rather than their souls not merely sinking into the depths, hurried by her own hand?

She persevered though, little choice remaining, and laid them carefully in the cold ground. As the old woman had instructed, she placed them head to toe, forming a fleshy ouroboros. In each of their clenched hands she placed a grape hyacinth and rubbed each eyelid with the balm she had been given. It smelt of summer and warmed her fingers with the glow of meadows in the sun. She swaddled them, as best she could with the small embroidered wrapping, and began to cover them over with earth.

Imagine—if you can—kind reader, her hands in the moist soil, moister with tears, covering the still warm bodies of her own babies. You may be the last to ever know how she stayed there all night, slumped over herself—somewhat foetal—mumbling words that nobody ever heard, or ever shall; arcane words that called a race forth who have long been hidden from us, dwelling in other worlds. You may be the last to hear how the delicate lights of other beings brightened the stormy night and assuaged the ruined soul of Elizabeth Lloyd, forgiving her dread deed. These beings, not without their own form of malice and cruelty (but of a different sort to ours), carried the little girls into their grassy home and gifted them with another sight. By dawn a ring of flowers had emerged around the low mound of earth—grape hyacinths—in full blue-purple bloom.

Imagine the unspeakable grief of that poverty that makes such murder possible. Imagine the belief that trusts infants to those half-beings such as fairies are. Imagine how those children dance now in fairy halls far from human lands, immortal and drunk on daisy wine, singing songs of the old gods and hidden to all cynical human eyes.

The villagers of Ystumtuen thought little of Elizabeth's disappearance and many believed that she had thrown herself, and the babes, to their deaths. Either that, or they had fled in hope of a better life, to one of the nearby towns, or perhaps even to England. So none were sent to search for her, and none reported her missing—not until the following spring, when a miner had decided to leave the village and head south to Lampeter. He had family in Tregaron and would stay with them a few weeks. He loaded his cart with belongings from the cottage and finally helped his wife, heavy with their third child, onto the front, lifting his other two children up to sit with her. The mule was old and had poor sight so the miner led it. They were seen off by a few of their fellows, but numbers were already dwindling and none really wished to see the truth of their plight: leave or die.

So the family made their slow way across the moor, heading for hope. None of them saw the flickering, dancing lights that darted in and out of the loaded cart, making mischief with their property, untying knots and mixing up the tattered clothes. One knot though contained a real undoing: a pick slid from the side of the cart and dragged along the ground a way before catching against a rock, jolting the vehicle and its passengers. In the wake of the anchored cart a great furrow had been torn.

The miner worked at re-lashing the cart, complaining at the poor job that had been made of tying their property down. Meanwhile the children played, as children will. As they danced along the path of the furrow, skipping back and forth across its earthy line, they came across the mound, ringed with beautiful blue-purple flowers. The pick had dragged across it and a great muddy gash revealed something white protruding from the ground. It was a piece of tattered cloth. Returning to their parents, dirty and excited with their new find, the mother cried and made them lay the muddy fabric down. It was not the usual cry that greets all dirty children though, for she had some knowledge of this cloth, and its uses. After some persuading, her husband helped her down, and with the children silently leading them to where they found the thing the family made a bizarre procession to the mound to discover the clean bones of Mary and Esther Lloyd.

Within days constables had arrived. Questions were asked and the facts assembled. That none knew the whereabouts of Elizabeth was not unusual and for some while the case rested with the authorities. Her final discovery would be by curious means.

The very vicar that had wed Ioan and Elizabeth had been called away from the depleted parish of Ystumtuen and was to visit his new flock in Dymock. A mile from Ross-on-Wye the carriage wheel broke, luckily only spilling the passengers into an embarrassed heap by the roadside. Being only a few miles from his destination the vicar decided he would lodge the night in Ross and then continue in the morning, by foot.

Now, this vicar was himself a troubled man. He had heard God's call and had been happy enough to go to Ystumtuen. Indeed, for a while, it had been his salvation. For despite his pious aspirations and love of the word of God, darker inclinations surged at the edges of his consciousness and seethed inside him in a turmoil of desire and decadent dissolution. Drink was the key which would unlock his desires. Ross was a growing town and it had all the vices which were absent from the small community of Ystumtuen. So that night, the world swimming with gin, the vicar found himself in a bawdy house, enjoying as many of the young professionals as the madam could offer. In the morning, and coming to his senses a little, he attempted to creep from that house of sin and make his journey on to Dymock, where perhaps he might find sanctuary from himself a while. Yet there, slumped against the door, lay a wench with a young lover draped across her drunken body. The vicar made attempts to move the pair but only succeeded in waking her. They looked long at each other, she recognising him before he placed her. It was Elizabeth Lloyd. Rushing past her he headed for his lodgings and gathered together his belongings ready to set out for his new life. But how secure might that be with Elizabeth knowing the truth of his most secret world?

After Elizabeth's arrest she was taken to Gloucester for trial but spoke not a word other than her confession to the killings. It became known that an anonymous letter had been sent to the magistrate in Ross. It told of the fugitive Elizabeth Lloyd and her deeds. She did not speak of the vicar. She did not speak of the old woman, the cloth or the balm. She did not speak of the other people that dwelt near Ystumtuen. She did not speak of Mary and Esther, who must surely be dwelling with them still. She offered nothing in her defence and gave no explanation.

This is, to us—knowing reader—quite understandable. Imagine how tired she was of this world, with its fretful desire for explanation, for the reasons behind everything, as though every deed were connected by strings that if you pick hard enough and long enough will finally reveal their cosmic order. It was that silence in the face of thirsty knowledge that condemned her. That, coupled with the general abhorrence of infanticide. For everyone loves a child, as the vicar would no doubt have informed you. So whilst in utero Mary and Esther were hers, and hers alone, untouchable and entombed (a tomb that she had recreated for them on that desolate moor), in the world they became the property of some disparate, dissolute polis that cared little for them save the fact that they were owned by a greater body than hers; a body of human numbers, a mass, which must be contained.

So within three days, from the 2nd to the 5th August 1831, Elizabeth Lloyd was tryed and executed for the murder of her two infants. It had been the talk of the city though. The famous William Calcraft was travelling from London to hang her. She would suffer dissection you know, after a short drop hanging—sometimes they suffered for minutes. It was commonly reported in the press that the prisoner had 'died hard', much to the reader's pleasure—imagine that!

And on that day, 5th August 1831, imagine the thousands assembled outside the prison gatehouse, with their food and drink and hatred. Imagine Elizabeth being taken from the prison house and led towards the gatehouse by the execution party, seeing the gallows silhouetted against the rising sun. Then after the short climb of the stairs they were out onto the gatehouse roof with the sun in their eyes. She heard only the yelling crowd, taunting and screaming. Then a hail of rocks and vegetables, dirt and rubble crashed into her. Her weak body slid down beneath its torrent and even the guards shielded themselves upon the ground beside her. Already she was bruised and bleeding from a hundred tiny wounds—nothing to the pain she would endure. Imagine how the vengeful mob was pushed back by attendant constables and after a few minutes had calmed enough for the execution to proceed.

Imagine—if you can—empathetic reader, the fear in Elizabeth's heart and the horror of impending death by hands so cruel and cold. Imagine the rub of the prickly rope upon her frail neck and the intonation of the chaplain's holy words, mixing with the rude jeers of an animal crowd. Imagine the trickle of urine that ran down her shaking legs as the white cap was slid over her head and the last image she would ever see—of leering, dirty faces—vanished from her eyes. Imagine the sounds collecting in her ears, intense now within that white bag. Then the thud of the trap, which stuck for a moment before Calcraft's booted foot set it free, and with it Elizabeth. Imagine how her body, so slight and withered, still dropped like a heavy sack of flesh—and then the terrible pain, the burning chafe of the rope grinding the skin from her neck.

Then there was the cheer—imagine the cheer from the jubilant wolves—resounding in the air, filling her last thoughts with terror. That should surely have been enough misery, but the crowd, in its passion, surged forward and overwhelmed the constables. They climbed the pillars on the gatehouse and massed on the roof, ripping at the scaffold and beating Elizabeth's swinging body. Then, for all to hear, a girlish laugh echoed from the gatehouse below and with it the giggling cries of newborn infants. A flutter of flowers—grape hyacinths—issued from the bloodied skirts of Elizabeth Lloyd and a ripple of silence rushed through the crowd, terrified by such sorcery.

What remained of Elizabeth hung there momentarily, twisting in the breeze, red with blood, emaciated pale white and flecked with fresh blue bruises: a flag of shame. With a crack the cross brace of the gallows snapped and her corpse was beaten into the ground by the ruthless mob, further enraged now by fear of the witchcraft they had witnessed.

∞

For a passing moment Stephen Sinclair tried to place the name, something about prostitution he thought, further details were not forthcoming. Imagine, if you can, dear reader (mindful, kind or otherwise) the infinite neglect of history by the historian. Imagine the millions of lives heaping up, untold, forgotten, yet undead in the graveyard of memory; begging, or praying, with skeletal hands to be brought back to mind, if only for an instant. At least the ghost of Elizabeth Lloyd, and her sad children, lingered a few moments in the flickering synapses of Sinclair's mind, straining into electrical existence because of her infamy. Then he turned the page and so many histories vanished.

Had anyone been at Ystumtuen they would have seen that ring of grape hyacinths fade to white and briefly flush again with red as though the land itself were bleeding.

'What an age to reach', all the neighbours had said of Miss Coulton on the day that William and Louise Hopkins moved into their new home in Sheffield, tanned and invigorated from a two week honeymoon in Mauritius.

'One hundred and ten years old, who'd have thought it,' they said.

'She was an old lady when *we* moved in, before we had the kids,' they said.

'She'd lived here for more than ninety years,' they said. 'Right from when her father died—he had the butcher's shop round on Rampton Road, you know.'

Louise and William didn't know, *of course*, but nodded politely as they carefully watched the removal men carrying their few possessions—gathered from two family homes—into the house (purchased with the help of Louise's father).

'We called her Miss Coulton for years,' they said. 'Miss Frances Coulton she was, 'til you was finally allowed to call her *Amy*—which was her mother's name, and the one she preferred.'

'She hardly went out you know,' they said. 'She hardly ever went out did Amy.'

'But, of course, she *did* go out,' they said. 'Once a year, for her holidays at the seaside, *you know*.'

'She loved her holidays at the seaside, did Amy,' they said.

William and Louise nodded.

'But, what an age to reach,' they said. 'What an incredible life!'

William was not so sure. He was a young man and he remarked to Louise that he didn't want to live *that* long. Indeed, that topic was part of the excited first night they had together in that house, sat on cardboard boxes in the living room sipping corked Bollinger (they didn't mind!) and laughing gently at the life Miss Coulton might have had in the many years she had lived there. They laughed too at the few items of hers that the clearance men had left. One thing, a chipped ceramic of a tramcar at Llandudno, raised a particular laugh, so absurd it seemed amidst the chaos of their modern possessions—sprouting like plastic fungi from their cardboard knolls. It didn't strike them as a particularly 'incredible' life, stuck in the house all year apart from a rainy few weeks at the seaside.

But then, isn't everyone's existence a mystery; the pointless hours edging by as the dust gathers on the senseless souvenirs. In years to come others would look upon William and Louise's small model of the ship *L'Astrolabe*, purchased on their honeymoon, and wonder at its ridiculousness, oblivious to the deeply encoded sentiments etched within its miniature timbers.

∞

It was a week before they explored the brick outhouse at the bottom of the garden.

They had busied themselves unpacking and making the main house more homely. The two bed-roomed terraced house began to resemble the student house they shared with Anne and David in Broomhall, just a little further North. But this was *their* house. They were married now. This was an important time in their lives together. Their years at Sheffield University were over and the time of *living* had begun, they thought. But then the reality of life always seems some few more paces over the horizon, as though the present were some hazy half-place awaiting the clarity of tomorrow.

What they found in the brick outhouse was certainly real enough.

They had dressed in their 'gardening gear' ready to make a first attack upon the weeds and grasses that had overgrown the thin rear garden. Hoping to find a few tools in this building, which was no more than a brick-built shed, they had broken the door down, having been unable to locate a key.

The wooden door gave in soon enough. William had been in the University rugby team. It did not strike them as strange that a weather-beaten crucifix was nailed to the door.

Inside they found plastic bags, stacked deep and high into the space, each stuffed full of newspaper. There appeared to be nothing else in there; no tools, garden or otherwise.

William grabbed a bag. It felt light, and he thought it could well be *just* newspaper. Looking a little closer he found that the paper was neatly arranged into parcels. He looked excitedly at Louise.

'I wonder what's in 'em,' he said.

Louise was less intrigued, more puzzled. She took one of the packets and unrolled it. Inside there lay a thick piece of decaying excrement.

Louise looked up at William.

'Cat shit,' he said.

Louise quickly discarded it and pushed past him into the building. She took another bag, at random, from deeper into the heap. Unfurling another parcel she found a similar offering, more decomposed.

She came out of the shed and threw the bag William was holding back inside, pulling the broken door closed, as best she could, behind her.

'It's cat shit, right?' William said, keen to convince himself.

'I don't think so,' she said, slowly taking off her new gardening gloves and heading back to the house.

What a vision of loneliness: a shed brimming with carefully packaged excrement.

William was a meticulous young man, Louise had always been impressed by his attention to detail—he was a good catch.

Imagine the average turd, William thought; perhaps five inches long and one inch wide and deep. Give a generous inch either side for the wrapping: 24 cubic inches per package. The shed was about ten feet by twelve, and about nine tall: one thousand and eighty cubic feet of available storage. Assuming the place was to be filled to the ceiling this offered space for almost ninety-six thousand packages. Assuming a regular bowel movement of once per day...

But had Miss Coulton evacuated herself as regularly as this? Or indeed, had she evacuated more frequently?

Let's be generous, William thought: two movements a day. That still gave over one hundred years worth of potential faecal storage here. But the shed was not filled to the ceiling, nor indeed did it reach to the door. A quick judgement of the dimensions, gave approximately thirty percent of the volume remaining. Allowing for holidays, and other absences from the house, he estimated that there was at least seventy-five years of excrement in there. Naturally, for a more detailed analysis he would need more data.

William was a tedious young man, as Louise would undoubtedly learn.

∞

It was a month before they investigated the loft.

As the boxes were unpacked—in between settling in at their new jobs—each was stacked in the second bedroom, and before long they needed to be stored. William was keen to keep them for the next move. It might save some money.

So, balancing on a stepladder that Louise held securely at the base, William pushed the hatch to the loft open. Shining a torch around inside it seemed very clear and spacious. He noticed there was no insulation. That would be another job to do before winter came.

'There's nothing up here really,' he called down to Louise. 'It's nice and dry though.'

She was pleased there were no more surprises like those in the garden shed. She has been dreading opening it to find further little gifts from Miss Coulton, but had said nothing to William.

'Oh, no, wait,' William said, turning around on the ladder and reaching back across the roof space. 'There are a couple of suitcases here.'

'Well, pass them down to me,' Louise shouted up to him. 'We can throw them out if they're no good.'

'I think this one's empty,' he replied, passing her a black leather case with a handle that had obviously been repaired a number of times.

'This one's got something in it though,' he said, pushing against the ladder as he struggled with the second case.

He came back down the ladder with a smaller brown case that seemed quite heavy. It appeared to be more of a vanity case, rounder and deeper than the other one.

Louise opened the black one to check it was empty. Again, she anticipated the worst.

A musty smell of lavender filled the landing, where they were sat. Inside there was a roll of scented drawer liner and a small leather name tag with 'Miss Coulton, 99 Vincent Rd., Sharrow, Sheffield' embroidered on it in pale brown stitching.

William opened the heavier brown case. A stack of about a dozen exercise books sprouted from the crammed case. Louise began flicking through them. William rifled through the rest of the case which appeared to be a jumbled collection of postcards and newspaper cuttings.

'They're Miss Coulton's diaries,' Louise exclaimed.

'Great,' said William, 'do they say why she kept her crap in the shed?'

Louise looked up at him disparagingly.

'Well, I'll put these in the back room,' William said, gathering the diaries together.

'No, leave them out,' Louise said. 'I'd like to read them.'

'Fair enough,' he replied, closing the cases up and storing them behind the packing boxes which he now began to thrust up into the loft.

Over the following months Louise relished looking through those diaries; so beautifully inked with that flowing hand that only the elderly can craft. It seemed like a secret graphic code to the mysteries of that time, almost a century distant.

But, as so often, the past only appears to be a sepia-tinted idyll. For in those diaries, of a child rapidly becoming a woman, Louise discovered a terrible story of cruelty. Miss Coulton's mother had evidently died young, perhaps when Miss Coulton was no older than five or six. Miss Coulton's father was a man easily given to drink and quickly succumbed to its more violent extremes. Entries spoke of the cold and darkness of the outhouse, and the whippings for not having warmed the bath enough on a Friday evening, or brought in enough coal to last the night. It seemed that the young *Amy* Coulton spent more time locked in the outhouse than inside the house itself. As the years went by the abuse worsened, to a sickening extent. Louise was forced to skip whole sections of the diaries, so terrible were the crimes perpetrated on the young girl. Yet, amidst the darkness there shone moments of deep love for her broken father. She spoke warmly of him at work, presumably less intoxicated than during the woeful nights. Amy wrote of how he taught her his trade, having no male heir. He showed her the art of the cleaver, block and carcass. He taught her to hang the meat and prepare the game brought in by local farmers. He instructed her on the sharpening and care of knives, and the correct blade for every cut; but most especially he taught her the importance of cleanliness. It was clear she loved him when the dark clouds of drink gave way enough for him to love her back, as a proper father.

Then the diary entries became shorter, and thankfully brighter, after his death. There flourished a young woman, with an independent income from the sale of her father's business. The days were filled with more usual records of meetings and conversations, of flowers in bloom and nature in abundance, or in wintery retreat. But behind it all the dark outhouse and its packages pressed on Louise's mind.

It was strange too that there were few entries in the diaries during the summer. But Louise recalled that the neighbours had said how much she enjoyed her seaside holidays. Perhaps she did not write her diary when away.

Marking the place in an entry from September 1899 was a faded postcard of Land's End. She turned it over to read, 'Dear Miss Coulton, Just a note to say I've done the first. More to follow, With love, Amy.' She placed it back inside the diary, saddened and puzzled.

From those diaries, Louise thought she understood a little more of Miss Coulton: with that lonely postcard addressed to herself and the years building up like dark lacquer. But increasingly, when she thought of her, all Louise could focus on was the shit heaped up in the dark building at the bottom of the garden.

∞

It was about a year before they returned to the brown vanity case.

William had been promoted and they had been away, celebrating in Bruges for the weekend, before returning to the house for a week of redecorating the back room. They had decided to try for a baby.

On the Sunday evening, after their return, they had had rather too much red wine and decided they should go through Miss Coulton's postcards in the case upstairs before putting them back in the loft. Neither of them wanted to part with the cases, or the diaries (Louise hadn't looked at them in weeks). Miss Coulton had been on both their minds. When no longer revelling in the dawn of their relationship—now gradually fading—William and Louise had even begun to dream of Miss Coulton. William's dreams were animated by proliferating turds innumerable, and Louise's by the image of the young, beaten Amy cowering in darkness, or the old, frail Amy heading to the shed at night with that day's package. They had discussed her less frequently though, as each dwelt on darker themes.

So, with the dregs of the wine bottle shared into their glasses they giggled their way upstairs, each a little apprehensive of their agreed task but too embarrassed to share their fears.

They opened the case and took out a handful of cards each, intent on reading them to each other. Underneath the cards and newspaper clippings there seemed to be a package folded in blue cloth. William lifted it out carefully.

'It's quite heavy,' he said, half-hoping Louise would ask him to take the lot straight to the bin.

He carefully unfolded the cloth to find a worn leather apron wrapped around a further piece of rolled leather, tied with cord. This package unfurled easily after a short fumble with its binding. With clanks and clinks a full set of knives and choppers revealed themselves to the couple. They were clearly worn down from many years of use. Inside the roll was a carefully folded set of diagrams, each listing the particular cuts of meat obtained from each animal; leg, loin, chine, belly, shoulder etc. These were clearly extracted from some old book, as each had a tear down one side. From the grubby brown smudges across each diagram, they had clearly been much handled and studied.

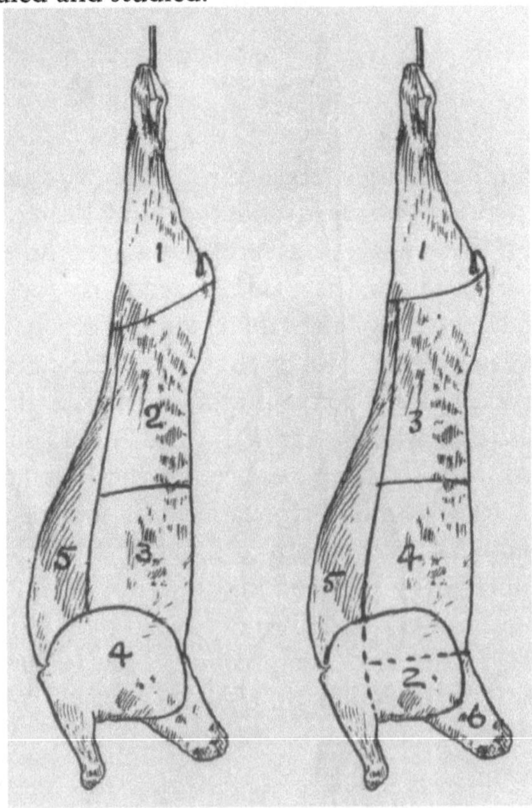

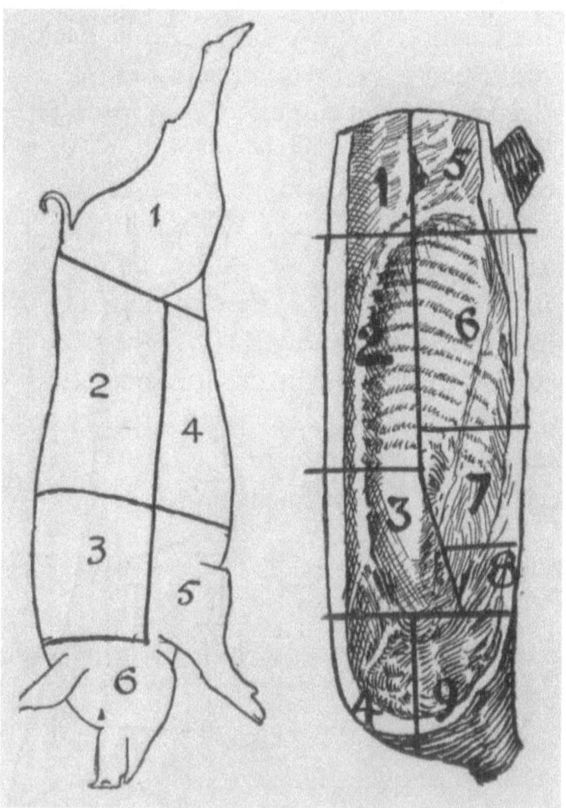

'What the bloody hell is that lot...' William began.

'Oh, they're her father's knives and butchery charts,' Louise said, attempting to mask her concern with plain facts.

'So she kept her shit in the shed and her dad's knives in the loft,' William said. 'That's just great!'

'Look, I'll tell you about it later,' Louise said. 'They're from his old butcher's shop and were probably quite precious to her. Let's just look through the postcards and then we can just put the whole lot away and forget about it.'

So they started to sort through the postcards. A number of them were wrapped in pieces of newspaper.

'At least they aren't hiding turds this time,' William sniggered.

Louise laughed nervously.

They read privately for a few minutes.

A rough picture emerged. The cards spanned most of the century; one each year from different seaside towns across the country. Each was addressed to 'Miss Coulton' and was signed 'Amy'. Each carried the same old script that Louise had so enjoyed in the diaries.

One card, dated the 15th of August 1921, carried an eerie drawing of the sea arch at Torquay. It read 'Dear Miss Coulton, There was a fine feast for the gulls at the archway this evening, With love, Amy.'

'What's she writing to herself for?' William asked, clearly irritated by Miss Coulton's eccentricities.

'But look at this,' Louise said, showing him the newspaper it had been wrapped in. 'It's the *Torbay Herald* from the same month: "A badly mutilated body was washed ashore by the Sea Road below Manor Gardens on Wednesday 17th August. The constabulary urgently seeks knowledge of any local man known to be missing. The dead man's savage wounds suggest a case of murder. Has *The Butcher* finally visited Torquay?" '

'Makes you feel like a proper detective doesn't it,' William said, still trying to salvage some humour from the increasingly disturbing situation that was unfolding.

Louise didn't respond. She just kept looking through the cards and papers, matching dates and places, bodies and holidays.

The stack of cards went backwards chronologically and most reports mentioned the murder of a young man at the hands of *The Butcher*, clearly a name coined for the killer by the popular press. Many of the newspaper clippings were taken from the *Illustrated Police News*, and featured gruesome line drawings of a caricatured butcher attacking his victims with various boning knives and cleavers.

Each message from *Amy* to *Miss Coulton* featured some cryptic remark which, when coupled with each report, suggested terrible things to the horrified couple. And still the pile went on.

Louise's hand shook as she unwrapped a card near the bottom of the pile. It was another *Illustrated Police News* 'shocker', from July 1905: '*The Butcher* strikes in Blackpool'. There was a shabby illustration of a moustached man, replete with chopper and striped apron, going at a well-to-do gentleman on the sea-front, with the tower illumined against the night sky in the distance. In contrast the postcard, also an illustration, depicted a cheerful couple enjoying some beach rendezvous under a similar Blackpool skyline, saucily entitled 'Oh Jack!!!'

Turning the card over, Louise read, in a shaky voice, 'Dear Miss Coulton...'

'It's addressed to herself again,' William interrupted nervously, ever eager to state the obvious.

'Dear Miss Coulton,' Louise said, gripping William's hand sympathetically. 'Do not think this is me on the other side, With love, Amy.'

That evening, having sorted through over eighty postcards, some with accompanying newspaper headlines, it became clear to Louise and William that it was not *The Butcher* 'wot did it', but rather Miss Frances Coulton: Frances 'Amy' Coulton—the butcher's *daughter*. Louise imagined the blades and the cleavers, carefully wrapped, in amongst the holiday cardigans and starched underwear, the lavender liner scenting everything with spinsterhood. She imagined Miss Coulton, every year, packing the same case with the same tools; and for every year a different resort, a new postcard home.

Louise and William stared at each other; their clammy fingers loosened their grip on the other's. The first gap of distance edged its way between them then—that inevitable distance, initiated by an unusual darkness. They each imagined Amy 'on the other side'; and without speaking about it ever again, they both knew exactly what that meant.

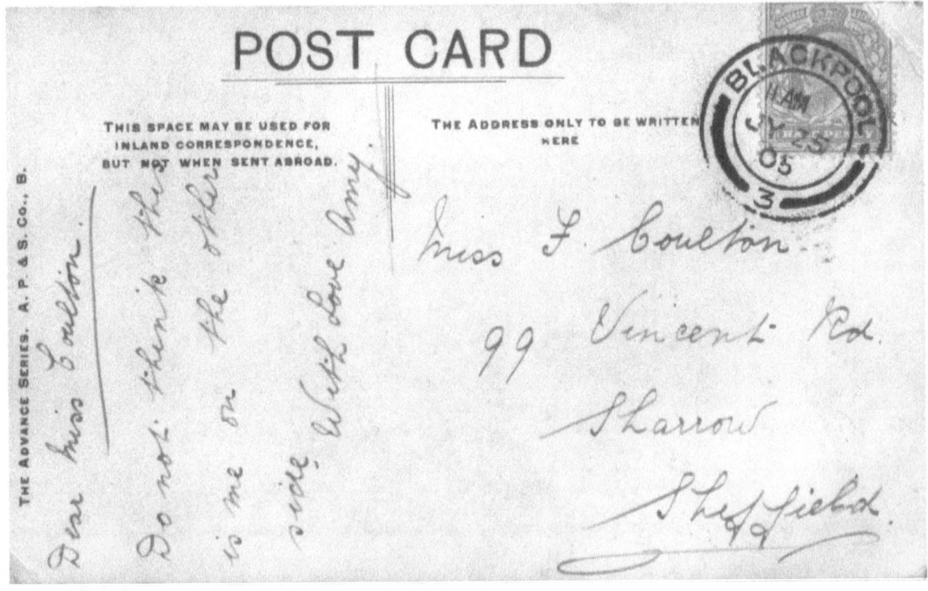

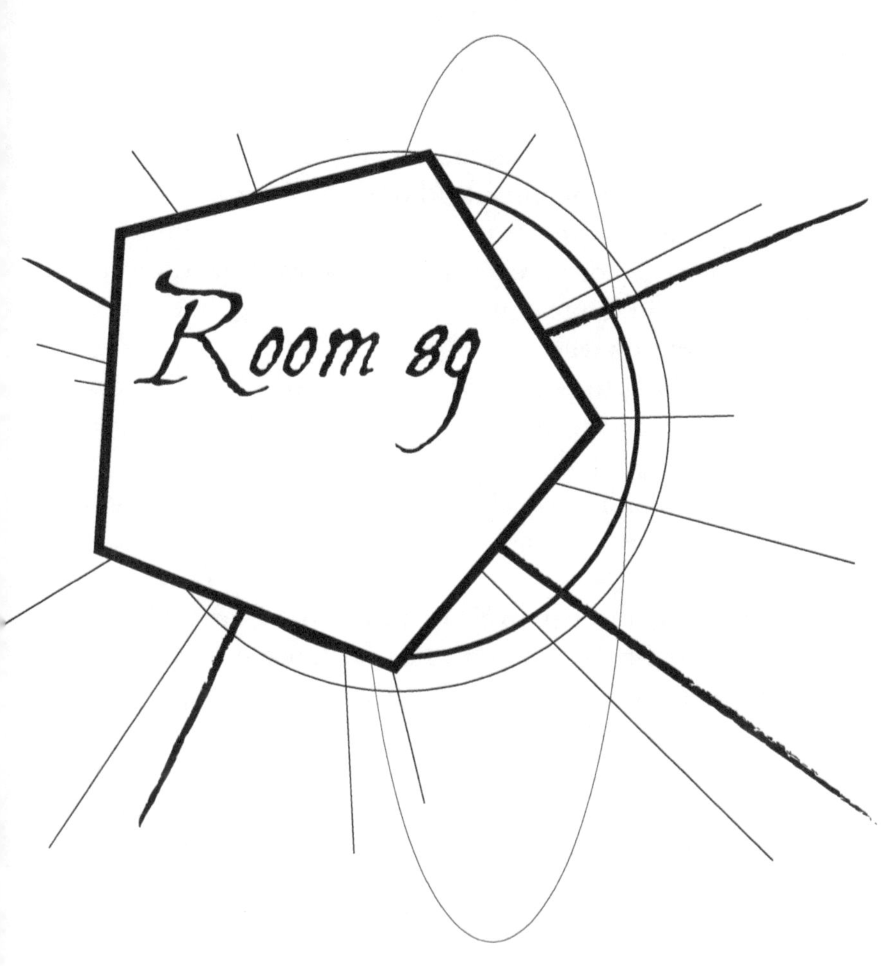

The hills are shadows and they flow
From form to form and nothing stands.
They pass like mist, the solid lands,
Like clouds they shape themselves and go.

Dr Alexander Weatherby had received a telegram from his publisher, Edward Arnold, informing him that his latest work, *Who are our Barbarians?*, had completed its print run and was ready for distribution. High sales were virtually guaranteed following the success of his 1908 lecture tour: 'Squabbles between Montesquieu and Gibbon with interruptions from Rousseau.' A verbose title, perhaps, but scandalous enough to merit press attention which, whether good or ill, is likely to secure public attendance.

The book had taken a further year to finalise and contained 'much new material' according to his publisher, although Weatherby—in private company—distanced himself from such claims. This was symptomatic though of his somewhat tedious propensity to diffidence. It was a smug modesty that most found quite repellent; encountering it early, and regularly, in any conversation with him.

'Will there be anything to return today, sir?' asked the delivery boy, who had remained standing by Weatherby's table in the lounge while he had read the telegram.

'No, No, I'm afraid all other acquaintances seem to have quite deserted me now,' Weatherby replied rattling his paper open loudly as the boy bowed briefly.

It was high summer, the last week in July; when Weatherby took his holiday. For the last fifteen years this had been taken at The Palace Hotel, Brighton—a town whose stately Victorian atmosphere had now degenerated, as Weatherby perceived it, into a populist morass of promenaders and seaside buffoons. He had loved to wander the pier each morning and evening, and even indulge himself with walks around the opulent pavilion. As the years had passed this one week had become more regular, with each day taken up with specific activities, until it had become as much a routine as his working life.

This year, however, Weatherby had elected to have a more extended rest at a different venue. After having read Hallam Tennyson's, *Tennyson, A Memoir*, he had become rather enthralled by the Isle of Wight. It seemed rather fitting that Queen Victoria had favoured the island with increased stays at Osbourne House in preference to the degradation of the Brighton tourist trap. So this year he had chosen The Royal Esplanade Hotel in Ryde as his destination. This time, rather than a week away he decided to take a month. With the publication of his book he had earned something of a sabbatical.

∞

The first week, as in any unfamiliar territory, was taken up becoming acquainted with the surroundings. Weatherby found Ryde itself to be a quaint town, with a serviceable bookshop and a number of curious emporiums trading in antiquities and memorabilia from across the empire.

He had not come to shop though but thought that towards the end of his stay he might find some items of interest to adorn his study. A coastal walk, which meandered south for many miles proved more than satisfactory for his requisite morning stroll. Even on these hot summer days the wind battered up against the cliffs making it a bracing and refreshing opportunity for after-breakfast reflection.

Weatherby had also visited other towns and villages mentioned in the Tennyson memoir. Shanklin, a small village on the south-east side had at first seemed idyllic. He had taken luncheon in a most agreeable inn and had taken the innkeeper's advice to follow the cliff-top walk that would then descend to a glorious beach. However, upon following this scenic route, which offered fine views across the sea and of the chalky cliff faces, he was disappointed to discover that the beach was quite awash with bathing machines and tourists of all sizes frolicking at the convergence of sea and land. Weatherby was not prudish; it was not the scene of bathing suits and naked legs that offended him. It was something more mean spirited in him; a sensibility that would see itself ploughed under soon by more liberal and fanciful ideologies. He merely resented people enjoying themselves. If there was no education to be had from a visit to a beach, or walk in the country, or no time for restful cerebration, then the exercise was vain and frivolous and to be abhorred. Bathing in the sea and cavorting on the sands fell firmly into this latter category of decadence and Weatherby was soon on the next carriage back to Ryde.

Newport had been a more interesting experience. He had enjoyed the short pier and the ordered arrangement of its town, with a wide market place dominated by the church spire. After a couple of hours there he had taken the steep walk up towards Carisbrooke where the ruins of the old castle overlooked the village. It was there that Charles I had been prisoner until his eventual execution and a gloomy atmosphere set in on his approach. This led to a thunderous storm from which Weatherby was forced to take shelter in the village. A wainwright at the inn offered to take him back to Ryde in his horse and trap, and Weatherby gratefully accepted.

During this first week, and with the onset of the storm that was to last for three days, Weatherby also became more familiar with the hotel and its guests. It was obvious that The Royal Esplanade had once been a family home, of some luxury, before being modified to accommodate guests. His room, number 86, was located on the third floor at the very height of the building. It had once been part of the servants' accommodation, as could be gathered by the sloping ceiling and the ungenerous size of the quarters and it was due to this that the room was offered at reduced rates. This fitted with Weatherby's parsimony and he was not dispirited by it. The room was adequately serviced otherwise, with an ample writing desk and sturdy chair, a large mahogany wardrobe and a comfortable single bed. Against the wall, by the door, there hung an enormous gilt mirror that reflected the entire room, beneath this there stood a low table spread with the periodicals and papers that Weatherby had requested be obtained for his stay. To the right of this table was an elegant Georgian wash stand with a wide bowl, unfortunately the water jug that accompanied this did not match and displayed some garish pastoral scene in a clumsy and faded blue glaze. The only other item in the room was a green wicker chair, positioned looking out towards the mainland. The wicker was quite worn and the seat crudely upholstered with a brownish paisley pattern that made it difficult to discern the grime from the motif. It also proved to be most uncomfortable due to badly distributed cushioning. From this seat though Weatherby had fine views afforded by two deep sash windows looking out across the sea towards Portsmouth. Another advantage of his residence on the third floor was the lack of guests plodding back and forth to their rooms at all hours. Altogether, and especially for the price, Weatherby was thoroughly contented with his situation.

The other guests in the hotel seemed a mixed crowd: a number of families on holiday who generally kept themselves to themselves, a small group of professional individuals who stayed for a day or two and then were gone again on business. There seemed to be a few residents of a more permanent capacity including an elderly medical Doctor by the name of Fisk, whose sanity Weatherby had suspected from the first evening when he had tried to engage him on a debate concerning the efficacy of leucotomy on deranged patients, not understanding, or listening to, Weatherby's protestations that he was a Doctor of philosophy and not medicine. After almost a full hour of a very one-sided debate Weatherby had excused himself and retired for the evening.

The next morning, at breakfast, he learned that the Doctor was something of a quack and had been barred from practising in London some years before. He had inherited a great deal of money though and had exiled himself to the Isle of Wight from where he wrote abusive letters to many of the finest Doctors in London. He was now rarely sober but was tolerated by the staff and most of the other guests as an eccentric addition to the hotel community. All this gossip was gathered from a Major Turnbull who dined on the table next to Weatherby. It was Turnbull who initiated the dialogue and divulged the information with the least pressure on Weatherby's part. Turnbull had observed Dr Fisk accost him the previous evening and merely tried to explain that he meant no harm.

During the course of that first week Weatherby and Major Turnbull became quite close friends and soon dined together, at breakfast and dinner, discussing the papers and world events. Turnbull had served throughout the Boer War, receiving a VC for bravery at the siege of Mafeking, and was now enjoying his retirement. He had never been married and had returned to Ryde five years before when his mother was taken ill at the family estate at Sandown. After she had passed away he sold the estate and elected to lodge here at The Royal Esplanade, feeling little inclined to keep the staff at the estate or to rattle around in 'a decaying old fortress' for any length of time. Life in the hotel was always interesting, he asserted; new people to meet and always a friendly member of staff to brighten the day. Turnbull was of similar politics to Weatherby, neither able to stand the new breed of liberalism and equality that now seemed so in vogue. They shared a belief in a social Darwinist model of racial supremacy promulgated in the 1880s and neither seemed equipped for the radical changes that the beginning of the century had brought. Whilst Turnbull was a great talker, he was not a bore. He could gauge when conversation was required and when it was not. So the two men complemented each other and also served to confirm, and deepen, their already worn out political obsessions.

Another of the more regular guests was a Mrs Fielding, wife of Charles Fielding: a wealthy botanist who was studying orchids on the banks of the Amazon. Mrs. Fielding was engaged in less dangerous research, she was cataloguing the rich variety of flora to be found in Parkhurst forest: a famous hunting ground of William the Conqueror. In particular she had identified an unusually rich and diverse selection of species at Firestone Copse. She was an amiable woman who took her work very seriously indeed. Her independence and forthright opinions shocked Weatherby, and by default Turnbull, for their ingenuity and radicalism. Whilst most of the guests were confined to the hotel for the duration of the storm she became the focus for some spirited debates concerning poverty, women's suffrage and the plight of the colonies. Weatherby and Turnbull decided that she was best humoured for the sake of the contentment of all concerned.

By the Friday of his first week Weatherby was well settled in and had found those with whom he could converse, and those with whom it was best to merely pass the time of day. Mrs. Fielding had advised him that Godshill would be a favourable destination for the Saturday, should the weather improve. She said he would enjoy the fine views afforded from the church that stood upon an ancient hill at the centre of the village. Major Turnbull had agreed noting that it contained a unique mural on the East wall of the South transept. This depicted a large figure of Christ crucified on a lily cross, and was believed to be the only remaining wall painting of its kind in Britain. That evening Weatherby retired, amidst the fury of the storm, which rattled and whistled at his windows, content that should tomorrow be fine he would be well served by a visit to this Godshill church.

∞

That night Alexander Weatherby slept very fitfully. The rain broke against his windows like volleys of shot from some old Spanish galleon come to pillage the island. He was continually woken by the casement as it was battered back and forth by the storm. The wind seemed to swirl and gather itself, forced forward in the interstice between each barrage of rain. At just gone midnight he had had enough and lit a candle. He considered reading some of the proceedings of the Harleian Society Annual General Meeting which he had received that morning and had not yet had chance to examine. Firstly, he decided, it would be prudent to attempt to arrest the wretched noise. To this effect he found a piece of cloth, from some ripped sheet, in the wardrobe and resolved to try to plug the gaps in the window to stop it rattling. Drawing back the curtains he saw the wild foam flying as the ocean endured the onslaught of the elements. The moon was nearly full and the clouds now seemed to be thinning having spent most of their watery fury now. The moonlight illuminated the long sea front with a glistening bluish gleam.

Weatherby began to push the rag into the wide gap between window and sill but after only a few moments a great gust blew his candle out. He was able to see perfectly well though and continued to plug the gap as best he could. Soon there seemed to be only the dullest of mumbles as the window pushed back and forth against its new padding. He would certainly be able to rest now. It was then though that the most unnerving feeling came across him. It must be recalled that Dr Weatherby was by no means a superstitious man, in fact he liked to call himself a political scientist. Any suggestion of a supernatural event was usually greeted with a snort of derision from him if it merited any response. However, he was sure that someone was watching him. Not from the street below, but from behind, in his own room. He turned around slowly in the pale light of the moon and allowed his eyes to become accustomed to the gloom within. There was nobody there. Of course there was nobody there, he had turned the key himself on the inside of the door, a habit which he had developed when a student at Oxford and one which he had continued to this day even at home.

He walked steadily back towards the bed, intent on relighting his candle and reading until drowsy. As his stubby fingers fumbled for the matches he glanced over at the large mirror and thought to himself how dark it looked. Standing as he was, almost in the centre of the room he could see how most of the room was bright with light from the window; the curtain to which he had not redrawn. The mirror did not seem to reflect this though. He struck a match, lit the measly wick and gradually approached the mirror in his tattered night-shirt.

The scene he beheld was extraordinary. He stood only a few feet from the surface of the mirror but it neither reflected the light he held nor even his own form, or even that of any of the furnishings of the room which, on turning, he confirmed were all alight with the pale luminescence of the moon's ambient glow. Instead the scene that greeted him was a bizarre duplicate of the room in which he now stood. It was shadowy and dull, the forms of the bed, writing desk, wardrobe and washbasin could be dimly made out by concentration, but there was no reflection of the odd wicker chair which he had found so uncomfortable. As he peered more carefully inside he gained the impression that he was looking into some kind of attic room, each of the furnishings having been carefully covered in dust sheets now dark with dirt. He shivered at the peculiarly familiar feel of the mirror scene, but also at its aberrant unnaturalness. He had stood there for only a few seconds, it seemed, before the feeling came over him again that he was being watched, not from behind this time, but as though he gazed directly into the eyes of some malevolent stranger intent on some injurious action. So strong was this feeling that he was forced to break his gaze from the mirror and rush to unlock the door, behind which he bolted, extinguishing the candle as he did so.

The hallway was quiet, only the ticking of a great grandfather clock on the landing below his room betrayed that he was not dreaming. The flight of stairs atop which his room was located was the last in the building and the door opposite was not numbered. He had seen the maid entering with clean linen a few times during the week and he presumed it must be a store cupboard. His room was, therefore, the last in the hotel and the building's geometry was such that it could not afford some view into an adjacent room; as through some two way mirror. Composing himself Weatherby reasoned that his nerves had been affected by his restless sleep and perhaps the intense brightness of the moonlight had altered his retina in some bizarre manner.

He entered his room again, paused a moment before relighting the candle and then turned briskly and boldly towards the mirror. He chuckled to himself, more with relief than with the plain confirmation that everything was as it should be. For there was the room reflected perfectly in the magisterial gilt frame, complete with wicker chair and also the image of what he thought to be a rather shabby and unkempt individual carrying a candle. For a moment he was startled before realizing that it was in fact himself, the comprehension of which brought forth a loud guffaw from the normally sedate Dr Weatherby. He berated himself for 'such nonsense' and resolved that a visit to the barbers was the first order of the day before venturing to Godshill.

∞

Weatherby awoke late the next morning feeling quite unwell. He was usually a very solid sleeper and the events that night had disturbed his regular eight hours sleep. Consequently he was the last to arrive for breakfast, in a despicable humour. Major Turnbull was just finishing his tea and about to retire to the lounge to read his paper when Weatherby stormed into the dining room pulling on his jacket as he came.

'Good Morning, Dr Weatherby,' began the Major genially. 'I trust you *weathered* the storm.' He chuckled at the forced pun.

'A good morning it is not, Major Turnbull,' replied Weatherby gruffly, gesturing for a waiter to attend him.

'I'm sorry to hear that, damned noisy last night I know,' the Major continued, trying to lift the mood. 'Nothing like the storms you could expect in the Transvaal though. Not a drop for months and then the deluge...'

'If you will excuse me Major I am ill disposed, this morning, for any sort of small talk,' Weatherby said dismissively, opening his copy of *The Times* without a glance at his friend. 'I need a little space in which to compose myself. I am little used, as you can tell, to a disturbed rest and would prefer to take a light, *quiet*, breakfast.'

The Major shrugged, noticeably offended, and departed in the direction of the lounge. Once Weatherby was sure he had gone he lowered his paper and placed his order for lightly poached eggs and tea. The dining room was still, a little murmur of conversation filtered through from the lounge but Weatherby noted how unusually quiet it seemed. He looked out through the great bay windows and noticed how calm the sea was, as flat as a newly pressed sheet. The morning was a bright, light blue and the sky carried thin trails of misty cloud as scars of the previous night's onslaught.

Weatherby jumped as a hand touched his shoulder. It was the waiter who had brought his breakfast. He flinched back as Weatherby reacted.

'Sorry, Sir, are you all right?' the lad enquired.

'Of course I'm all right,' Weatherby grumbled, slightly embarrassed to have been caught in some kind of reverie. 'Your accursed bedding and the wretched state of disrepair of my room have kept me up half the night. Apart from that I'm perfectly fine.'

'I'm sorry to hear that. I shall mention it to Miss De Lisle,' the waiter replied.

'Yes, you do so. Nail the damned window shut if necessary to stop the infernal rattling,' Weatherby said, stabbing contemptuously at his eggs with a fork.

'Will that be all, Sir,' the waiter asked, bowing.

'Call a carriage for me, to go to Godshill,' Weatherby said, cooling slightly.

'Very good, Sir,' he said retreating to reception.

Weatherby pushed his plate away and poured some tea. For a few minutes he turned the pages of his paper mechanistically, he eyes hovering on the blur of print as each page passed. He was occupied in considering the real causes of last night's incident with the mirror. He presumed that the angle of positioning may account for the phenomenon, for he was little disposed to admit the fault might have been with his own eyes. He shook his head as though to clear away such befuddled thoughts and alighted on the obituaries; a section of the paper he read with keen interest. No notable reformers or fuzzy liberals today, he thought, shame.

Tucking the paper under his arm, and draining the last of his tea Weatherby made his way to reception to enquire what might be done of his complaints. As ever the petite figure of Miss De Lisle was there feverishly collating, stamping and filing documents. Weatherby had frequently seen her engaged in this activity during the week and he wondered what could produce such mountains of paperwork for her to be so occupied. She glanced up from the desk and noted his presence with a nod. She lifted a great heap of documents and whisked them across to a smaller table on which six great spikes were positioned. She impaled the papers on the furthest spike from her in a gesture that Weatherby found rather uncomfortable. She rose and bustled towards him with a great rustling of crinoline and lace.

'Good morning Dr Weatherby,' she began with a wide smile. 'I understand your sleep was disturbed last night.' Weatherby made to speak here but Miss de Lisle continued raising a hand. 'No, no, Dr Weatherby it is our responsibility to see that our guests are kept in the best of comforts. We shall change your mattress and I shall see to it that the caretaker attends to the window at the first opportunity.'

Miss De Lisle had a habit of disarming her most bellicose guests, leaving them flushed with confidence in her abilities as Hotel proprietress. This was the state in which Weatherby now found himself and he stood for a few moments quite unable to muster any kind of response to her efficiency, so used was he, in the many establishments he had stayed in, to state his case clearly and forcefully to some member of staff (and usually a number of times) before any action was forthcoming.

'Well… er… yes,' he stammered, greeted in return by her broad smile and inclined posture, eager as it seemed to accommodate any other complaint he might propose. 'Very good and might I compliment you on the efficient organisation that you run here. It has been a pleasure to see such a methodical approach from a… er… a hotel.' Weatherby was, of course, going to mention her membership of the fairer sex but thought better of it, recalling the brutal impaling of the paperwork a few moments before. Her face clouded a little as she realized the blunder that he had almost fallen into. Searching for some other issue with which he might prolong, divert, or end the engagement Weatherby enquired into the nature of the third floor of the hotel.

'There are no other rooms on my floor are there Miss De Lisle?' he asked, moving over to a large and ornately calligraphed family tree that hung, beautifully framed, by reception.

'No, Dr Weatherby, why do you ask?' she replied, a little nervously he thought.

'I merely wondered what lay beyond the door opposite my room,' he said, removing his pince-nez to examine the genealogical chart more closely.

'It is nothing but a store cupboard for the hotel linen. Is there something else that troubles you?' she asked, with a developing edge of urgency.

'Oh, no, not at all. I thought it was a store, having seen the maids going in and out performing their duties,' Weatherby replied, happy to have regained control of the exchange.

'Oh, good,' she offered, with some relief, 'because I hope you feel sure that if there are any problems we will be…'

'No, Miss De Lisle,' Weatherby interrupted. 'Everything else is more than satisfactory.'

'Are you interested in family histories, Dr Weatherby?' she asked, gesturing to the chart which he was examining.

'No, not particularly, it just seems a beautifully presented piece, wonderfully drawn,' he responded.

'Yes, it took my grandfather four years to compile and draw. As you can see down there it doesn't record his death: Ambrose March-Phillips de Lisle,' she said, pointing towards the bottom of the chart. Weatherby bent down and found the name, born 17th March 1809, married Laura Mary Clifford 25th July 1833.

'Yes, I see,' Weatherby said, recalling the family name. 'Wasn't there an estate in Leicestershire?'

'Why, yes there is Dr Weatherby,' she said, pleased that he was familiar with her family. 'Grace Dieu Manor, it is a wonderful building. My brother owns it now.'

'When did your grandfather pass away then Miss De Lisle?' Weatherby asked.

'March 1878, I had considered adding it to the tree, along with my father and other aunts and uncles,' she explained. 'As you can see there were sixteen children from the marriage. However, I have decided to begin a new tree rather than disturb this one.'

The main doors of the hotel opened and a driver strode in towards the reception.

'A carriage for Dr Weatherby,' the driver called to Miss De Lisle.

'I shall be there presently,' Weatherby said and the driver returned to the carriage. 'Yes, I think it a wise choice to begin again, there is no knowing what damage new inks might do to the quality of this one. If you will excuse me then Miss De Lisle, it has been a fascinating conversation and one that I hope to resume again during my stay.'

'I wish you an interesting day Dr Weatherby,' she said as he took his overcoat and stick from the stand.

Weatherby informed the driver that he wished to visit Godshill and was told it would be a two hour drive. He was content enough with this having taken paper and pen with which to write a sort of journal of his visit. With a jolt they were away and soon Weatherby felt himself becoming drowsy with the rhythmic clopping of the horse's hooves and the fresh sea air.

∞

He awoke some time later and observed that the carriage had become altogether gloomier; outside a thick mist had descended, entirely obscuring the surrounding countryside. The carriage came to a gentle rest and the driver appeared at the window, startling Weatherby for a moment.

'What seems to be the trouble?' Weatherby asked, sliding the window down further.

'I'll just have to light the lamps, with this fog, sir,' the driver replied. 'It should only take a moment. We're about halfway there.' The driver retired, buttoning his coat against the chilly mist.

After a few minutes the carriage was away again, and Weatherby was writing a few notes about Ryde. He peered absent-mindedly at the white shrouds drifting past the windows—as though the vehicle were gliding through clouds—and was soon asleep again.

He came to with a frantic urgency, his body shaking with a panicked urge to flee. Looking outside it seemed the mists were thinning and occasional cottages loomed and vanished again. They must be nearly at Godshill, he thought. His alarm on waking had seemed to occur from some dream he had been having, which now nudged suggestively—but elusively—at the limits of his consciousness. He looked down at his paper and saw, to his horror, a ragged trail of half-formed words etched across the page in chaotic fashion. It was, without a doubt, his own handwriting—albeit distorted and deranged—and that familiarity provided further horror for Weatherby as he deciphered their matter. It appeared that he had repeatedly written, in a spidery palimpsest, 'the face, the voice, from room 89.' Poor Weatherby hadn't the slightest idea what on earth this meant, or what shadowy dream-thought might have provoked it. The style of the script—whilst certainly his own—reminded him of the degenerate practice of automatic writing which had become popularised by mediums, fortune tellers and other repugnant charlatans. He had been present at one of these 'séances' given by Lady Lambert in Kensington, and had proved for himself that it was mere quackery. To be confronted by a similar event, here in his very lap, was most disconcerting. He was about to call for the driver to return to Ryde, when the door was opened by the man.

'We're here, sir: Godshill,' he said, unfolding the carriage steps.

Weatherby was desperate to hide the paper from him, and in his hurry to crumple it he managed to drop the entire contents of his small case. Periodicals and papers slid across the floor and his fountain pen only narrowly avoided having the nib broken.

'I'm sorry, sir, did I startle you?' the driver asked, beginning to gather some of the articles together.

Weatherby merely nodded, relieved to have maintained a grasp on the infernal sheet of paper, which he now slid into his pocket as the driver collected the last of his things and put them on the seat opposite him.

As he alighted Weatherby saw that the mists had almost cleared and he was granted a wonderful view of a square Norman church high on a steep hill rising from the centre of a huddle of thatched cottages that formed the main part of the village. The driver had stopped opposite The Red Lion Inn which seemed, even at this early hour, to be the lively hub of village life.

'Wait for me here,' Weatherby said, composing himself. 'My visit will be short for it is only the church that interests me.'

'Certainly, sir,' the driver replied. 'I shall wait for you in the inn.'

Weatherby nodded and strode off purposefully in the direction of the hill. A series of steep steps led upwards from a side lane and seemed to head towards the church grounds. Weatherby followed these, noticing that the chill from the fog still lingered. Halfway up he buttoned his coat against the cold and gained his breath. On reaching the summit he was rewarded by a fine view across the surrounding countryside, whose gentle hills rose from the wisps of mist that persisted in the valleys and hollows. The brightening sun would soon clear those vapours and Weatherby thought the scene would be much improved after he had visited the church itself.

Before heading for the porch Weatherby took a moment to wander a way around the tower to take in some of the outer structure. On the uppermost stage of the tower he noticed a series of ornate pinnacles and on the South-west of these a grotesque carving leered out at him. It depicted a bearded face with bared teeth and wide, staring eyes. It seemed quite a curious adornment for it appeared to be quite the only feature of such ornament anywhere on the tower and the asymmetry it gave to the building seemed most irregular. He headed back round and entered the porch where he found a massive mediaeval door whose sturdy surface was studded with large nails. He struggled a moment with the stiff latch but finally gained admittance.

What struck Weatherby most was the bright and spacious feel of the church. He was also impressed by the impact of a large and colourful Rood Beam which depicted the figures of Our Lady and St John. Also of interest was the double nave which was separated by an arcade of six bays. Weatherby's main intention was to see the Lily Cross recommended to him by Major Turnbull and so he headed first to the South transept where it was located. An ornate iron grating divided the South transept from the rest of the church and it had a large, rusted, padlock to secure it. Through the twisted iron bars Weatherby could see the pale and strange painting of Christ, crucified on a triple-branched flowering lily. Despite its great antiquity the gentle green of the flower, and the delicate hue of Christ's skin could clearly be seen. It was undoubtedly a very peculiar and intriguing work and Weatherby was certain he had never encountered its like before.

He wandered both naves leisurely before heading for the North transept where no bars prevented his access. The area had been rebuilt in some pompous Classical style with marble busts either side of a small altar and the whole surmounted by a military trophy. Weatherby found the entire effect rather conceited but could find no clue to those that had built it other than their initials, R.W. and H.W. emblazoned over each of the busts. He decided to head back to the main church to sign the visitors' book which had lain open on a table as he entered.

After a cursory glance over the last few entries, placed there over the last few weeks Weatherby entered his own comments in a flowing confident script: '31st July, 1910. Enchanting views from the hill and interesting mural of obvious cultural value. Whole effect slightly spoiled by somewhat obscure and indulgent modern addition to the North Transept, Dr Alexander Weatherby—political scientist.' Content that he had established the right tone of commendation for the works of antiquity and mockery of modern affectation Weatherby began leafing through the previous comments to confirm his own analysis. Amidst the awed praise and tourist celebration he could not find a single interesting comment until he arrived at an entry from exactly one year previously. It read: '31st July, 1909. Enchanting views from the hill and interesting mural of obvious cultural value. Whole effect slightly spoiled by somewhat obscure and indulgent modern addition to the North Transept, Wilfred Jarry—political reformer.' Quite apart from the bizarre iteration of words it was the name of the individual who had written them that most concerned Weatherby. Wilfred Jarry was the most radical of contemporary political agitators, always involved in some faddish scheme or other to reform working rights, to change whole social systems which had run (very effectively in Weatherby's opinion) for centuries. To find his own words copied by such a man infuriated Weatherby to the point of apoplexy. However, as he soon realised, Weatherby's statement had not been copied by Jarry, but in fact the reverse was the case—or so it would appear to anyone reading the entries chronologically. This fuelled his anger even further and he hurriedly turned back to his entry with a view to striking it through so that none would be able to discover the eerie echo. Calming slightly it seemed to him that this course of action would not be entirely satisfactory, for however much he scribbled it would not completely erase the evidence and a great blemish of black ink would be sure to raise suspicion—and therefore an attempt to uncover the words which lay beneath. No, the only sure method of obliteration lay in the removal of the entire page from the visitor's book. This, unfortunately, meant the removal of almost a month of previous comments, but the price of a few vanished tourist burblings did not concern him too much. As Weatherby took the page firmly, and gazed about a few times to confirm that there was no stern gaze watching his desecration, he tugged the paper from its binding with a loud tear accompanied by a guilty cough on his behalf—as though to disguise the sacrilege from the ears of the Almighty, whose home he was now defiling. Weatherby headed for the heavy door with eyes cast down, like some sheepish schoolboy retreating from scornful admonition, and hurriedly exited the church.

He crumpled the page into his pocket as he ventured into the brightening daylight that now illumined the churchyard as though to highlight the fugitive. He took the exit straight ahead which led down a steep flight of crooked steps back to the village. Their mossy overgrowth suggested that the villagers used this pathway, although more direct, infrequently. Weatherby gripped the decaying wooden rail to give himself some support in the descent. Within a couple of minutes he was back at the inn, expecting the driver to have somehow guessed that he was ready to depart. It was still barely past midday and Weatherby waited a moment outside the squat thatched building. After composing himself for a few moments he knocked loudly on the door. A hush came over the voices, which had previously been quite audibly animated at his approach. The landlord opened the door, smiling through a thick brown beard.

'You're welcome to come in, sir, there's no need to knock,' he said, with a brief ripple of laughter applauding him from behind.

'I have no need to enter,' Weatherby replied sternly. 'Could you tell my driver that I am ready to depart now.'

'Certainly, sir,' the innkeeper bowed, rather too low and with somewhat fake affect Weatherby thought. 'I shall send him out immediately.'

The driver appeared quite quickly, rushing over to the carriage where Weatherby now stood by the steps to the compartment.

'Sorry, sir,' he said, pulling on his greatcoat and adjusting his cap. 'I thought you might be sometime longer than you have been.'

'I have seen all I wished to,' Weatherby said. 'Now, I think it will be straight back to Ryde, as speedily as possible. There is some urgent business I must attend to.'

The driver nodded as he opened the door and unfolded the steps for Weatherby. Within a few minutes the carriage had turned and headed back at a jolting pace for Ryde. With the number of strange coincidences and odd events of the previous evening, and that morning, Weatherby did not feel inclined to doze but merely gazed out of the window at the green and brown patches of land that slid past, attempting to find some adequate explanation for these occurrences.

∞

After paying the driver, without a tip as was his custom, Weatherby headed into the hotel to find Major Turnbull. He was, as usual, to be found in the lounge digesting every word of the paper. Weatherby sat in the creaking leather armchair opposite him, feeling quite uncertain of how to begin.

'Afternoon, Weatherby,' Turnbull called from behind the paper, still somewhat put out by the surly mood Weatherby had offered him that morning.

'Good afternoon, Major, I trust you have had a pleasant morning,' Weatherby offered in an attempt to appease him.

'Why yes, it has been quite enjoyable,' Turnbull said, lowering the paper. He was not the sort of man disposed to unpleasantness and with this *almost* apology he considered the matter to be done with. 'I've certainly given every page a thorough analysis and found it all to want some rather serious remedial action.'

They both laughed for a moment, perhaps at the realisation that the world was quite outpacing their own antiquated involvement in it.

'I trust you had an interesting trip to Godshill,' The Major enquired, filling a pipe from a faded leather pouch. 'Did you see the Lily Christ?'

'Yes, I saw it from some distance. A locked gate barred my entrance however and I could only peer through at it,' Weatherby said, wishing to discuss the issue of Jarry's presence at the church.

'Oh, I know, quite unfortunate really. The vicar had to lock it up after some of the villagers began talk of moving it back to its *rightful place*, whatever that might mean,' Turnbull said through puffs of his pipe.

'Well, that is a shame,' Weatherby said, not in the least concerned for the mural or its fate. 'I was wondering if you had heard of that agitator Wilfred Jarry.' At the mention of this name Major Turnbull looked quite surprised and leaned forward in his chair expectantly.

'What, have you seen him then?' he asked urgently.

'No, not seen him, but noticed that he was here last year,' Weatherby replied, interested in the Major's sudden interest in this fellow. 'He had signed the visitors' book at Godshill church and I wondered if you'd encountered the rogue during his stay here.'

Major Turnbull sat for a while, sucking on his pipe, which had now extinguished itself. He looked concerned, and glanced over at Weatherby guiltily.

'I haven't mentioned what happened last year to you?' he asked, genuinely puzzled that this information had not been shared with Weatherby. 'I mean, what *happened* to Jarry when he was staying here?'

'He stayed here did he, indeed?' Weatherby said indignantly, as though the man were unfit to room in even a pigsty.

'I should have told you about it before, considering our shared political positions,' the Major said. 'Well, perhaps it was just that, such common ground, so many topics to discuss, that meant it quite slipped my mind. He stayed in the room you now occupy, about the same time last year I think it was.' The look on Weatherby's face was as one who has just discovered his home to have been used as a brothel beneath his very nose.

'He arrived with a big trunk of books and papers, making quite a fuss about how it was to be carefully carried to the room,' Turnbull continued. 'He announced at reception that he was going to be staying for quite some time, that his genealogical research had brought him here and he would remain for some months until it was concluded. Well, Miss De Lisle—amiable and welcoming as she is—took an immediate dislike to the man; as did most of the other guests. I was, of course, familiar with his brand of soapbox revolutionism but there seemed to be something else quite repellent about his complacency—as though it were aimed at making Miss De Lisle uncomfortable. If that was its purpose then it certainly succeeded for she was always wary, and watchful, of him and seemed quite unable to talk to him about her family history—which is why he had come here—or even to look him in the eye as he passed in the hallway.'

Here Major Turnbull stopped and attempted the relighting of his pipe. Weatherby was eager to hear more and leaned forward in anticipation. The Major took out his pocket watch, and ever able to pace and time a good story he interjected here with an aside calculated to heighten the impact of the tale.

'I know its early Weatherby, only just gone one o'clock, but I could fancy a brandy, how about you?' Turnbull asked, rising and ringing a small bell on the mantelpiece to call for service.

'No, not for me please, I'm afraid that with the journey it would send me quite to sleep,' he said. 'But, please continue, while we wait for someone to come.'

'Certainly, old fellow, where was I?' the Major said settling back into the chair. 'Ah, yes, Miss De Lisle couldn't abide the fellow, and as I say I was already set against him from the start. The strange thing is that his arrogance actually led him to believe me some kind of confidant to whom he could unload all kind of bizarre ideas he had floating in that bog of a mind. Of course, not being one to alert the enemy of my animosity until I have fully reconnoitred his offensive capabilities I was not going to let on that I was other than a sound ally.'

The Major paused here a moment to confirm that his stance had been morally sound rather than plain nosy. Weatherby obliged with a courteous: 'Why naturally, of course.'

'It seemed that amidst his dubious political preachings and half-baked theories he had some interest in matters of religion, or should I say of old religions,' the Major continued, waving his pipe with authority. 'You know the stuff, ancestor worship, trees and druids and other sorts of occult poppycock.'

It was at this point that the tale was interrupted by the waiter who asked what they required.

'Yes, my boy,' Turnbull broke from his story. 'Could you bring me a brandy, please. Now you're sure you won't have one Weatherby?' A slow shaking head was his reply. 'Well, just the one for me then, better make it a large one to save troubling you again.'

'Very good, Sir,' the lad replied.

'Jarry had some kind of occult interest, you were saying,' Weatherby began, in an attempt to get the Major back to the heart of the matter with as much haste as possible.

'Yes, a most unhealthy interest in it to be sure,' Turnbull continued. 'Well, all of us here saw the effects on him within a couple of weeks. He started looking very pale and unkempt. Hardly seemed to shave, and always seemed to turn out in the same set of clothes, which after his frequent walks in the countryside were becoming torn and muddy. I almost mentioned it to Miss De Lisle in case she could coerce some change in his habits, but considering her own dislike of the fellow I let the matter rest.

Well, after the first few days he had confided quite some amount of his interest in Miss De Lisle and her family. He had apparently uncovered some kind of evidence—pah! What *evidence*?—that her father was involved in some kind of Catholic heretical cult which dabbled in some form of ancestral soul exchange! These were his *own* words Weatherby—I'm not making this up, as preposterous as it sounds.'

'No, I'm sure you're not, but what exactly brought him to this hotel?' Weatherby asked.

'Well, Jarry had known some chap who was involved in some queer goings on at the estate owned by Miss De Lisle's father: Grace Dieu Manor. This chap had informed Jarry that after some terrible evening at the manor Ambrose De Lisle had fled here to the Isle of Wight to escape some terrible fate that would consume his family. What this was, Jarry would not detail precisely, but it involved some artefact that could "bridge the shadow-world" as he put it. So the De Lisles came here and soon after her father's death Miss De Lisle's mother, Laura, converted it into a hotel after she returned to the manor house. Jarry had come here to find out about this artefact and any other information he could draw from Miss De Lisle—the insidious little pest! Of course, at the first opportunity I communicated his dishonourable intentions to Miss De Lisle who said she would be on her guard in the future. Well the dislike between the two of them became even more apparent over the few days that followed and Jarry looked even more dishevelled than usual. Then one night, pop! He disappeared.' This last line was delivered with great gesticulation from the Major and coincided with the arrival of his brandy.

'What do you mean, he disappeared?' asked poor Weatherby, increasingly perplexed.

'Why just that, Dr,' Major Turnbull said after a large gulp of his drink. 'The chap just vanished. All his belongings were there in the room, all the wretched books strewn around the place and clothes everywhere. I was one of the first into the room. Miss De Lisle had to call a locksmith out to chisel the lock. He'd locked the thing from the inside. Better than Houdini he must have been Dr Weatherby: to have crawled out of a third floor window in just his night gown and vanished off the face of the earth.'

'What happened to his belongings, the books and papers?' Weatherby asked urgently.

'I think Miss De Lisle kept charge of them, in case he returned. In fact, that wicker chair in your room belonged to him, apparently he couldn't write anything without being seated in his *favourite* chair,' the Major pondered. 'Of course, she'd have every right to sell the lot because he left his bill unpaid you know.'

Weatherby nodded in agreement. The Major was packing another pipe, quite contented at having delivered an adequate performance of one of the more spooky tales in his burgeoning repertoire.

'Please excuse me Major,' Weatherby said as he stood. 'Thank you for a very interesting piece of information. I must go and enquire about my room with Miss De Lisle.'

'Certainly Weatherby, see you at dinner,' Turnbull replied, turning back to his paper.

∞

Weatherby waited in the hallway a few minutes. There was no one at reception, which was highly unusual. It had almost felt as though Miss De Lisle ate and slept there for never before had he encountered the area without her managerial presence. Finally he gave the bell on the desk a sharp tap and the shrill pitched note echoed a few moments before the step of her purposeful shoes and tired sigh of many layered skirts could be heard advancing from the dining room.

'I'm sorry to have kept you Dr Weatherby, how may I be of assistance,' she announced after taking her place behind her desk.

'I wondered if you might still have some of Mr Wilfred Jarry's documents that I might be able to see?' Weatherby asked, entirely unsure as to how she might view such a request.

'Mr Jarry,' she said, pausing a moment as though to affect an attempt at remembering him. Weatherby, a keen observer of the way people pretend to each other was not in the least fooled but thought it rather odd nonetheless—perhaps she wished to distance herself, and consequently the hotel, from any involvement in the disappearance. 'Yes, the gentleman who left so rudely last year leaving his bill unsettled. I believe his belongings are now in the cellar. What is your interest in them?'

'Well, I... I thought,' Weatherby stammered, uncertain of his own motives for wishing to see any of Jarry's papers. 'It is just that some of my own interests seem to have somewhat overlapped with his and I thought there may be something of interest to be found there.'

'It seems rather unusual to me Dr Weatherby,' she replied, flicking through a few invoices on the desk. Then her tone changed from icy distance to sudden friendliness, a change that threw Weatherby off his guard completely. 'If you wish to view his papers then I'm sure I can trust in your confidence over any details you might find there. I shall have one of the boys fetch the trunk in the morning.'

All set to put his point more forcefully and suddenly greeted with such an immediate acquiescence he stood for a moment unable to say anything.

'Will that be satisfactory, Dr Weatherby?' Miss De Lisle asked, glancing up at him.

'Yes, Miss De Lisle, thank you, that will be most satisfactory,' he replied, nodding automatically.

'You will also be pleased to know that your window has been fixed and the mattress changed for one of more even padding. I hope that you rest well in it this evening,' she said, turning to another pile of documents.

'Why thank you again for your, your…' Weatherby paused a moment, '…efficiency.' With that he made his way up to his room to formulate some ideas concerning exactly what it was that he wished to discover in Jarry's trunk.

As he wandered towards the final short flight of stairs that led to his room Weatherby fumbled in his pockets for his key and found it beneath the crumpled paper on which his hand had scribbled those odd words and into which he had also crammed the page from Godshill Church's visitor's book. Still feeling ashamed for this action he glanced back into the hall to check that nobody pursued him for that crime. He turned to his door and fitted the key in the latch. The bronze numbers that designated the room read 'Room 89' and he stopped a moment, concerned that he had taken some wrong turn. Yet his was the last room in the hotel, Room 86, he could not possibly have been mistaken; there was no room 89 in the hotel. On closer inspection he understood what had happened. The stud that held the upper curve of the 6 in place had come loose allowing the numeral to slide round to its present position – becoming 89, with the 9 positioned slightly lower than the 8. The whole place was falling apart Weatherby thought moodily. He would inform Miss De Lisle of the problem in the morning.

With all the fresh air, and the Major's story, Weatherby must have fallen asleep on his new mattress for when he awoke it was quite dark in his room. He felt quite disoriented by such a sudden and long sleep and he fumbled to light a candle to check the time. It was past midnight. He had slept through the entire afternoon and most of the evening, missing dinner as well. All of it had been due to the previous night's restlessness. He resolved that by spending the rest of the night asleep he might recover those energies which were now so out of balance. He changed grumpily into his night shirt, annoyed at having missed dinner; a dinner that he had paid for. Before climbing into the bed he remembered to turn the key in the door as he had done all these years.

∞

Perhaps it was hours, or only a few minutes, later that Weatherby awoke. The room was in darkness but he could hear something; it was a faint, but steady, whispering. Thinking initially that the window had not been repaired properly and that some infernal draft was causing it Weatherby hastened to the window muttering to himself about incompetence and laziness in the working classes. On checking the window he found that it had been stoutly hammered shut with long nails and that not the slightest breath of air seemed to be issuing from it.

Then the odd notion came over him, as it had the previous evening that someone watched him from behind. His skin crept, a feeling that must, obviously, have been due to a sudden coldness in the room. He whirled around, breathing heavily. There was, again, nothing to be seen. Precisely that in fact, for he gazed into the mirror on the other side of the room and it reflected nothing at all, merely a solid black surface which rippled gently like some lake reflecting a dark sky, stirred by a gentle breeze. It was also then, as he stood still and afraid, that he could discern the origin of that persistent murmur he had heard on waking. It was coming from the mirror. He approached on shaking legs and the sound seemed to increase by tiny fractions as he came nearer. The surface of the mirror was still and black but Weatherby felt some curious urge to examine it—no doubt a scientific propensity. But there are other things that fascinate besides the ordinary ticking and tocking of this world's machinery; matters that speak to our dark and corrupt souls, things that promise and threaten at the same time. Such a thing spoke to Dr Weatherby at the instant that—against his reason and the pounding ache of his terrified heart—he touched that moist black surface undulating with delicate alien waves of movement. He felt a sigh rush past him, as though all the last breaths of humanity's legion of dead had been collected into one.

He knew then that he was on the other side of the glass.

There behind him was a dim room, similar to that he had occupied just moments before, pervaded by a feeble grey light which seemed to have no discernible source. All items were there; the bed, writing desk, wardrobe and washbasin, but no wicker chair. Looking into the mirror from here he saw his few books and periodicals on the desk, the clothes he had quickly changed from a little time before and a figure crouched by the wicker chair rocking maniacally back and forth. It was a man with a long beard and hands that were torn and broken, completely destroyed as if from repeated blows. It was then that Weatherby began to bang his own, for now intact, fists against the glass. It was of no use, the figure beyond did not cease from his incessant backwards and forwards motion, and the mirror would not break. Weatherby decided that a stout blow from the chair by the writing desk would reunite him with that human space beyond, but as he grasped the edge of the seat his hands glided through air. Those shadowy moonlit objects that inhabited the place he now dwelt in were mere simulacra, or hazy ideals, of that which existed in the room he had left: his room. As the hours passed Weatherby tried everything until his bruised and tired body slumped finally to the ground before the shadow mirror that so tortuously reflected the real.

∞

Weatherby awoke in that grim grey world some hours later and found that the mirror revealed a bright day beyond. The man, now obviously a gibbering and insane Wilfred Jarry, was still there rocking and muttering. Finally as he stood in silent wonder at the scene beyond, Major Turnbull and Miss De Lisle, accompanied by an ordinary looking man with hammer and chisel entered that room beyond. The Major was obviously appalled and gathered some of Weatherby's own clothes to cover Jarry, who seemed neither to acknowledge their existence nor shield himself from their gaze. Miss De Lisle gave the locksmith a few coins and turned to the mirror to check her hair (as always, neatly gathered into a bun at the top). Weatherby leaped at the loathsome glass, smashing his knuckles against its cold surface and screaming as loudly as he could endure. But few people can hear the voices from other worlds, although Weatherby was sure he saw Miss De Lisle incline her head slightly and smile, as though watching a small child at play.

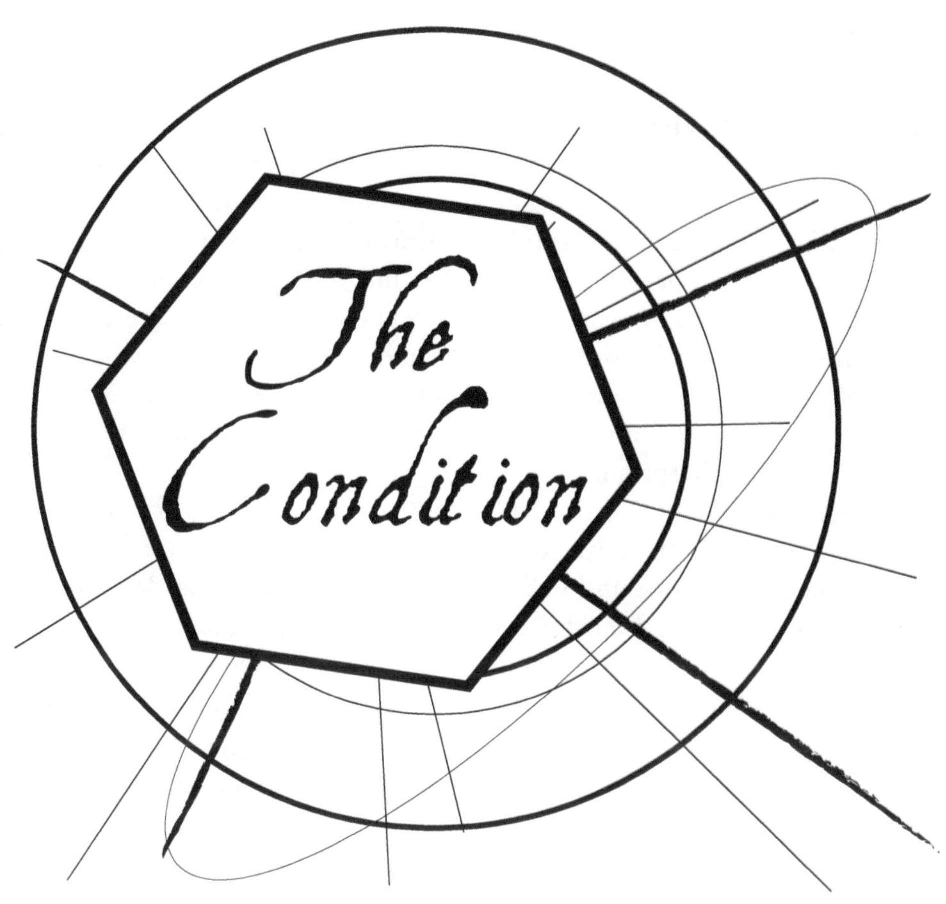

The Condition

'All art constantly aspires towards the condition of music.'
Walter Pater, *The Renaissance*

I had not been back in the country long, but long enough to have felt the faint oppression of that malaise which had forced my departure three years before. To have received a letter from Bertram Wilson was the last thing I was expecting. We had been good friends at school—quite contrary to our interests—but had not maintained the friendship after leaving. I had been a precocious and arrogant exile from my peers. My interest in Eastern antiquities and anthropology had always ensured my exclusion from the mainstream pursuits of my contemporaries. Bertram Wilson was quite the opposite; a keen cricketer, the head prefect and a member of the national badminton team. He was everything that I could never be, nor wanted to be. I skulked gloomily around the school buildings with my obvious hatred of all they represented seething within me. It gave me a sense—misguided of course—of some power within me; a power to control their simple emotions and subjugate them to an ancient will that seemed to be surfacing slowly, and painfully, within me. These were the fantasies and megalomaniac impressions of an adolescent whose abhorrence of the ordinary, the mediocre every day, had set him on a path to remote and unwholesome self-absorption.

My brief career at university had sealed our separation. I found the confines of the city destructive to my work. Libraries had never been a particular passion of mine and so I gradually forgot my studies for more carnal pleasures. In 1936 I left for Borneo and spent four incredible years drifting through the Indonesian Islands, living with the people and sharing their rituals and customs. Then the world broke in and with the arrival of the Japanese I caught one of the last boats back to England. Soon I was conscripted and the war worked its horror upon my mind. After being present at the liberation of Bergen-Belsen my brittle mental state finally collapsed and the years following the war were spent between institutions, the names of which I have forgotten. I gradually recovered my interests and spent a slow decade becoming more bookish; researching the occult from the comfort of an armchair rather than in the bowels of its practice. However, the books and articles could not long keep me contented. I was eager to return to travel and discovery, and after a serendipitous inheritance I departed England's dull post-war shores in the hope of permanent escape.

Those three years had been most rewarding. I had seen practices of unbelievable power; conjurations of ancestors, spirits and demonic powers; bizarre sacrifices to deities long forgotten in the West and magical incantations from the mundane to the extraordinary. The time vanished and the money did too. Like many men of my age, with relatively minor financial means, I had become a decadent; whilst others undid themselves—and hid from their memories—with drink and drugs, I had tried to vanish into an unreal other world of barbarism. Finally though, with little money left, and a mind filled with ancient terrors I returned to England: a country that was as alien to me now as those strange lands I had visited were to most of my countrymen.

So there I stood, in a beachfront boarding house, reading a letter from Bertram Wilson. It was short enough: 'Dear Miles, I'm glad to hear of your return, and trust your expedition was worthwhile. I am sick. I would ask a favour of you, in memory of our old friendship. Please call on me here at St Agnes' Hospice at your earliest convenience, if you are so inclined. Your old friend, Bertram Wilson.' It was also clear enough. I did not know what had happened to Bertram during the war but had a terrible feeling that his illness must be somehow connected to it. Perhaps seeing him again would help me settle back into the miserable greyness of my homeland. As it was imperative that I establish some form of income, and soon, it seemed sensible also to see if Wilson might know of a suitable position. I admit that my initial thoughts were of myself. Any remaining vestige of European social conventions had vanished from my thoughts, so immersed was I in alternative communities. I would discover soon enough what condition troubled him.

∞

The hospice was located in London, a short enough train journey from Hastings, where I was boarding. I believed that sea air would at least give me some feeling of freedom. I approached the city with foreboding though. It was the symbol of all I had wanted to leave behind: security, civilisation, progress, and most of all, knowledge. What had we discarded in this rush for technology and capital? All our old gods had withered now, laying bleeding and abandoned amongst the scrap-yards and dole queues of Europe. Hah! What did this wretched society know of values, of love and hate, of true sacrifice? Everything was reduced to numbers, to clocks, workloads and formulae.

I had to break my hatred of modernity, or I was lost again.

I concentrated on the gentle rumble of the train upon the tracks, soothing myself into a trance.

A short taxi-ride from Victoria station saw me to St Agnes' hospice. It was a curious place, hidden inside a large private garden behind a tall hedge. Without the driver showing me to the very door I would never have found it.

It must have been run by nuns when first established, over a century before. But now it was staffed by modern nurses. In a way they seemed no different to a religious order. They were silent, almost devotional. They passed through the corridors and wards in their navy uniforms, dutiful servants to a higher order; at least it was to pure human compassion rather than the hollow God of the Holy Trinity.

One nurse showed me to Wilson's room before rushing away to the sound of a bell from down the corridor. There was some clamour and a man began to scream. I was intrigued and followed the commotion. I stood back from the doorway and watched as a nurse struggled to hold a grey haired man down upon a bed whilst the one that had shown me to Wilson's room rushed to an old gramophone on the far side of the room. The man was screaming at the top of his voice, crying out against some kind of threat he imagined above him. The first notes from the record began to play and the man immediately relaxed, as though he had been sedated. His face settled into a calm composure but his eyes still stared towards the ceiling, filled with a terrible void that I knew well myself. He was clearly much younger than the grey hair had suggested.

The nurse that had restrained him talked briefly with the other nurse and then left the room hurriedly.

'Excuse me, Madam,' I said. 'Might I trouble you to tell me a little about that patient?'

She eyed me suspiciously for a moment.

'Why,' she asked. 'What is it you wanted to know?'

I could hear the music through the door and was sure I recognised it.

'That's Elgar, isn't it?' I asked.

'Yes, it is,' she replied. '"The Nursery Suite." It is the only thing that will calm him when he starts.'

'What happened to him?' I asked, recalling the short composition which had been dedicated to the royal princesses some years before.

The nurse shook her head and sighed. 'The poor man lost his wife and child in the blitz. Direct hit, whilst he was struggling with the shelter door. The gramophone and a set of disks were in the shelter, and they are all that remained of the house and the family's belongings. He's been here ever since. When he remembers the event, which happens most days, the only way to quieten him is to play the entire suite. Alice will be in there now for the next half-hour or so, changing the disks. If you miss one, or don't change them rapidly enough, he has another fit and you have to begin again. Sometimes I wonder if it wouldn't be best for him to go and join his wife too.'

She stared at me a moment, perhaps regretting telling me so much. But I assumed he had no family left that might object to her indiscretion, and I was unlikely to tell anyone.

'Thank you,' I said, rather quietly.

'Yes,' she nodded. 'Now I must attend to my duties.'

I stood there, outside the door of the shocked man, and listened for a few minutes until the first movement finished and the nurse had to change the disk. It was indeed a child's sort of music, filled with moments of frivolity and gentle menace. Perhaps one might call it theatrical. I could image his child animating his or her dolls to the tracks whilst the loving parents looked on with joy. But those days of lightness were dead to him now. I felt they were dead to me too, with all that I had seen.

I headed back to Wilson's room and knocked lightly.

'Come in,' a voice said.

On entering the room I was struck by how homely it seemed. The patient next door had been here many years and yet his room was stark and bare. But Wilson had obviously been here some time too. He had filled it with books and paintings and even had a violin on a stand by the window. There was even a drinks cabinet in the corner by the washstand.

'Ah, it's great to see you Miles,' Wilson said, easing himself up in his bed which, despite the more cosy surroundings, looked particularly clinical. There was a drip on a frame beside him and a number of hypodermic needles nestling in a kidney bowl on the bedside table. 'I had a feeling you might come today.'

He certainly looked ill. Or rather, he looked old. Not in the startling fashion of the man in the adjacent room. Wilson was thin and haggard. In fact the skin seemed to hang from him as though he were an elderly man. Gone was the robust physique of the sportsman I had known. A cruel pang of schadenfreude welled within me.

'Hello, Wilson,' I began. 'It's a pleasure to see you again... I mean not in this state... but it is good to see you again.'

I was so unused to speaking with Europeans, with all their tedious evasive etiquette, that I didn't really know how to discuss his illness tactfully.

'Don't worry Miles,' he smiled. 'You never were any good at the small talk. It's one of the things I liked about you. You're an honest man, even if that is somewhat hurtful at times. It's because of your honesty that I asked you to come.'

I entered the room a little further and deposited my coat and umbrella on a low chest at the foot of the bed.

'I'll take a seat if I may,' I said, settling into a comfortable chair beside the window.

'Certainly,' he replied. 'Would you care for a cup of tea or something? I can call for some.'

'I'm fine thanks, Wilson,' I said, eager to find out why he'd called me here. 'What has happened to you?'

He stared at me with his gaunt face and I saw how much he had changed. His eyes were dark and distant. I wondered what they had witnessed in these past years. My own eyes must have betrayed a sadness because a single tear fell from his eyes and rolled down his cheek.

'I have a condition that the doctors are unable to diagnose,' he said, still holding the firm gaze. 'They believe it to be some sort of wasting disease. They are wrong. I am indeed wasting away, but it is not a disease and there is nothing in this world that will ever cure it.'

'I am sorry to hear that, Wilson,' I said. 'But how can you be so certain, perhaps they will...'

'They will not!' he interrupted. 'They cannot! Because what ails me also ails them, and you. It is the condition of all humanity. In me it has found physical expression and I will make sure it is concluded.'

There was a short silence. There had been an aggression in his voice which I had not expected, and had not experienced in all the years that we had been close.

'You have not really been able to recapture your love of other cultures and their odd beliefs since the war have you?' he said, bluntly. 'I mean, you've travelled. You've no doubt seen surprising and unusual things. But nothing can quite erase the memory of what happened in the war.'

He was right. He just stared at me with those black, unchanging pupils, and spoke the truth that I hadn't had the courage to confront yet.

'I am the same, my old friend,' he continued. 'I was captured after my ship went down and spent the last three years in a prisoner of war camp. I worked in the Sosnowice mine. There in the darkness I discovered something, something that has been with me since.'

Again there was a long silence and the solid, unblinking, gaze.

'What? What did you discover?' I asked, absorbed now.

'Not what you are thinking. Not some object...' he said, shifting his gaze finally towards the window. 'It is a *sense* of things that I found, or rather, the sense *within* things. I began to hear how the basest elements sing with the sound of the first eruption of life.'

I was used to hearing all manner of beliefs, of theories and philosophies that proposed strange celestial orders and cruel fates for humanity and its verdant earth, but I never expected to hear them from a man such as Wilson.

'Do you know what holds the most beautiful song?' he continued.

I shook my head.

'Works of art. Pass me a book from the shelf if you will,' he instructed, pointing to the bookcase nearest to him.

I extracted the nearest one I could find and was pleased to see that it was Sarban's *The Sound of His Horn*. It had only been published a few years previously and I had read it only recently, finding it one of the few books that had accurately captured the perversity and true horror of the awful regime we had fought against. But thinking again now I wonder if there was not a deeper meaning in my selection of that book, for it revealed a hidden lust and barbarity which lurks within us all, waiting for its bestial moment to come.

I handed him the book.

'Yes, an ideal choice,' he said, gripping it in his left hand and clutching it to his chest.

I stood by the bedside waiting for him to say more but he had closed his eyes and seemed to be breathing slowly and deeply. I waited for what seemed like minutes and was at the point of calling for one of the nurses, fearing he may have slipped into a coma.

Then it began.

It seemed as though Wilson became blurred. That is the only way I can describe it. It happened only for a brief moment, as though he had become a sort of gossamer being, as thin and fast as the wings of a fly. I blinked my eyes a few times but this odd haze still persisted around him. The rest of the room, and even the bed in which he lay were clear and focused. A moment later I heard a tingling noise, much like a tuning fork, clear and sonorous.

He turned to me and spoke. 'There, that's that.'

'What's *that*?' I said, rather frustrated at this increasingly obscure charade.

'There is no more Sarban,' he said, handing me the book.

I took it from him and placed it back on top of the bookcase. I must have looked thoroughly perplexed because he viewed me with what could only be called pity.

'You'll see,' he said. 'I am rather tired now. Might I trouble you to visit me tomorrow—just to witness the last movement, you understand. Then we can resume our distance again.'

I wanted to say no. But I suppose I owed something to our history.

'Of course, Wilson,' I said, gathering my things. 'You get some rest.'

∞

On my return to Hastings I felt unusually tired and considered that the brief episode of Wilson's shaking fit might have had some form of psychic effect upon me. I had experienced similar during my travels and slept until the early hours of the following morning. I watched the sun slowly penetrate a gloomy morning over the block of terraces my window looked out upon. I had resolved to visit Wilson as early as possible to conclude the matter, which now seemed quite absurd. It was clear that he had become obsessed, as so many had, with the awful scenes he had endured. It would be a short time before he would pass away, and I would have done what I could to ease that passing.

As I gathered some bread and cheese to make a small breakfast on the train I thought again of Sarban's short novel and pulled out my copy to browse through. Leafing through the pages I discovered that they were all empty. Not a single word was printed in them. This must be some elaborate hoax, I thought. I had only read the thing a couple of weeks before. Wilson must have dreamt up the scam believing me to be some credulous moron who would accept any form of spiritualist trickery as evidence of the supernatural. I would take the book with me and demand an explanation.

I was striding purposefully down the corridors of St Agnes before 10am, determined to discover who was involved in this charade.

After a terse knock I entered Wilson's room to find him on a respirator. The patio doors were open to a small balcony overlooking the back of the gardens. A gentle breeze passed through the room.

Of course I was unable to vent my disgust and headed over to his bedside. He removed the mask and croaked a greeting to me.

I responded as politely as I was able. Then I opened the book before his face and flicked through it.

'Yes,' he nodded. 'Mine is the same.'

I flicked through his copy, still where I had left it the previous day. It was exactly the same—blank. I even removed the dustjackets to check the spines, in case he had had some other notebook swapped for the originals. But there on the spine was written the title and author, identical on each copy.

'What is going on, Wilson,' I said, as calmly as possible.

He seemed to have gained a little energy and was now propped up against his pillows.

'I showed you yesterday, Miles,' he said. 'It's all gone now. Not a copy remains in the world. I have liberated it.'

'But surely this is some joke...' I began.

'A joke! You think I would lie here and joke with what has been revealed to me in the squalid darks of the earth's depths,' he said, with a growing anger. 'From darkness I extracted light. We no longer deserve all of culture's gifts, which people have worked for years to reveal form the core of our being. There is nothing remaining that has not had its song darkened by this century's deeds. The world will have to begin art again. And from what it has lost it will realise the value of everything.'

'But what do you mean, Wilson?' I asked, struggling to understand his insane diatribe. I dropped the two books on his bed.

He picked one up and flicked through it smiling.

'Don't you see? There is no more Sarban,' he whispered, 'and soon there will be no Rembrandt or Shakespeare, no Stoss, Turner or Mozart. This world no longer deserves such wonders. I will extract them. The galleries will be empty; their canvases bare. The concert halls will be silent; their scores evaporated. The libraries will be unused halls of nothing; their books blank. Art will finally attain its condition.'

He closed his dark eyes and I saw his body shudder with that strange vibration that I had seen the day before. This time it was quite noticeable, even violent, but so entirely unlike any shiver or tremble of the body in even the most evolved and practised shamans of the bizarre tribal rituals that I had witnessed in my travels. It was as though every atom of his body had begun to oscillate making his entire form into a steadily accumulating blur. And from that haze a luminosity emerged whose origin was indiscernible, but without a doubt present, and then I began to hear it. It sounded like that last prolonged sigh with which all beings die, yet at the moment I had caught it the sound vanished and all the peripheral sounds; traffic, the breeze in the trees outside, the voices of passers-by and the general hum of existence, entirely evaporated. I felt enfolded within a tangible silence which wrapped me in its quietude so completely that I questioned my entire existence as separate from that supreme calm. The event of this quiet could have been only the most slight division of a second before I heard again Bertram's breath, and then again the quiet, the breath, the quiet, breath, quiet, all within an instant. Finally a rushing breath of sound, as of a gasping final trumpet call, seemed to enter through the open patio doors and I collapsed.

On coming round I found Wilson lying there unmoving. I presumed him dead. His eyes stared upwards, and had regained their original piercing blue colour. His face was contorted into a rictus, indiscernibly dreadful or joyful.

Before I was able to cry for assistance the patient next door began a screaming fit. I was beside the low bookcase at Wilson's bedside, and, through my horror, thought to check the books. I pulled one volume after another from the shelves. Blank. In my panic I scrabbled on my hands and knees amidst a growing heap of literature, checking each one before discarding it. Every word had been erased, from the greatest poems to the cheapest of potboilers. My cries joined those of the patient next door; him for his lost loved ones, me for a world of loss.

Gathering myself together and drying my streaming eyes I rushed to the room next door and found the same nurse struggling with the agonised man in the bed. The other nurse, Alice, was there too. She watched with amazement at the gramophone record revolving. The speakers emitted only a faint crackle from where the needle touched the blank revolving disk.

'It's not working,' she yelled, turning to me and appealing for assistance. 'The record's broken.'

'No, it's not broken,' I said, my words flat and hopeless. 'There's nothing on it to play. There is no more Elgar. There is no more Shakespeare, Turner or Mozart. This is now our condition.'

The patient thrashed about in the bed still screaming at the top of his voice. I could hear calls from down the corridor as other nurses gathered to lend assistance. I left Alice and her colleagues to do what they could for him. But, from that incredible day of judgement, there remained nothing in the world that would quieten him.

All His Worldly Goods

'To have no yesterday, and no tomorrow. To forget time, to forget life, to be at peace.'
Oscar Wilde, 'The Canterville Ghost'

Alan was gazing out of the shop window as he often did on rainy days when people preferred the comforts of the new coffee shop over the road rather than the shelves of The Nelham Hospice Charity Bookshop that exuded, as all such shops did, an air of obsolescence and the gentle sadness of bereavement.

It was April now. Late March had promised so much with sunny days and the lengthening evenings. But now the rain was back, and the first two days of that 'cruellest' month had already whipped the local press into apocalyptic warnings of floods. He need not worry though. His mother's house was up on Hill Road, a few minutes from the shop but up a steep enough rise to protect it from even the most extreme deluge. He would be safe if it came.

His mother's house; well that was what he'd been used to calling it these past forty-odd years. It was his house, now that she was gone. But it had only been a few months since her death, just before David—and his computer—turned up at the shop. Bad things often come together Alan had thought (or was it in threes?).

Alan had never been ambitious. His father died when he was a teenager—and with him all of Alan's drive, even for the simplest of pleasures. That was when his mother, Susan, took increasingly to her bed, with various ailments and one undiagnosed condition after another. He had taken care of her throughout and gradually witnessed his world shrink to the drudgery of a day's cleaning and food preparation. A few years ago there had been a change in her though—when she met Bill in the waiting room during one of her frequent visits to the doctor's surgery. He was an energetic man, just retired from the army, and keen to take her out and see some sights. They went to the cinema, the theatre, on short breaks to the coast—even for meals at the local Indian curry house (a thing unthinkable before, her delicate stomach being unable to take the spices apparently).

That was when Alan had volunteered at the charity bookshop, to give himself something to do—having been relieved of most of his duties at home. It had been Bill's idea, his sister Gladys having enjoyed working there for some years, before she had passed away.

But Bill, with all his vitality, died the following year from a heart attack, at the birthday party Susan had been planning for weeks. And she slowly retreated back into the old mother he had known for many years before the beautiful hiatus of Bill and Susan. He continued working at the shop though—as you do when things become habitual—it didn't occur to him to leave. He was also happy there, if such an emotional state remained within him. He never read books though, and all the staff that passed through the shop, from the old ladies to the young students getting work experience, always remarked how odd it was that Alan was never interested in literature. It had almost become a matter of pride for him, a little enigma to retain his own mystery.

But then David had arrived, with quite some impact, last July. He brought his laptop and with it all the bookdealers and bookshops, traders and collectors, prices and profit margins. It had changed the shop radically. Liz, Alan's boss (although it seemed less so David's), adored the young lad—as did most of the other volunteers. He was taking a year off before studying economics at university (and everyone he met was told in detail about it). He was writing a novel too. And he collected first editions of Agatha Christie—Alan never asked why, although he found it a strange hobby.

David was there today. He came in every Thursday to price up stock. It was normally Alan's duty to open the shop each day (Liz liked a lie in). But David had his own key now and would arrive at least an hour before the shop was opened to 'do some catching up, in peace'. Alan found his presence in the backroom terribly unnerving; and the endless tapping of the computer keyboard was a further irritant.

The shop door opened, and a man walked in with a large, and clearly heavy, box. He was in his late sixties and was quite drenched from the rain. He had a grey woollen coat (now almost black with the wet), a soaked tweed hat that dripped steadily from its rim, and a pair of black leather gloves. The day was wet, but it was not exactly cold, and Alan found the man's attire rather over the top for the season. An umbrella would have been more use.

Alan lifted the box from his arms and took it to the counter. It certainly was heavy. People who donated books always underestimated their weight and would try and cram as many as possible into most unsuitable boxes and bags. Many books were damaged in that way, losing the shop money. But what could anyone say? People were donating them and they never failed to assert their moral superiority on that front, Alan found; best to smile and get them to fill in the 'giftaid' form and then deal with the books later.

The man had unbuttoned his coat and shaken himself down on the way to the counter. He was removing his gloves in a very practised and methodical fashion. Alan noticed how dirty his hands were. His right hand had long fingernails, beneath which a layer of brown dirt had collected. Even the palms seemed coated in soil. He must be a gardener, Alan thought.

The man noticed Alan staring at his hands and he looked them over himself.

'Oh, I do apologise,' he said. 'I was just putting in some runner beans this morning. I like to get them going in two batches, early and late crop.'

Alan nodded. He had never been interested in flowers, or vegetables.

'I have brought in some of my brother's effects,' the man said cheerily, drumming his grubby fingernails on the counter. '*Effects*. It is a peculiar term, don't you think?'

Alan looked at him. He did not know what to say.

'I mean, what are *effects*?' the old man said, taking his hat off and wiping his brow with a pocket-handkerchief. He gestured to the box, chuckling. 'Are these books about to be set free into the world to enact some chain of causality? My brother would have found it amusing, you know, to think his things—he was such a retiring and private man—would be beginning new lives, and affecting other lives, in such a way, *effects* indeed!'

'So you want to gift them?' Alan asked, finding the funny man's speech hard to follow.

'Oh, certainly,' the man said, having begun to clean his spectacles with the handkerchief. 'It's what my brother would have wanted. He so loved his books. I'm sure he'd be pleased to know others were enjoying them. There are some more back at his flat, but I have to take it easy myself these days, what with all my own *aching bones*.' He affected a comical voice for these last couple of words, although Alan was unable to place whether it was meant to be a pirate or a farmer.

'Are you a guitarist?' Alan said, pointing to the man's long nails as though it was a straightforward inference.

'Oh no...' he said, clenching his fist self-consciously. 'I used to enjoy playing the flute though. I love the call of wind instruments. You know... they beckon, don't they?'

Alan didn't really know what he meant by this, or indeed how an instrument might 'beckon'. He thought of all his prog. rock albums at home and the electric guitars that hummed throughout. Was that beckoning? he wondered.

An awkward pause.

'But, they're not fashionable are they?' the man said.

'Prog. rock bands?' Alan said. He had, having been so silent and alone for so long, begun to believe his thoughts externally manifest. Perhaps they were. Perhaps all ideas and inner dialogues are externally manifest, in some fashion.

'Oh no, I mean wind instruments; the flute, the pipes, the *bassooooon*,' Eli said.

He said this last word with a long, deep, somewhat gleeful elongation, followed by a cheeky smile.

Alan laughed; he didn't know why. He liked this man.

'Anyway, I'll leave these with you,' the old man said. 'I may drop some more in soon. As I say, there's quite a collection. Oh, sorry, I hadn't introduced myself. The name is Wood, Eli Webb. My brother was Kenneth Webb. He was a professor.'

He held his hand out to Alan, who shook it. There was the grain of the dirt and the scratch of thick calluses on the fingers. It was a hand that had seen much physical labour.

Wrapping himself back up against the weather he then gave a short bow and left.

Alan took the first few volumes out of the box. There were some story collections ranging from the prosaically titled *Ghost stories for Christmas* and *Horror Tales* through to the weighty *The Mammoth Book of Thrillers, Ghosts and Mysteries* (this had an interesting embossed bat on the cover, flying against a full moon). Others had more enticing titles; *Tales of the Dead*, *Ghostly Tales to be Told*, *Tales from Beyond the Grave* and *The Hell of Mirrors* (that sounded different!). They were in a terrible jumble though and he began trying to sort them into some order (David was always so particular about receiving the books in a designated order—by author, size and age). A handful of tatty paperbacks appeared next, Pan and Fontana collections, and a stack of Dennis Wheatleys. Alan's father had been a Wheatley fan. He remembered a small collection of red hardbacks on the shelf (maybe a dozen or so), with titles that had fired his young imagination; *The Devil Rides Out*, *Strange Conflict*, *To the Devil-A Daughter*, *They Used Dark Forces*. They had been part of a mail order offer his father had subscribed to a few years before he died. Volumes would appear occasionally in the post and cause an argument between his parents—his mother found their subject matter abhorrent. A few months after his father passed away the books were gone, and an ornamental clown jug of most repellent design replaced them on the shelf. Alan resolved that the jug should go out now, at the first opportunity. These Wheatleys were just assorted paperbacks though, badly damaged, and would likely end up being recycled.

There were also a few books on theatre—but more technically focused, and all clearly out of date; *Costume for the Stage*, *Stage Lighting for Beginners*, *Props: Their Acquisition and Maintenance*. Near the bottom of the box there seemed to be a good selection of larger art books, and artist's biographies, but tucked amongst them there was a stout yellow volume.

Fishing it out it declared itself as *The Supernatural Omnibus*. He inspected the tattered paper cover, bright yellow with large varied fonts announcing the horrific contents; Witchcraft, Were-Wolves, **Diabolism**, *Necromancy, Satanism,* **Divination**, Sorcery, Goety [he had to look that one up], Voodoo [which he knew all about from *Live and Let Die*], **Possession**, *Occult Doom & Destiny*. This last line quite captivated him: *Occult Doom & Destiny*, and in italics—portentous indeed! At the top of the front cover 'Great Reissue!' was proclaimed in bold red and, in the same colour, at the bottom 'PRICE: 620 Pages 25/-'. He found it revealing that they had felt it necessary to remind the customer of the number of pages before listing the price—a costly 25 shillings! He supposed even the writing of books—always such an arcane and hallowed occupation, to his mind—was reducible to pages per penny, each one exchanged for leisurely reading (if such this was) to while away the hours.

25/-. He stared at it for some time. 25 shillings. The cover stared back at him, as only inanimate materials can—arrogantly immortal in their abject servitude. The value shone like a hieroglyph from some past life. He remembered shillings as a child—beautiful round emblems of value, filling his palm like a promise of power. And it was thus, by the facile regularity of 'pocket-money', that he had been delicately inculcated into the phantasms of exchange.

He flicked to the inner pages of the book to find the publication date—at least he knew that much about books, after all these years: ninth impression, May 1969; first published June 1931. He turned back a page: Victor Gollancz Ltd; edited, with an introduction, by Montague Summers. The names meant nothing to him, but he liked the sound of *Montague*; he imagined a tall man, from Oxford University, with a monocle, in a tweed suit. Victor Gollancz, Victor... an Eastern European gentleman, of means no doubt (another suit, wide features, stocky frame—an investor, with a hat, which Alan's imagination rendered in indistinct style).

David appeared from the backroom with his Acer notebook in hand.

'What's that?' he asked, pulling the book out of Alan's hands, plundering its front matter for facts.

'Er, it's from this box a chap... erm... Mr Eli Webb, just brought in...' Alan mumbled, '...from his brother. His "brother's effects", he said.'

David was already tapping away at search engines and the like, scrolling through webpages of bookdealers.

'Two quid, it looks like loads of sellers have it,' David said with finality.

He pulled his retractable pencil out of his top pocket and scribbled in the top corner of the first page. 2.00, 2/4. He always marked the date in the books. It allowed swift identification of those that weren't selling. They could be sent to the central depot to be distributed to other stores to see if their customers matched the book's 'target demographic' more effectively—well, that's what David said anyway.

David turned the book over in his hands and gauged the spine width.

'Shame...' he said, with the air of a practised—although soulless—assayer, '...it's rather thick. It'll take up valuable shelf space. We'll give it the twelve weeks though, just in case. Don't know why anyone would want it though; it's just silly fantastical nonsense.'

He skimmed the book back across the counter at Alan—for him to shelve—and then departed.

It was then that Alan determined to read the book. He did not know what *fantastical* nonsense might be, or indeed what *unfantastical* nonsense might be. But because it seemed so abhorrent to David he resolved that it might hold some interest to him, and, at the very least, would perform some minor rebellion against the tyranny of his 'notebook' and its infernal judgements.

David had quite destroyed the nostalgic reverie of Alan's encounter with the book. He tried to recapture some of his day-dream, but to no avail. The price, '25/-', seemed only a dull mark of passing time, and the words on the cover (so, richly provocative only moments before) now vanished back into unintelligibility, rather than a delicious strangeness.

Despite the magic having vanished he would read it, even if it took the rest of the year. That evening, although it was completely against the shop's policy, he smuggled the book into his 'bag for life', hidden beneath his Tupperware lunchbox, and dashed home—his heart beating as though he had just pulled off a major jewellery heist.

He did not get on well with it, determined though he was. The collection contained nearly forty stories, admittedly none of them that long, but he had not read properly in years. And there was that daunting figure on the front cover: '620 Pages'. It was there to entice the eager reader, but to him it seemed—especially in its garish red—more a warning, or even a taunt. The titles on the contents page did not calm his trepidation: 'Malefic Hauntings: Mixed Types', 'Malevolent Mystery', The Dead Return', and overleaf: 'Black Magic', 'Satanism', 'Contracts with the Demon'. He was clearly heading into deep waters.

The list of authors of no further reassurance; only two names had any familiarity. There was Charles Dickens. Everyone, he assumed, knew who Charles Dickens was—although Alan had never actually read anything by him. He'd seen the old 1950s *Scrooge* film over countless Christmases. He had also heard of Bram Stoker, and *Dracula*, from Bill actually—after one of his weekends away to Whitby with mother. But again, he hadn't read anything by him. He was quite taken by one of the section titles in the book 'The Vampire', a story called 'Carmilla'. But looking at the page count he saw it was quite long, nearly seventy pages, and might be tough going to start with.

He resolved to take a random approach. He closed his eyes and flicked through the pages until he thought he was some way in, and then stopped: 'My Brother's Ghost Story' by Amelia B. Edwards. It sounded ok, and was only twelve pages long. It might get him in the mood for the vampire one.

It began, 'Mine is my brother's Ghost Story'. Alan immediately thought of the old man, Eli, who had brought the book into the shop as part of his 'brother's *effects*'. He smiled to think that in a way this was something of Eli's brother's ghost story, as the book had passed to him now and something endured of the man here, although they had never met. But he couldn't even finish the tale. Each time that wretched narrator said 'my brother said', 'my brother exclaimed' or 'my brother' did this or that an image was conjured in Alan's mind. It was Eli, wandering back and forth up the highstreet, aimlessly peering into windows. And it was Eli's voice that spoke inside his head as he read each of these lines, slowly transforming them into 'my brother's *effects*'.

He couldn't get the thing from his mind. He put the book down and turned on the radio. He was tired anyway. If he got some sleep, took the book back in the morning (in case anyone noticed), he could bring it back the following evening and try again.

∞

The book was back on the shelf well before anyone showed up at the shop. In fact Alan had already had two coffees and sold a few books before Liz arrived. She was asking him all manner of questions, and running through some of David's plans for the shop. Alan wasn't listening. He just kept hearing those few words over and over in his head: 'my brother's *effects*.'

Alan had a tendency to wander off both mentally and physically, and he left Liz mumbling away in the backroom as he headed out to watch the street from the window. It was one of his favourite activities: people watching.

As usual the coffee shop was busy, with the mums coming and going with their bright buggies and prams. There were the elderly with their shopping trolleys, off for their pension. It seemed a street of stereotypes, or characters from a story, he thought. If only he could write he thought. Perhaps he should start a novel, like David.

But there was one person that didn't quite fit the behaviours he had come to expect from his watching the highstreet. It was Eli. Alan couldn't remember having ever seen him before the previous day and found it odd he should be there now. As in Alan's thoughts from last night he was walking up and down looking in the shop windows. At each he seemed to pause and stare in for quite some time.

A customer came into the shop then, and the new electric door buzzer woke him from his ponderings. It was a small middle-aged man in a battered leather jacket and jeans. Alan recognised him as an old regular at the shop, although he had seen less of him recently. He was a book collector and casual trader on one of those trading websites, Alan recalled. The man smiled at him and began his systematic scan of the shelves, like some ruminant beast returning to familiar, fertile ground.

Alan missed these people: dealers and collectors. They had not been such regular customers since David's reign had begun. The prices in the shop were now similar to those they would charge themselves, and when a rare book came in—worth tens, or even hundreds of pounds—David would contact head office and it would vanish to an auction, or their 'posh shop' in London. So there was very little left for these clients. They had been replaced by others though, and many of them; customers keen to get celebrity biographies—stout hardbacks—for a fraction of their original price. And there were people with very specific requirements; ...anything on outdoor photography... ...books on beginning birdwatching, for my son, I don't want to spend too much on it—he'll be onto the next thing in a week... ...something about spirit guides, if there is such a book... ...Hitler's last hours in the bunker... etc. etc.

Steadily the shop had become a place to actively find books, rather than a repository of volumes that no longer belonged anywhere. The jumbled shelves had been ordered properly, and bright new spotlighting installed (guiding the customer on their 'journey'). They started selling a range of scented candles, incense, and metallic bookmarks with filigree butterflies. Although Alan had helped in the remake of the shop (frequently assigned the heavier tasks) he had felt increasingly lost in these new surroundings.

It was in such a distant state that he found himself again that day, until the customer placed a stack of books on the table.

'Not often I find anything affordable in here these days,' the man said, with a nervous laugh, rubbing his hands together in an exaggerated attempt to warm them. 'Bit chilly out there, and in here I might add.'

'Yes, the heater's broken,' Alan replied, keying the books into the till, being sure to assign them to their right 'department': *Magic, Myth and Medicine* (Science, or maybe History—History, he resolved), *Great Masks* (Art), and *Dolls and Dollmakers* (Crafts). Then, *The Supernatural Omnibus*. That bright yellow cover again, the book he had returned to the shelf that morning.

He looked up at the customer, who was now shifting back and forth from one leg to the other as though the cold had spread to his entire body.

There was a long silence. Alan looked at the book and back at the customer.

'Is everything ok?' the man said, eventually.

'Do you really want this one?' Alan asked, in a confrontational manner quite unlike him.

'Well, yes,' the man said, almost apologetically. Another pause. 'That is *ok*, isn't it?' And he now assumed an indignant tone to match Alan's odd challenge.

It wasn't ok. This guy was stealing his only chance to get back at David. He had hoped that over the coming weeks he'd have armed himself well enough even to have an argument about the merits of fantastical nonsense. But there was no use resisting. It was absurd. This was a bookshop, and this was a book.

'Sorry, sir,' Alan said. 'Of course it's ok. I just wasn't sure it was your taste.'

The man paid, but looked rather annoyed, and hastened out without saying thank you, or goodbye.

And who should be staring in the window as he watched the annoyed customer depart. It was Eli, again in his heavy coat, hat and gloves—although the day was almost warm (Alan hadn't understood why the customer had felt so cold—it was quite nice really). Eli was not looking at the window display but rather gazing through the shop, beyond Alan, and beyond even the wall at the back. It was just a relentless, fixed stare, and it lasted minutes. Then, he departed.

The book was gone. Eli was gone. Things gradually returned to normal.

∞

For a few weeks Alan was annoyed that he had not purchased *The Supernatural Omnibus*, so determined was he to have some means by which to get back at David, if only in his mind. But as time went by he forgot about it and looked forward to the day in September which marked David's leaving for university. Alan hoped it was far away, even abroad.

But it appeared university was not all it was might be, and David came back home at the weekends, and each Saturday found him at the shop.

Then, early one Saturday morning, as the leaves on the trees turned brown, Eli returned to the shop, with another box.

Again, Alan helped him in with it.

'Hello there,' Eli said, going through his routine of removing his hat and scarf and undoing his coat. 'Now these ones might not all be to your liking, or anyone's for that matter. Many of them belonged to Kenneth's wife—romances mainly.'

Alan reached in and took the first book that came to hand.

There it was: *The Supernatural Omnibus*, and surely the very same copy that had been purchased a few months before by that book collector. There was no mistaking it—even with the same pencilled in price and date, in David's hand.

'That one's quite special, I think,' said Eli. 'Such a lovely bright cover don't you think?'

Alan nodded.

'Anyway, I'll leave you to sort through them,' Eli said, wrapping himself back up in the gloves, scarf and hat he'd just removed. Alan noticed that his hands were just as grubby as they had been before, in fact the soil seemed to crumble from his fingers, and from the gloves as he prepared himself for the elements. It made a crackling sound on the shop floor. 'There may be some more books back at the flat, but I like to spread them all around a bit, to the different shops. As I say—fair's fair.'

And he was gone.

David emerged from the backroom with a long list. He had planned a good clear out in preparation for Christmas stock.

'What's that lot?' he asked, pointing to the box.

'Oh, Eli just bought them in, Eli Webb,' Alan said. 'He donated some books earlier in the year.' He was about to say 'his brother's *effects*' but thought better of it.

'But we're not open yet,' David said incredulously. 'How could anyone have come in?'

'What do you mean?' Alan said.

David tutted impatiently and plodded over to the door to give it a dramatic tug: locked. He smiled his irritating 'I'm right and you're wrong' smile and stood there waiting for Alan's explanation.

'Sorry,' Alan muttered. 'I mean these are *mine*. I brought them in from home. I've been trying to clear out some of mother's things.'

David looked unconvinced, but after a moment just shrugged and headed towards the back shelves to begin the cull of malingering literature.

'You might also give the place a bit of a clean up before opening up,' David said on his way by, pointing to the counter.

Alan was perplexed by what had just happened. On the counter, near where Eli had been standing, there was a scattering of dirt. Alan brushed some towards him. It was moist, rich soil; dark and freshly dug. Alan recalled the first meeting with Eli, and his dirty gardener's hands. However this seemed to be an unusually large amount to have been brought in on a pair of gloves, or even the dirty hands inside them. The box must have been sat in the boot of the car, Alan thought. Gardeners' car boots were no doubt full of mud.

Quite how Eli had got in, and back out again, was still confusing. But Alan was more thrilled to have the book back than to focus on such a mystery. He resolved to purchase it immediately, rather than attempt to smuggle it back and forth between shop and home, with the attendant risk of someone purchasing it again.

Alan rang the book into the till, under the 'Fiction' department, and threw his two pound coins loudly into the cash register. David sighed and shook his head.

∞

That night, with the book legitimately in his possession, he resolved to prepare himself properly for it: a milky coffee and propped up in bed with three pillows. Once adequately ensconced he took a deep breath and started at the beginning, with the introduction. This was by Montague Summers, and he still couldn't shake off the image of someone with a monocle. He only got a few pages in and was struggling. It all seemed rather academic. He wasn't that interested in the history of the writers and their work. He got to a bit about ancient Egypt, Assyria and the Greeks and decided that perhaps one was meant to read introductions after the rest of the book, so you knew what they were talking about.

He went back downstairs for another coffee. This required patience.

Back in bed again he thought he'd try another approach entirely, or rather the same approach but from the opposite direction. Start with the last one first: 'Toussel's Pale Bride'. It was in the 'Voodoo' section and he hoped for some tarot cards and attractive women in white dresses, like in that Bond film.

He finished it, but it came with a wound. The last line lingered in his mind, 'and when she looked into the faces of his four other guests, she went mad.' He saw the anniversary table of the poor Camille and he imagined the faces of her dead guests peering back vacantly as she sat in her beautiful dress.

Perhaps these were not the sorts of stories for him. Mother may well have been right in asking his father to banish the Wheatleys to a high shelf. He thought they were of similar subject matter.

But, this was the stuff that David detested so he must strive to enjoy it.

He picked the volume up again and scanned its contents for something that might appeal.

One title leapt out: 'When I was Dead' by Vincent O'Sullivan. It was the temporal discontinuity that appealed to him, and the fact that it was only four pages long, like the Seabrook had been. This was the last chance. If this one went sour then he'd have to declare that supernatural stories were really not for him.

It began with a description of what was to be assumed was a grand house, Ravenel Hall and the owner—he must have been some Lord or other gentry Alan assumed—engaged in some bizarre research concerning hidden qualities of blood that could bring back the dead. Alan knew, or at least surmised from the films he'd seen, that many horror stories contained wealthy, educated individuals engaged in the quest for some form of arcane knowledge—scientific or spiritual. From the beginning there was something familiar: 'The passages were long and gloomy, the rooms were musty and dull, even the pictures were sombre and their subjects dire.'

Hmm, how like here, he thought; well, not long passages, but certainly gloomy, and the windows—he'd always felt—were rather too small for the size of the rooms, giving a dull twilight on even the brightest of days. And those pictures his mother had bought; faded prints (even when new) of agricultural landscapes, Scottish mountains and lochs, portraits of people who, if famous when they were alive had now vanished in the collective memory, and brittle papery prints of Dutch still life paintings that got stiller, and greyer, with every year. I'll take them all down in the morning, he thought. It would be a relief.

It carried on with a meeting between the Lord, Alistair, and his friend debating his experiments, and the friend coming to the reasonable conclusion that it was all somewhat unhealthy to be cooped up in that vast house with all that playing on his mind.

Alistair resolved to continue his experiments—a requirement of the story no doubt.

But then there was a terrifying description of the apparition so conjured, '...an old woman with her hair divided in the middle, and her hair fell onto her shoulders, white on one side and black on the other. She was a very complete old woman; but, alas! she was eyeless, and when I tried to construct the eyes she would shrivel and rot in my sight.'

That was tough, but he persevered.

It appeared that poor Alistair died at some point, and was energetically consumed by trying to make himself seen, and heard, by his servants. The tale came to its grim conclusion with his funeral (after an evening spent lying in his own coffin). The last lines were, again, haunting: ' "I'm not dead!"... "Sweet God, I am not dead." '

He put the book down and allowed those brief pages to work their effect. He had often heard from others that the act of reading was some form of calmative, or remedy for life's ills. He did not feel that at all. The book had so far been a battle; from the difficulties of the introduction to the horrifying final story (he wondered if he'd started at the first story—as surely one ought—he might have been gradually prepared for such an image of dead guests at a celebration dinner). This short tale by O'Sullivan was a different matter entirely. It seemed to echo within him in a manner he could not describe. It was a feeling so unfamiliar that he was quite unnerved. As he lay there in the semi-gloom of his room he thought of his mother again. Was it possible to be 'not-dead' in the fashion of 'Alistair' of Ravenel Hall? Was it possible to conjure the image of some spirit guide just by cogitating on some drops of blood in a vial? Did the spirit linger, so tormented and lonely, after the body was gone? And if so—if all this were true, or even part of it—then might his mother be next door, in her bedroom still, invisible to the living eye? Or worse, might she be here with him now, in *his* room, leering at him across the bed; or chiding him with her shrill demanding voice, admonishing him at a pitch alien to living ears? And what things would he have done over these last few months that would have incurred her wrath... things no mother, least of all his, would approve of.

He jumped out of bed and hurried into his dressing gown, looking desperately around the room for a glimpse of her ghostly face, eyeless or not. He raced down the stairs and into the kitchen.

It was a long room, with a wretched brown carpet in awful paisley pattern—that could also go soon, he thought. He was beginning to assemble a list in his head; the awful clown jug, the pictures, this carpet! The stark light of the striplight (installed for her weak eyesight) that usually annoyed him so much was now quite comforting. It banished grim spirits and silly phantasms raised by stories. Perhaps David had been right—a painful thought!

The kettle whistled and he had a tea in his hand in moments. Tea and bright lights—always powerful tools of exorcism, for an Englishman at least. As the minutes ticked by it became clear there would be no frightful apparition, none of the 'undead dead', 'malefic haunting' or other spectacular *nonsense.* Something more disturbing happened, or might we say 'took hold of' him.

At first it was simply a sense of loss; loss of his father and his mother. Then it became the emptiness of a house with three bedrooms, a lounge and dining room (with table and chairs for six); the emptiness of such a house with one occupant. And then the sadness of his lack of siblings; he couldn't share the memory of those leather books by Wheatley on the high shelf, he couldn't joke with anyone about the years of mother's hypochondria or laugh about old Bill and her during their happy months together. It was all inside him, a lost cargo of memories, slowly rusting into oblivion. Where could they all go? He began to shake, like a body possessed. And he muttered, 'I might as well be dead. Sweet God! I am already dead.'

∞

Weeks passed again but the burden of alienation crept steadily upon Alan. Not as dramatic as the night he'd read O'Sullivan's story, but no less debilitating. It was coming up to Christmas. Alan usually loved Christmas at the shop but this year it was different. David—having returned from university for the holidays—had organised a marketing meeting to plan their 'strategy' and now there were all manner of targets to meet and events to organise, including a local author reading from their book and signing copies in the shop, with mince pies and coffee (provided free from the coffee shop over the road—along with a stack of leaflets about their loyalty card).

Alan's first task of the day, after opening up, was to rip off the 'Shopping Days 'til Christmas' sheets in the window, designed—of course—by David. 'Only 7 Days to Go' it announced.

He was happy the shop was making money. They'd earned twice as much for their charity this year than last. He hadn't really joined for that reason though he realised. He had volunteered for some company and for a sense of belonging. But now something was deeply wrong. It didn't feel real anymore. He watched the customers darting around the shop as though they were on video fast forward, or he had been reduced to half-speed. He felt like a glitch in David's smooth computer program; what did they call it; a 'bug'! He felt like a bug.

Part of him just wanted the old Christmases back; when people didn't come to a charity shop for gifts. They wanted new things from the other shops in town. They wanted coffee and cake over the road and 'Santa's Grotto' in the department store. Now the shop was more like one of *those* shops. Scented candles were doing a 'roaring trade', as David described it.

A familiar voice spoke.

'Hello, Alan.'

Alan turned to find Eli, wrapped in his usual grey woollen coat, gloves and tweed hat.

'Oh, hello,' Alan said, thinking to himself how short Eli was. He didn't recall him being so short before.

'Just thought I'd check up on how things are going,' he said, picking up one of the books from the box Alan was restocking the shelves with. 'Ahh! *A Family Christmas*, "easy festive crafts for all the family".' It was a large book on decorating the tree, doughcraft and other such Christmas pastimes that nobody has any time to do anymore. Eli slid it onto the shelf next to Raymond Briggs' *The Snowman*.

'Why don't you take a little break,' Eli said. 'We could go for a walk.'

There was a soft depth to his voice that Alan found calming, even soporific. Again, he had that sense of being slowed down, as the customers and staff whizzed around them, blurring into lines of fuzzy coloured energy.

He watched the Christmas shoppers rushing back and forth in the snow. They were hurrying to get gifts for loved ones, for siblings, for husbands, wives and lovers, for parents, for children. He had nobody left. Even for all her 'illnesses' mother had anchored him to the world; she needed him, and he realised now how much he had needed her.

'I'm sure we could slip away for a while,' Eli continued, 'for a chat. You've earned a little time off I should say.' And he walked out into the street, as the streetlight outside began flickering into life. It was that late afternoon winter darkness, darker still because of the snowstorm.

It didn't even occur to Alan to get his coat, even though the snow was coming down in thick flakes—the kind of flakes that had heralded such excitement when he was a child. Something told him he didn't need a coat.

Eli took his hand, the icy leather glove gripping him firmly. Alan flinched a moment; how odd this would appear, a man in his late-forties hand-in-hand with a short grey-haired pensioner. But then his new friend looked up at him with an understanding smile and it felt comfortable. In fact, it seemed to satisfy some deep yearning that Alan had not realised he had.

Then, relinquishing himself to that comforting grip, Alan allowed himself to be led on. And that kindly old gentleman set off at a steady pace, clearly intent on a very specific destination.

Mikhail Kuzmin had recommended the name to him. Yes, that's right, Kuzmin the poet; the one they found in the Volga last year with a Punchinello puppet stitched to his hand and a string of sausages dangling from his frozen mouth. It was Kuzmin who had given Dr Dapertutto his name, at a sycophantic, drunken party to celebrate the first performance of his troupe of Commedia dell'arte players, if such they were. So many tales have been told about Dr Dapertutto that it seems he has earned that epithet of 'ubiquitous doppelgänger'.

Ah, poor Kuzmin, I heard they never found his legs.

∞

On the gloomy stage of The Interlude House sat Dr Dapertutto, one of his white gloved hands resting upon the arm of a faded green velvet armchair, the other hand twirling a black cane lethargically between long fingers. Had there been anyone there to see him they would have remarked that Dr Dapertutto looked weary, staring out into the auditorium with his heavy, sullen, eyes. These observers might also have said that he appeared impatient and indeed on occasions glanced languidly at his pocket watch; the face of which bore a gibbous moon-face with crazed eyes, its contorted mouth releasing two spindly tongues which formed the hands of the clock and with each sonorous hour its gemstone eyes would roll around in their silver sockets. However, Dr Dapertutto was not inclined towards impetuous agitation for he had no emotion of any kind. It would also have been quite incorrect to suggest his tiredness, for Dr Dapertutto never felt the urge to sleep, or to eat; he was of an entirely different order to you or I. So there he waited, alone, in his tattered theatre, watching the idle moments of human time pass around the face of his comical timepiece. He sat and waited for The Inspector to arrive.

On that cold December morning the only mail The Inspector had received was a bulky package wrapped in brown paper. Upon opening the curious thing—which bore the address of The Investigations Bureau in a strange archaic script—he discovered a large, round, metal tin. There was also a small business card in the shape of a crescent moon, along the curve of which he read: 'Dr Dapertutto: Direktor, Entertainer, Reveller, Charlatan and Misanthrope. The Interlude House, 57 Sadovaya-Sukharevskaya Ul., Moscow'. Below this, still following the sharp curve of the crescent and in the same outdated style that had appeared on the wrapping, was written: 'My dearest Inspector. For your enjoyment. With kindest regards and seasons greetings. Dr Dapertutto'. Within the metal tin The Inspector found a short reel of film. Since his participation in the glorious revolution, having passed from being a farm hand to an influential member of the NKVD, The Inspector—who had never used his real name since—had not encountered such a blatant and insolent manifestation of bourgeois decadence.

'How dare this *Dapertutto* waste the resources of the State by sending such a package—a film—to the Investigations Bureau,' The Inspector thought. 'I shall send Comrade Ovslovsky to bring this deviant in.'

So Comrade Ovslovsky was sent. And Comrade Ovslovsky returned.

Comrade Ovslovsky reported that there was no such place, no building at all in fact, it had been pulled down the previous November after the authorities had learnt it had staged 'theatre of a form unfit for the education and betterment of the Soviet State.' There had indeed been a theatre by the name of 'The Interlude House' but now all that remained was rubble and the plan for a new Proletkult meeting house in its stead.

'I shall have to watch this film to discover the purpose for which it was sent,' The Inspector reasoned, with a precision of mind that had evidently secured his powerful post at the Bureau. Comrade Ovslovsky was, as ever, impressed.

So, The Inspector donned his great coat and fur hat and set out to visit the State Institute of Documentation, where he knew there was a cinematographic projector. His boots crunched through the snow and great clouds of vapour blew from his mouth and nostrils as he cursed and grumbled, repeating, over and over, the insolent words on the card that had been attached to the film reel.

None of the beleaguered minions in the Institute dared block The Inspector's path. He was obviously here on serious business, and these poor souls had enough to concern themselves with without incurring the wrath of such a mighty man.

The Inspector, after some violent encounters with petty administrators and worried bureaucrats, had made his way down to the screening room where a man named Pietr catalogued the reels of tape. Reaching the door of the room he had been directed to The Inspector felt a pulse of nervousness overcome him, a kind he had not experienced since his days toiling on the farm. He paused at the door a moment to collect himself and heard the faintest murmur of laughter from within. It was a child's laugh, a gleeful chuckle that inhabited the moment so entirely that one could not help but smile too. The Inspector opened the door without knocking, his face contorting to suppress his happiness.

Within the room sat an ancient man of diminutive build, wearing a greasy waistcoat and trousers that were hoisted by great braces nearly to his chest and over this bizarre attire was draped a torn leather apron. He crouched over a Steentable which shone light directly up towards his decrepit eyes as his papery hands fed film through the entire machine. His face flickered as the images passed before his eyes. Against one eye he had a long black lens which reached almost to the frame of the Steentable and from his gap-toothed mouth there came a breathy, rasping, laugh like a midnight breeze that awakens fallen leaves. A few moments passed as The Inspector looked about the dim room for the child whose gentle, fairy laugh had so enchanted him from outside. But there was no one else, only stacks of metal tins, identical to the one he carried under his arm.

'Pietr?' The Inspector, asked, with the unbelieving tone of a son who returns home to find his parents have turned into wolves.

The old man looked up from his work and smiled broadly. His plastic face seemed to shudder with joy at encountering another person. He peered at The Inspector through the long black lens, which gave The Inspector the unnerving feeling that he was being examined by some great tentacled eye.

'Yes, Sir,' Pietr said, wiping a burden of saliva onto his apron. 'May I assist you?'

The Inspector was desperate to view the film reel so thought better of commencing a tedious disciplinary affair with the cretinous projectionist.

'You will project this reel of film for me to view,' The Inspector stated, thrusting the box into Pietr's hands.

'Certainly your comradeness,' Pietr said, climbing down from his stool. He motioned for The Inspector to follow him through a curtain into a smaller room whose back wall was whitewashed to enable the showing of the film archive. A row of ten wooden chairs faced the wall in a crooked fashion. Behind them was the apparatus to project the pictures. Pietr was already fiddling and positioning the film into its reels and so The Inspector took a seat. The chair was uncomfortable and dug deeply into his back. The Inspector was hardly a large man and it seemed to him that the chair was far too small. With a click the lights went out and the whirr of the projector began as a streak of grey, dusty light hit the white wall.

A dim picture flickered for a few moments showing a tall figure in a cape, with a tattered top hat, retreating from the camera into a large auditorium whose lights were already going down. This fading illumination offered enough to see the figure mount some steps onto the proscenium and bow with a grand revealing gesture towards a figure that lay just before the curtain. Candle footlights remained to illuminate the action on stage, although given the distance of the camera and the fluttering candlelight the whole scene was difficult to discern. It seemed to The Inspector that the figure was bound and gagged, and was obviously a male who had been stripped down to his evening shirt and trousers. For a few moments he struggled before the curtain was opened with a slow sweep of its torn fabrics. Beyond, from the gloom of a stage devoid of scenery, long dark drapes dropped in swathes across the stage. The bound man turned and paused a moment before renewing his struggle.

The Inspector heard a brief, childish titter behind him and he turned a moment to see if Pietr was still there. The brightness of the light issuing from the projector prevented him from seeing beyond but he was just able to make out a low stooped figure that seemed to be moving feverishly about the machine. Hearing the cracked wheeze of Pietr's breath and a burst of his hacking cough The Inspector was confident that the peculiar projectionist was still there.

Returning to the screen he was pleased to see some advance in the entertainment. A number of figures had emerged from behind the stage drapes. Each carried a short, stout stick and was clothed in bizarre tattered garments that gave them a shaggy appearance. Mounted on each of their heads was a twisted crown of branches from which hung various types of skull, masking their features. The Inspector moved uneasily in his undersized chair. He then noticed a further strangeness to these approaching figures. In comparison to the man, still struggling in the foreground, these figures seemed unusually small. As they came even closer to the figure on the proscenium their diminutive stature became even more apparent. It must be a troupe of performing dwarves The Inspector assumed, having seen a similar clowning troupe before the revolution. These figures, now totaling about twenty, had gathered in a semicircle around the figure and began to beat their sticks against each other in rhythmic patterns. They started to dance, jigging their unnaturally small frames up and down and from side to side in a movement that evoked an oddly familiar feeling in The Inspector. The process seemed so formalised, yet at the same time The Inspector could make out no overall system to the dance. After attempting to discern each individual's systematic manoeuvre in relation to the overall chaos of their gyration The Inspector rubbed his eyes, which now blurred and ached with the strain. As this uncanny jig reached its conclusion, The Inspector had a sense that he was witnessing a ceremony of some description rather than a stage entertainment.

It was then, as all the figures sprung into the air bringing their staves together, that this pack of midget mummers descended upon the bound figure, beating, scratching and kicking like a vengeful lynch mob. The Inspector had witnessed, and been party to, incidents of extreme violence during the Revolution but the savagery of this, and its presentation on a stage, appalled him. The group had surrounded the trussed man and was dragging him into the darkness of the drapes when the curtain closed rapidly and the caped man returned to take his bow. With the final gutters of the candlelight The Inspector made out the shadowy forms of spectators in the front rows whose arms were raised in adulated applause of the sinister, top-hatted compère.

Then, the screen went blank, accompanied by a flutter of loose tape as the film uncoiled from its reel in the projector.

Pietr turned the lights on and stood subserviently by the curtain as The Inspector gathered his thoughts. He stood abruptly and strode to Pietr, pulling on his gloves and beating open his fur hat with irritated swipes of his hand.

'You will document this reel and return it to The Investigations Bureau, labelled "Dr Dapertutto, exhibit one", is that clear?' The Inspector demanded.

Pietr nodded and pulled the curtain back. The Inspector stopped a moment to observe this decrepit individual and wondered if he had been similarly affected by the viewing.

'What are your opinions on the decadent crime portrayed on this tape?' The Inspector asked. 'Do you find its content an affront to our very society?'

'Oh, no sir,' Pietr replied. 'You see, I am almost blind, I am unable to make out even the brightest of images.'

'And you, virtually blind, work *here*, cataloguing the great achievements of our comrades?' The Inspector said angrily.

Pietr nodded shamefully for a moment, but then looked up gleefully. 'But I have my lens, sir,' he said, screwing the black telescopic prism back against his eye as though it were a light socket. This reproduced the strange spectacle that The Inspector had first encountered on entering the editing room. Pietr's right eye seemed to bubble and bulge at the end of this device giving a eerie perspective against his face: it were as though this one eye were on a vegetable stalk, peering at him as the crooked mouth grinned and salivated behind.

Exiting the screening room The Inspector was compelled, by force of habit, to pause a moment to devise some rebuke for the projectionist; to comment on the contemptible state of both Pietr and his editing room. However, for the first time in many years The Inspector's unassailable confidence had quite ebbed from him and he exited The Institute of Documentation hurriedly and with great relief.

He fuelled his indignation, and embarrassment, converting it into his usual angry misery as he cracked through the icy streets in the direction of where The Interlude House once stood. He was certain that some aspect of Dr Dapertutto's theatre must endure, either in the figure of some hoaxer or a more threatening presence that he was bound, through a collective duty, to investigate.

It was, of course, Comrade Ovslovsky's idle nature that had overlooked the small passageway that led from Sadovaya-Sukharevskaya into a small courtyard, cluttered with weeds and ivy—but discernible nonetheless. It had escaped the snow entirely, a fact that The Inspector put down to the high sided buildings that enclosed the yard on all sides. What an acute mind the man had! He was equally unperturbed by any of the noticeably ornate rococo features that adorned the courtyard's arches and columns. In fact it resembled an arbour of some European country home and would have made a lesser man than The Inspector feel quite disoriented. However, The Inspector had already noticed a painted sign at the end of the courtyard that read 'The Interlude House' and he headed for it, with regained confidence, ready to unburden his frustrations.

The door to the theatre was of a rickety construction, more befitting a shed than a place of entertainment. It gave in to The Inspector's forceful advance and stood open a few seconds, shaking, before creaking back against the frame with a weak crunch. The Inspector found himself in almost complete darkness, so little light seemed to penetrate into this vestibule. After a few moments he could make out the thick folds of a dark red curtain only a couple of feet from him. He pulled one side, which gave way with an elaborate swish, releasing the thick pungency of damp mould.

The Inspector entered the auditorium with a grand gesture, one quite fitting to the theatrical environment he found himself in. There he discovered the same stage, with its long auditorium, that he had watched only hours before in The Institute of Documentation. There too was the figure he had seen walk the length of that cursed auditorium to mount the stage and take a bow before directing his malevolent performance. He was seated on that green armchair, dressed in top hat and tails. In one hand he twirled a cane, slowly, in his white gloved hand as the other rested on a high table beside him. There was an identical armchair on the opposite side, facing the auditorium, obviously intended for The Inspector. 'How dare this man,' repeated in The Inspector's mind as he approached the stage, but, ever opportune himself for the gratuities of theatrical indulgence, he walked purposefully toward his allotted seat and took it.

Time passed. The Inspector was unsure of its duration. He seemed to dwell in that performative moment so naturally that he did not want to harm it by the violence of speech. As one, The Inspector and Dr Dapertutto turned to one another and smiled nonchalantly; two comedians well versed in their act.

'So, where is the body Dapertutto?' The Inspector began.

'Am I to assume that is an ontological question inspector,' Dr Dapertutto nodded, pure gesture. 'Or the tedious rhetoric of your profession?'

The Inspector, as you might expect, was unsure how to reply. He forgot his lines, but Dr Dapertutto, ever the performer, was happy to oblige.

'I would have welcomed you with... well, a welcome...' Dr Dapertutto said, with a wave of his gloved hand, that had rested for incalculable moments upon the table. 'It seems we have begun badly inspector.'

A ripple of laughter passed through the auditorium, but The Inspector dismissed it as the acoustics of a draughty communal space. They're all so similarly dark, brushed clean by the lonely stagehand that lingers for a last cigarette in the space between work and family or work and loneliness. The theatre is the loud inhabitation of silence.

'The theatre is a loud inhabitation of silence, wouldn't you agree inspector?' Dr Dapertutto asked, his black eyes demanding a response.

From somewhere within him The Inspector discovered a voice, one that had been given him.

'Why all these prologues, Dapertutto?' The Inspector asked. 'I am here on your invitation to investigate a crime recorded on your own cinematograph.'

Dr Dapertutto nodded, one of those sagely momentous agreements that absorb the delicate interstice allowed between communication, making it into a mockery of performance; revealing the truly monstrous demonstration within our every word. It seemed that The Inspector had watched Dr Dapertutto's nodding agreement for so long that he had become some dancing clown whose vaguely animated corpse had been played into motion, never to cease. The Inspector would stop this charade.

'I will stop this charade, Dapertutto,' The Inspector affirmed, rising from the table, amidst an assertive commendation of applause.

'You have asked why my theatre needs all these preludes,' Dapertutto said, rising to face The Inspector. 'Will the scenario itself not suffice? Well the answer, my inspector, is *no* it will not. There are moments played out for the delectation of spectators, as vacuous as they are [some laughter here and a cheer from the back, I believe] and others for the pleasure of the players. The man you enquire about is already dancing the joys of the Cabotin in the lanes of a world you'd imagine had died. It *is* alive inspector, here in the sold out seats of the travelling stage. Don't you think it remarkable how tradition endures?'

A low rustle sounded behind The Inspector, as of that midnight breeze that awakens fallen leaves. The drapes that formed the backdrop to The Inspector and Dr Dapertutto's show rippled with life. The midget mummers emerged, with their short wooden staves and skeletal masks. One strike of their wretched props was enough to awaken The Inspector's cultivated sense of danger.

'I will have no more engagement with your fantasies Dapertutto,' The Inspector assured himself. 'Your theatre is a decadent obsession, and one that will be consigned to the errors of history.'

'Theatre is a *passion* of mine, Inspector, not an *obsession.* A passion that has become *all consuming*,' Dr Dapertutto said, the gentle beat of the diminutive mummers approaching with each word.

'You can call off the dwarves, Dr Dapertutto, the authorities are involved now,' The Inspector appealed, knowing somehow that he was a witness to an event as old as humanity.

'Oh, they are not dwarves my dear inspector,' Dr Dapertutto smiled. 'They are *my children,* and you know how children love to dance.' Dr Dapertutto produced from his jacket a sheet of papers, clipped together neatly at the top. 'My latest work, inspector, enjoy its denouement.' And he departed.

Turning the pages, as the rhythmic beats of the staves advanced behind him, The Inspector read every word of the dialogue that had passed between himself and Dr Dapertutto written out in the, now familiar, flowing script of Dapertutto's hand. The final line, inscribed in beautiful Copperplate italic read: '*The children advance, smiling and dancing to that ethereal murmur they so love, and they make of their guest a Cabotin who shall play in the byways of those dark lands where we linger.*'

∞

So Comrade Ovslovsky made the usual enquiries. And Comrade Ovslovsky did not understand.

Pietr, a young and earnest party activist, who catalogued the film archives at The Institute of Documentation could not recall any visit that winter by a man meeting the description of The Inspector.

And so, Comrade Ovslovsky would be promoted to Inspector that spring. Then later that year, on a crisp winter day, Inspector Ovslovsky would receive a bulky parcel in brown wrapping with his name, and The Investigations Bureau address, written upon it in a flowing archaic script. He would store this, without opening it, in a box file marked 'The Interlude' and return home early to drink vodka with his loving wife Natalia, who always smiled and loved to dance.

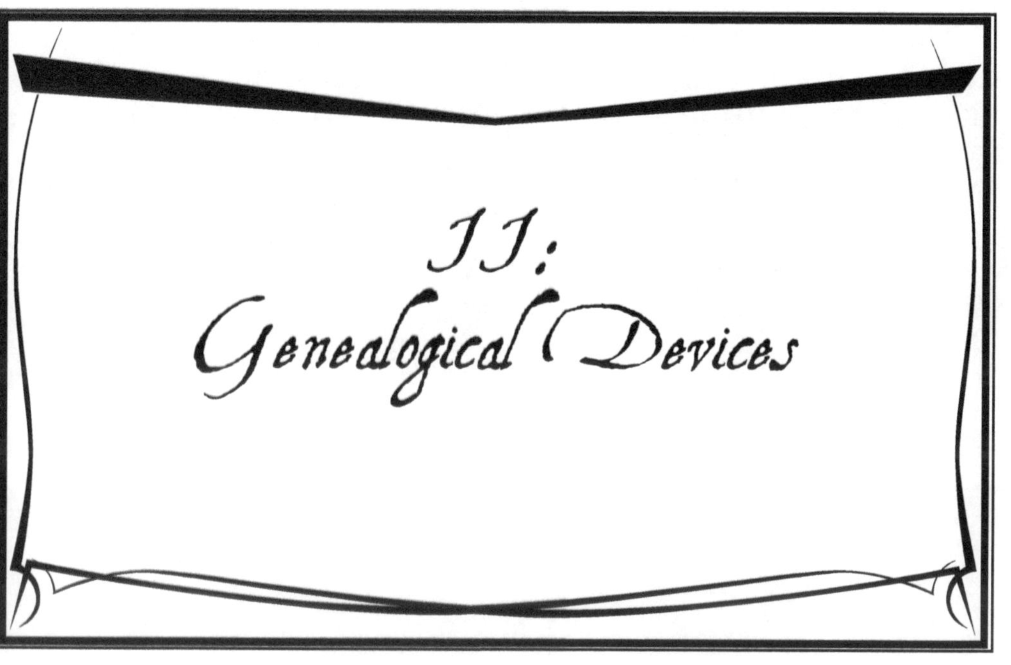

II: Genealogical Devices

This building is very old, it has lasted for centuries, with curious additions and renovations every few decades. Each transformation I have witnessed, or heard, or felt, as it echoed through the aged hallways of this almost ruin. I have seen the owners born and I have watched them die. All of them? Well how can I be sure? It would take too long to be certain of a word such as all. *I have lived too long to use a word like* all. *What is most definite—indeed, a solid rock of fact—is that such as I have seen, and heard, and felt, I have retold so many times that what I have not seen or do not know I will invent. It has been said of me, not unkindly (or with kindness I should add), that sometimes I understood all, and sometimes I understood much, and sometimes I understood little, and sometimes I understood nothing, as now.*

So let it be apparent right from the start that I am another incarnation in this infinite charade of inhuman oppression. I understand it is called a figment, a phantasm, a ghost; the exercise of some grey matter. I understand it can relieve the boredom, it is a tendency in the human, a fallacy, a stumbling block perhaps: the proclivity to boredom. Yet I *burn with a desire to be bored into oblivion; to sense that equidistance between despair and joy, to understand everything as commonplace and not to care whether anything either is or is not. In a word to have done with it all and carry the whole thing back off into the whiteness, where I belong.*

Yet having existed here, briefly, despairingly, joyfully, bright eyed with wonder at it all as though witness to some paginated miracle, I will attempt (I'll keep it short, don't worry) to articulate an environment, something accessible, readable, demonstrable. None of the old arcane bullshit; the figures and symbols, half-light and fancies, the resurrection in wolf's clothing, your alpha and omega and kingdom come. Forget that, that's all dead in me now—if it ever breathed at all (I have my doubts).

I am the dust on a dressing table that the carpenter never built. I am the clinging sweat of a foreign heat, the scattered ashes of a forest campfire, dried ink on the letters from a friend, and invisible tears. I have been the peeling paint of a neglected merry-go-round, the tingle of morning frost on bare feet, the ache of time in growing roots. History? Pah! *I am the lost thread buried in everything woven, I am a contagious rumour; the civility of cognac,* sir. *I was an old grey raincoat hanging, neglected, in an empty hall. I am forever the subtle pulse of blood through time. I am infested with so many crawling entities that writhe in joy across my surface—for that is all I shall ever be: an infinite surface of erosion and invasion, an expanse of incredible possibilities and unbridled fantasies. I am the pornographer's dream and the puritan's.*

I have been called a ghost—that may be true, no matter—I have been called worse. I have died so many times, then resurrected, reborn, dug up and left out to dry or freeze my dusty bones in differing climes. There is no doubt I am some monster living on all sides of circles, so far ahead that you know how to forget me. So much the centre I shall always be effaced, behind these words, inhabiting them until they learn to vanish.

Here I shall be a crackle of silence in a telephone line and if you find me stretched along some limit I will be elsewhere.

∞

Lady Lotherington had been in mourning for her husband for the past fifteen years. She seemed to like to dress in flowing black garments that rustled and crunched as she walked along. Her grey hair was neatly arranged in a bun on top of her sour, thin face. Long black gloves, that lent themselves more to a soiree than to sorrow, graced her slender arms. She had a servant; a young woman from the nearby village, and a gamekeeper for her large estate. Both were treated courteously if a little sternly. Lady Lotherington certainly gave the impression that she was not to be taken lightly.

If someone had taken a look beneath Lady Lotherinton's skirts of lamentation (a place visited infrequently even when the Lord was alive) they would have had quite a shock. Adorning her feet were not the highly laced Victorian black boots one might have expected but instead a pair of fleece lined slippers (in quite terrible repair) with a fading blue velveteen finish on the upper. If you had known the Lord though you would have forgiven her this little indulgence, for he had been worth less than the dirt the maid would wipe from the step—as useful as old pink buttons in a jar. He had been, for years, an idle drunk and wasteful gambler and was chiefly responsible for the slow decay that the estate was falling into from lack of adequate funds for its upkeep.

It was in these comfortable slippers then that Lady Lotherington glided through her draughty corridors to answer the black telephone hidden in a dark recess beneath the stairs. The two piece telephone almost shook the ear piece loose as it trembled with each beckoning ring. The Lady lifted it and listened, a rare smile creeping across her face as she recognised the familiar voice. This voice belonged to a middle-aged man who lived in a town twelve miles away. He made all people's business his own and often rang the lady at strange times, when she would talk, and sometimes laugh, with him for hours.

The Lady: Hello, is that you?

Man: It is madam.

The Lady: Have you found out? Is it true?

Man: Well there are elements of truth to it, but I have discovered more, much more than you would have dreamed of. Such details to make our hearts leap for joy. Oh, you cannot know how much this will please you.

The Lady: Yes, yes, out with it. I want to know.

Some would have said that she wriggled and squirmed like a schoolgirl eager for gossip, others would have said like a trapped worm on the hook. For myself I neither know, nor care, and would prefer to offer the description that she moved awkwardly; a broken machine anticipating repair.

Man: Be patient Madam, for the full story shall be told and the designs we shall engineer will need careful thought and much deliberation. Do not be too hasty, this is after all some kind of life we are toying with.

The Lady: I understand. Have no fear, I shall be most careful.

Man: Then I shall begin...

And it was here, in the excited pause, as The Lady was listening most intently, that he let out a rasping, grating, cough that echoed down the phone line. I shuddered, The Lady winced. It is my suggestion that these coughs (for they happened frequently) were deliberate and served only to attempt to distract her. Hell! How do I know? being only the memory of some burnt photograph.

Man: It came all of a sudden. So unexpected that there was not time to get to the hospital. The others arrived in the hospital. For this one though there was the comfort of home, initially at least. Swift and painless someone called it, as often things can be in the depths of night. I'm sure I heard those first screams as I slept. Still it has arrived now, and only eleven months after those twins you know?

The Lady: Oh, I know very well. She's a machine, churning them out like there's no future without them.

Man: Or with them.

They both laughed; I ventured some cruel chuckle and almost broke the connection.

The Lady: What was that?

Man: Some disturbance, the weather is bad here.

The Lady: It is fine here, even some sun in the late afternoon.

Man: Perhaps it is heading your way?

The Lady: What?

Man: The weather.

The Lady: Perhaps.

Man: Where was I?

The Lady: Only eleven months since those twins you said. Then we must remember the two she had before. The girl and the boy, how old are they now?

Man: She is six and he's about three, Roberta and...

The Lady: (*sharply*) Don't use their names. I hate their names.

Man: Fine. I shall not use their names if they displease you. Well, it seems they have had second thoughts now. They are quite happy with the four of them and this fifth seems to be unwanted.

The Lady: Are they Catholic do you know?

Man: Now there's a point, I don't know. I shall have to write that down for later investigation.

The Lady: It would be useful to know now, it might have some bearing on my decision you understand.

Pause.

Man: Hmm, it may well do. Still I do not know. I could hazard a guess?

The Lady: No there shall be no guesses. We will have to do without all the facts.

Man: Well, the child was born on Ascension Day. If they were Catholic they would be obliged to attend Mass, I don't recall them leaving the house.

The Lady: They might be non-practising Catholics.

Man: Then what would it matter?

The Lady: It still matters to me. Anyway don't worry about that, I shall make a decision without all the facts!

Man: And you think that is wise?

The Lady: Not wise but a necessity, given the circumstances. Now please continue.

Man: Very well...

The terrible cough was unleashed again, would you not agree that it was deliberate; after his icy words with The Lady concerning these questions of religion? I think he secretly hated, or loved, her. Can you bring yourself to accept the words of a deaf old worm such as me?

Man: They have already made enquiries about adoption.

The Lady: Adoption?

Man: That is what I said. They have even gone so far as to fill out some forms.

The Lady: Some forms?

Man: Indeed, and they have had a meeting with some government group, some sort of charitable institution. They have a low income you see.

The Lady: People of very little means.

Man: People who mean very little.

They laughed and laughed and laughed. For me it is difficult, as you may have gathered, to gauge these blocks of time but if it is an issue then I think they laughed for days or weeks. It certainly was not for seconds; I have some bleak memory of those. Ah, seconds, those were the days! Funny how vast gulfs of time, huge gargantuan aeons, immense intractable millennia, have given me only an inkling of a moment—enough said, they laughed long (and loud).

Man: *They are making enquiries* shall we say?

The Lady: Yes, let us say 'they are making enquiries'.

Man: *They are making enquiries* into different possibilities concerning their new infant's welfare.

The Lady: That is good of them.

Man: So having heard all I could from valuable sources, and gathered information from those who know of these things...

The Lady: What *things*?

Man: The *things* which we have discussed.

The Lady: Oh, the delicate discussions of *those* things.

A reverberating clearing of the throat battered The Lady's ears at this point and it seems opportune to point out that I have not the slightest knowledge of what this conversation concerned. It seemed to me—having heard all of the words ever exchanged in the shady confines of this mansion of woe—that they delighted more in the irrelevance of speech and its futile, beautiful, undercurrents of death. You accuse me of exaggeration, of dramatic hyperbole, well perhaps that's true. True? Yes, of course it is true. I am the most brazen liar that life has ever known, the most shameful charlatan, a giddy fool sick of this ageless dance. I should never deny though it is hard—as hard as a blood-stained oak club in the teeth—to tell tales.

Man: Having made my investigations I am certain that we can make other arrangements to confound them.

The Lady: Yes, I quite agree. What was the mother's name again?

Man: Charlotte, but I thought you hated their names.

The Lady: I hate the children's names. Charlotte is a beautiful name. I believe my own mother, or grandmother—I forget which—was called Charlotte. I might be wrong but something in the name appeals to me.

Man: Then you have something planned?

The Lady: That is an astute assumption. I think I might be able to find a place for him in the new school in the swamp.

Man: It has been finished then, so soon?

The Lady: Yes, completed last month with all the little touches to frighten lonely boys. It seems marvellous from what my cousin told me in his letter. The place reeks of all that's ancient; there's even an armoury.

Man: Wonderfully mediaeval!

The Lady: Yes, a remarkable creation for the lost. It is thrilling to realise that there are still those dedicated to the enduring agony of life. I quote some favourite words of my dear departed husband, 'worse than death is to vanish before one's own eyes'.

With that Lady Lotherington kicked off her slippers beneath her long grim skirts and played with a thin gold ring she had worn on a toe for fifteen years.

'We're all going to die, Jamie,' Roberta said, pouring another draught of vodka into her glass, 'and when it happens it doesn't seem to bother some people. It's what you leave behind that counts; the record of it. However dismal you might think life has been you've got to record it all, or as much of it as you can manage.'

She stood up and walked over to the fridge and took out another bottle of coke to have with the vodka. She stood a while puzzling over the label on the plastic bottle.

'I hate this company you know,' she said, walking back to the pine table, 'but I still carry on drinking this crap; diet, caffeine free, cherry flavour, I'll have any of it.' She smiled at Jamie. It was a true, warm, embracing smile.

Jamie had sat there for the last two hours, steadily working his way through the bottle with Roberta. This was the first time he had been invited to her flat. It was a bed-sit, in a grim area of town, and above the notorious Vishnu Palace which had been closed down a year ago but was now doing good business again. A pokey window in the far end of the room looked down on a flashing neon light below, and the car park beyond. Occasionally Roberta would peer out of the window as though she was expecting someone. She had managed to fit quite a lot of furniture and items in the room without it seeming overcrowded.

Jamie's eyes were swimming though, and the occasional wafts of scented meats and spices from the restaurant below caught him, making his stomach churn with nausea. As he looked at Roberta's smiling face, the room began to spin and he decided it was time to get some fresh air.

'Do you mind if we go outside for a moment?' Jamie asked, he clipped his words sharply in an effort to appear less drunk. 'I need to get some cigarettes too.'

Roberta seemed absorbed in thought and absent-mindedly replied, 'Yes, let's go and get a coffee at The Junction.'

The Junction was a cafe that never seemed to close, often Jamie stopped there after a night out in town. It was about five minutes walk and should sober him up enough to continue the evening talking to Roberta. That was what he wanted most of all—to talk to her. They had already spent three hours together after meeting by chance in the High Street and going back to Roberta's. Jamie had been surprised by the invite, and by her talkativeness. It made a change from her usual yes and no answers. They had once spent a night at The Golden Crown and she had said only seven words to him during the entire evening. Jamie spent a lot of time thinking about Roberta, she seemed to require careful consideration. He had almost given up any hope of understanding her, until today's meeting.

They brushed past a group of young lads who looked as though they had just come from the pub. Jamie looked at his watch, the pubs were just closing and the Vishnu Palace would start to get busy now. The biting winter night woke him instantly, and a harsh wind was blowing up the street. After a few staggering steps he was walking confidently and felt able to cope with another bottle if they returned later. Roberta's head darted about, searching every shadow for something Jamie could not see. She seemed to be anxious about something, turning occasionally to look behind her. 'Don't be afraid,' Jamie said, with a grin. 'I'm here to protect you.'

Roberta did not catch the ironic note in his voice, 'I'm not afraid Jamie, I just feel a little sick,' she said sternly.

He nodded his head in agreement, thinking she referred to the bottle of vodka that they had nearly finished. This was not the case though, Roberta was a capable, although infrequent, drinker and she did not feel nauseous from alcohol. It was instead the feeling that beneath the pavement, behind the concrete facades, between each crack in the walls and floors, there was the pulsating life force of the organic, bent on revenge for the monstrosity of building that had usurped its role. Roberta found a deep satisfaction in the artifice of urban sprawl; as it generated itself from necessity, and found itself inside the aesthetic. For Roberta it was the perfect paradox: she loved the town because it operated as nature, but was not natural, and she loathed the organic world because it could not be other than itself. It had taken on the horror of a disease within her mind; a pest to be eradicated. Some solution must be found—it had become terrifying. She had never been like her brothers, or sister Rebecca, revelling in the illusory freedom of Sorham Wood. She had always wanted to be at home, safely inside the bricks of the family dwelling; a family she could never understand or feel a part of, but which was *hers* nonetheless.

They wandered through the empty subway that took them under Six-Ways Junction, the bright yellow lights shocked their eyes, which had grown accustomed to the moonless night. The subway unnerved Roberta even further: it was underground. Soil and roots surrounded them, held back by a veneer of tiled concrete. The monotonous rush of the traffic echoed behind them, easing her mind, and soon they emerged surrounded by the confused lights of the main street, which never seemed to sleep, the shop windows still bright with special offers and empty aspiration.

The Junction was on the next corner, next to the bus station, and they could smell it from halfway down the street. An odour of greasy chips and stewed tea drifted in the night air. Luckily a table still remained, by the window, and Jamie grabbed it immediately. The walk had completely sobered him up, and he was looking forward to one of Albert's bacon rolls and steaming mugs of tea. A mixed group were in that evening, as was to be expected. Some were obviously on their way from the pub to a nightclub and had succumbed to the drunken hunger that provided most of The Junction's trade. Other people were less easily defined though; a few trampish looking individuals cradled warm mugs, but a man in a pin-striped suit read *The Times* by the cooking hatch, occasionally taking a bite from an unappetising roll on a plate beside him. Two plump women laughed and joked with Albert as he cooked them some egg and chips, and a bemused looking man with a suitcase played with some matches on his table, glancing frequently at his watch.

'So what's this book about?' Roberta asked, passing him his cup of tea and roll. She sipped at a large Espresso. 'The one you've been working on for the last couple of years.'

'Well, I'd rather not try to explain it,' Jamie replied. He had never told anyone about the ideas behind this novel, they changed too much. 'It'll all be different next week.'

'Okay,' said Roberta, so unconcerned by his refusal that it bothered Jamie.

In order to keep her interested he decided to outline the original idea he had started with.

'Well, it's a modern attempt at Frankenstein,' he said, as Roberta turned to listen. 'You know—what you create rebels and attempts to destroy the creator, the failure of man as God. I'm using genetics as the basis for the book. The main character sees weakness in his children, he becomes annoyed that he cannot change them, control them, force them to do the things he didn't, to correct the mistakes he made and so on. He doesn't trust the changes that society puts on his children and begins developing an artificial environment for them to exist in. It's taken a turn towards science fiction, so I suppose it'll have to be set quite some time in the future. I can't be sure whether to make him a researcher for an established programme or an independent scientist, a sort of renegade.'

Jamie sat back for a moment, absorbed in thought. This was why he never tried to explain the book. The ideas evaporated as rapidly as they came, displaced by newer thoughts, and always the doubts. Even when he actually sat down to write something he found his mind racing with so many possible scenarios that he could not begin. Roberta sighed, and looked at her watch.

'You see,' Jamie continued, 'the main point I want to develop is the effect of rapid change. In this case he becomes dissatisfied with the results of environmental manipulation and decides to opt for rapid restructuring of genetic code. Change of any type affects us, as human beings, and here I see that the change that he sets off affects language—that which seems to be most human. After three generations he had produced offspring that no longer understand death, for themselves or for others. The creatures that he breeds have recalled some primeval instinct that had always remained dormant in their genes. As speech is lost, so too civilisation becomes lost and human life begins to slip away. The final aim of humanity is its own destruction by experiments that...'

His words dropped away, to join the buzz of voices that surrounded Roberta. She was staring at a noticeboard behind the serving area. After a few moments Jamie stopped talking, having noticed that she wasn't listening to him. Shrugging his shoulders he hunched over his tea and slurped loudly from it in the hope of catching her attention.

It was of no use though, she had seen a black and white photograph pinned to the board. It was a portrait, probably taken at the turn of the century, of a woman in a shirt and trousers with a kind of helmet on her head. The costume reminded Roberta of someone on safari. It had obviously been taken in a studio though, with thick drapes behind her and a large plant, with palm-like leaves, beside her. The woman had an air of defiance and determination about her that excited Roberta's imagination. She had a good use for that photograph and was determined to have it.

She stood and walked over to where Albert was serving. She peered intently at the picture and said in an automatic voice, 'Can I have that photograph please?'

Albert turned around with a confused expression on his face. The two ladies he was serving seemed equally puzzled by her abrupt demand.

'What photo's that then, love?' Albert asked, rubbing his stumpy hands on his apron.

Roberta pointed to the noticeboard, there was a desperation in her eyes, something deeply absorbing that seemed to have taken control of her. Albert walked to the noticeboard and fumbled with the pin that held the picture up. He walked back, gazing fondly at the picture, and placed it on the counter in front of her.

'That's not a photo, my dear,' he chuckled. 'It's a postcard from my brother, said it reminded 'im of our mum. I couldn't see it myself. You have it if you want it.' He grinned, and winked, at the ladies he had been talking to. They giggled and whispered to each other.

Roberta looked intently at the postcard. She seemed to want to know every detail of the picture. 'Thank you,' she said. 'Thank you very much. This is such an important thing for me.'

Albert shrugged and watched her walk back to the table where Jamie was. He was already talking quietly with the two ladies at the counter, and occasionally one would turn around to look at Roberta as subtly as possible. She was still studying the picture when she sat down opposite Jamie.

'So what was that all about?' Jamie asked, still annoyed that she had not heard all the details of his work, especially as she had been the first to ever hear about it.

'It's nothing really,' said Roberta, slipping the postcard into her bag. 'I'll show you later, maybe.'

Jamie was intrigued now but thought it best not to press for an answer. Roberta seemed so serious about many things, often what appeared to him to be the most mundane or commonplace occurrence. She could silence him with a few words, as she had done last week when discussing her strange dream. Jamie felt aware that he was always at risk of breaking some unforeseen limit of tolerance she had when in company. Their relationship intrigued him, not least because he longed to know what she thought of him. He recalled something she had said to him earlier in the evening, before they had become too drunk: 'I never want to hear about your family, just leave them to be discovered.' It was the type of comment that seemed typical of Roberta, when she spoke more than monosyllables. Her comments were icy, almost to the point of being hurtful, but always mysterious and thought-provoking.

She was looking through Jamie. It was an unnerving feeling. Her contented smile had appeared again and she was happy—in some hidden moment of perfection. Jamie intruded with a cough that brought her back from her trance. She looked at him with sympathetic eyes as though she had understood some gentle pain.

'What are you thinking about?' Jamie asked, worried by her detachment.

'You're a lovely boy, Jamie,' she said, reaching a hand out to stroke his cheek. 'Let's not spoil it, shall we?'

She stood up swiftly, swinging her bag over a shoulder and waving goodbye to Albert. She turned to Jamie and asked, 'Ready to go now?'

He nodded and drained the last of his tea, still pondering her previous remark. Spoil what? It was another of her comments that seemed to arrest further discussion. His head began to ache. Another drink might help him understand her more.

'Back to your flat then?' he asked, making certain that he was still welcome, considering the strange mood she seemed to have sunk into.

'Yes,' she replied sharply, already on her way to the door.

They returned through the subway and few quiet streets that led to the Vishnu Palace. The midnight silence had descended; that time after the pubs had closed and before the nightclubs had. Jamie enjoyed this time of the night—peaceful, yet menacing—and neither of them spoke a word on the return journey, both involved with their private thoughts.

The Vishnu Palace was occupied by a few late night diners, talking and laughing. Jamie could still hear the murmur of their voices as Roberta opened the door to her flat. Hearing the voices from the restaurant below had irritated him earlier, but now he felt the soothing effect of their tone, a strange sense of belonging came over him. Perhaps this was why Roberta liked living here, he thought. She had already placed the second bottle of spirits on the table and gestured for Jamie to sit down, 'Help yourself,' she said, draining the dregs of the first bottle into her glass. 'You know where the coke is.'

He poured a large measure of vodka, swigging it back in one gulp, watching as Roberta carefully opened the top drawer of her chest of drawers. She took out an old wooden box—looking like mahogany in the dim light—and came over to the table with it. She sat opposite Jamie, who quietly watched her. From the box she took a bundle of letters and a pile of photographs. She took a blank sheet of paper from the box and a pair of scissors and proceeded to cut a square of paper that fitted the size of the postcard which she had just obtained from Albert at The Junction. Jamie poured himself another drink, not daring to interrupt her task, which she carried out with an air of solemnity and ritual. He was soon feeling the haze of alcohol blurring his thoughts, and he thought it best to mix his third vodka with some coke. Besides, he would then be able to get a better view of what Roberta was doing with the postcard. She glued the paper over the writing on the back of the card and smoothed it down. Jamie took the bottle of coke from the fridge and stood behind her, peering over her shoulder as she wrote carefully on the back of the card, 'Sarah McIntyre, taken in Baghdad, whilst on the Koldewey dig at Babylon.' She was writing in a copperplate script which seemed alien to her own style, and she struggled slowly with each letter to achieve authenticity.

'What's that then?' asked Jamie, puzzled by her writing and the reason she had asked for the card.

'It's a friend of my great grandmother,' Roberta replied, with satisfaction. 'She was an archaeologist.'

'That was Albert's postcard though, it's a modern copy of the original photo,' Jamie said with a chuckle, pouring coke into their drinks.

Roberta's eyes stared into him accusingly.

'I'm not concerned with the original, Jamie,' she said, taking a gulp from her drink and making her way back to the chest of drawers with her box. 'It doesn't need to be the original to document the past.'

'It can't be your great grandmother's friend though,' Jamie said, with slight sarcasm. 'That would be too much of a coincidence.'

'Precisely,' Roberta replied. 'We can't rely on coincidence, it never happens. All that remains is to invent it. What do I know of this woman in the picture? At least now she has an identity again—a completely new history for someone who has been forgotten.'

Jamie did not want to say anymore about the postcard, it was obvious that Roberta was becoming irritated by his comments. He walked over to the chest of drawers where she was sorting through the drawer. He looked inside and saw a collection of items: a pile of files, bulging with papers, a leather glasses case, a battered wallet, a number of watches of varying age and three old books. He recognised the top one, a small book of poetry: *Palgrave's Golden Treasury*. It was the first poetry he had ever read, and had loved it so much that he spent a whole weekend reading and rereading it when he was eight. Seeing the book again brought back a flood of sentimental feeling, heightened by a second wave of drunkenness that began to overwhelm him.

'This was my grandmother's book,' Roberta said, picking up the slim volume of poetry.

'Was it?' Jamie said, reaching out for the chest of drawers to steady himself.

'It may well have been,' Roberta said impatiently.

'What do you mean?' He said, wrinkling his brow in confusion, defensive over his own personal association to the book. 'Either it is or it isn't.'

Roberta looked at him blankly.

'I don't think you have to know either way,' she whispered, as though to herself. 'It is useful for me to think it was hers.'

Jamie was perplexed by her collection of old photographs and memorabilia, which was clearly a complete fabrication of her family history.

'It's not true though,' he said, taking the book from the table where Roberta had just placed it. He leafed through a few pages as though it might provide some insight into Roberta's thoughts. 'That's completely false. Surely you could trace your family's past? It isn't natural to just create a new history for them.'

'What do you mean?' she asked, looking equally as confused as he did. 'It doesn't matter, we're all part of some fantastical script. Don't cling to ridiculous concerns like truth. There is nothing natural about any of this, and the only history there is, is *new*, inventive and changing. There is nothing for us phantasms but the dream of ancestry and the hollow fictions that belong to it.'

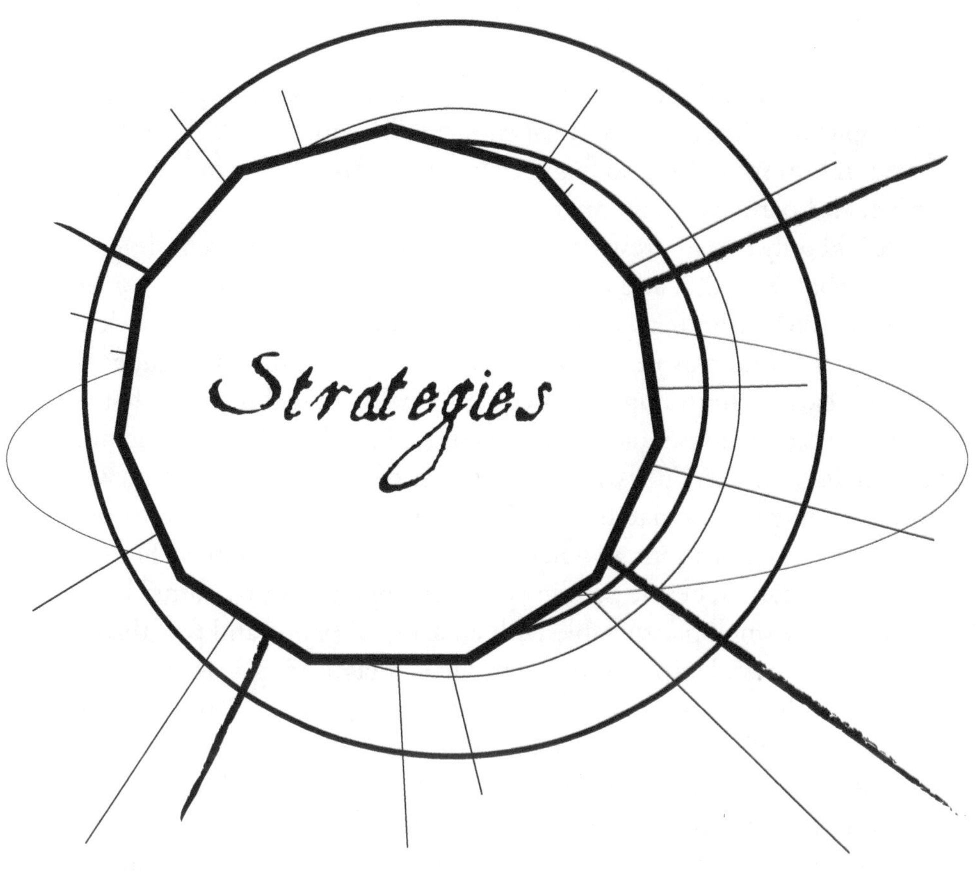

Samuel Wood was in his late fifties although he appeared to be much younger to those few who saw him. He had a chubby face, with an uneven growth of stubble that had never really grown often enough for him to be concerned with shaving regularly. When he was younger he had delicate blond hair. Now though it had taken on a slightly darker colour; an 'almost brown' he called it. There was very little on Samuel Wood's face that suggested age, he had not acquired any wrinkles on his forehead, although a few lines had developed around his eyes. Those who knew Samuel Wood though would have been able to identify that these lines were due to his interest in painting small military figures until late into the evening. If anyone could have seen him at the window of his eleventh floor flat they would have found him hunched over a low plastic table handling these delicate figurines. His voice did not display any form of age either; it seemed as though his entire person had become trapped somewhere in late adolescence. His manner was always jovial and there seemed wonderment in everything he said. The few people who knew him were always careful with Samuel Wood; there seemed in him something so fragile, some innocence that would have been terrible, and perhaps terrifying, to destroy.

He had only two interests: painting model soldiers and assembling them into large battle scenes, and gardening. It might seem unusual for someone who had lived without a garden for nearly fifty years to enjoy gardening but Samuel Wood was determined that his city life should include some pleasant, leafy surroundings. Consequently he had filled his small flat with an abundance of household plants, including Azaleas, Chrysanthemums, Weeping figs, Yuccas, Fuchsias and a number of carnivorous varieties whose nastic movements fascinated him. The only room that was free from the undergrowth was his lounge where a great table stood, almost filling the room. In the corner, beside a sliding door that opened onto a flimsy looking balcony, was a small plastic table with an array of paints and paintbrushes, miniature figures clamped into small vices, magnifying glasses, and jam jars filled with various chemicals now coloured by paint. Beside the chair there was a small pile of thick books which detailed the patterns, colours and proper dress of every army or military organisation that had ever lifted arms to fight another; every possible uniform was there from the Roman Triani to a modern American Marine. On the larger table was a landscape modelled exactly to scale. He was working on a diorama of the siege of Alesia in 52 BC. Each detail was carefully researched before he completed a section of the landscape. Sometimes a full recreation of a battle could take over a year to finish. Then he would take photographs from all possible angles of the diorama. It would then be dismantled and Samuel Wood chose another battle that he wished to recreate. His principal pleasure in this came not from the appearance and perfection of the finished battle scene but from the months of reading and cogitating over the roles and decisions made by the generals or commanders in question. He considered it a responsibility to the finished piece's authenticity that he should assume the frame of mind of both the victor and the vanquished.

Standing at his kitchen sink, gazing out across the urban sprawl of an industrial estate, with huge vehicles depositing and collecting pallets of mysterious commodities, he considered Caesar's options as he surveyed Vercingetorix's camp at Alesia. He was repotting a small spider plant whose roots had become tangled and choked inside its constricting pot. Samuel

Wood liked to be able to control nature in this way; if he left the plant it would die, if he moved it into a larger pot with new and rich soil it would grow and thrive—but only as far as he allowed it. When a plant became too big he would simply throw it away in one of the large metal bins in the basement of the block of flats. Then he would devote his attentions to his smaller plants, training and pruning them, carefully watering and nourishing them and tending their tangled roots, until they too became too large for his liking and were elected to become waste. Samuel Wood was supremely urban: he decided everything, nothing need disturb him and if it did he could dispose of it. He could be as isolated as he wished. Behind the door of his flat anything could happen. Nobody ever need know him.

His office door at the Department of Recovery—a shady government body whose purpose was difficult to discern even for those who worked there—displayed a small brass plaque bearing his name and warned those under him that he was the Director of that department. A number of myths had developed concerning Samuel Wood—although he did not know of them—because he was so seldom seen and communicated so rarely, even with his secretary. She would receive a bundle of dictation and errands for the coming week at precisely 3pm every Friday. She talked to him via an intercom and saw him only occasionally. People speculated about his superiors and why they had employed him. They even discussed how long he had worked there. The oldest member of the department was Anthony Timms who had been there for nearly eight years and when he had been pressed over Mr Wood he had informed everyone that Mr Wood had always been the Director for as long as he had worked there and probably for some considerable time before that. Mr Timms had been recently provided with his own office near to Mr Wood's and he was seen less frequently by everyone, leading them to wonder if it was the Department itself that slowly engulfed its employees in secrecy. But that, they all agreed, was a ridiculous idea.

On one October morning Samuel Wood stood near his door, observing his staff as they walked along the corridor outside his office, heading for their partitioned cubicles further down the corridor. He watched them through a thin blind that covered a small window by the side of his door. He was able to see them but they were unable to see him. Samuel Wood preferred it that way.

Walking to the grey metal cabinet he opened the top drawer and leafed through a few files until he came to the one he wanted. He had looked at this file everyday for almost a year. The file contained information on one of his employees: Miss Roberta Reid. Samuel Wood found this woman fascinating precisely because she was not fascinating at all. He saw her arrive for work each morning at half past eight. Now that it was beginning to get colder she would arrive wrapped in a brown sheepskin coat that was too large for her. She would walk slowly up the corridor undoing the coat and absorbing the warmth in the Department building. Some mornings she would pause for a second and look at the plaque on Samuel Wood's door. This morning Samuel Wood stood by his door, waiting for her to arrive, peering through his blind with her file in his hand. Clipped to the top of the file was a passport photograph she had been asked to provide 'for the records'.

That morning it had been raining and Roberta Reid had stopped off at the market cafe for a cup of tea and a cigarette. She was a little late and hurried up the corridor towards her office. As she passed the Director's door she paused for a moment, turning to glance at the brass plaque glinting beneath the humming strip lights: Mr S. Wood, Director. She felt as though she wanted to reach out and touch the plaque, to trace the name with her fingertips so that somehow she might know who he was. Her hand reached out slowly, but—perhaps nervous of some impropriety—she quickly withdrew it and walked on towards the office.

Samuel Wood had watched her as she reached for his office door. He treasured this employee. He was so interested in her that he had given her an office to herself within three months of starting. Most of the other workers were lucky to get their own office after even three years of employment. It did not have a brass plaque; instead there was a black plastic plate on the door: 23.

He was sure she would be pleased with it.

Roberta had not even thought twice about it on the day she had been moved to her new office, she merely gathered her belongings and moved from the large room, partitioned into workspaces, into her new isolated space. Samuel Wood had watched her reaching for his door. He reached for the door handle from the inside and as he was about to touch it she looked away and moved hurriedly up the corridor.

A strange thing happened: Mr Samuel Wood—Director of the Department of Recovery, keen reconstructor of ancient battles, and amateur urban gardener—became very angry. He threw Roberta Reid's file across the room. It hit a large Fuchsia 'Boliviana' by the window. The plant toppled to the ground, its long-tubed scarlet flowers scattering amongst the pages of Roberta Reid's file. The pot cracked, spilling soil and white roots like tentacles across Roberta's passport photograph.

That evening Samuel Wood returned home. He was rather disturbed by what had happened that morning. He had carried the broken fuchsia back in a plastic carrier bag. Looking over its damaged leaves and broken roots he decided to leave it to die. He placed the bag and contents on the draining board for later disposal in the waste bin and moved through to the lounge.

He poured himself a large glass of whisky—normally an indulgence only allowed at Christmas—and looked over the battlefield before him, knowing that the Siege of Alesia was almost over.

That night he began work on the figurines needed for the final part of the conflict between the Gauls and Romans. Caesar's plan had been simple: to wait until the leader of the Gauls was forced to make a foolish manoeuvre out of desperation. Samuel Wood wondered when his wait would be over.

I pulled the handbrake on and let out a sigh. It had been a hard day, not at work (I have no formal employment) but from worrying. Had I made the right impression on her? Why did she never want to meet my gaze? Roberta Reid was certainly a very peculiar woman, but I felt attracted to her—somewhat obsessively—nonetheless.

I gathered together a few scraps of paper I had been writing notes on. Underneath them on the passenger seat was a copy of Freud's *The Interpretation of Dreams* that I had been trying to grind my way through. I have just finished the short section entitled 'Why Dreams are Forgotten'. It seems that in the process of recalling the dream in the morning we subject it to a process of logic that does not fit with the absurd nature of the dream itself. The copy I have borrowed from a friend has a rather serious looking picture of the analyst on the front. I assume it was taken of him when he was in his late thirties, yet his eyes seem so young, almost infantile; small black marbles with a gleam of light at their edge. I smile at his beard and moustache though. They look false. It as though a black rat has curled around his mouth. I can almost see it breathing; that young black rat.

The car door refuses to shut, again. Even when it does I can't seem to lock it. I decide to leave it unlocked and only just on the catch. Any thief is quite welcome to the old sandwich wrappers and coke cans, and certainly nobody would think of stealing the car itself. It's almost impossible to start it, even with the key. Turning round I head towards the lonely door in the side of the brick building. A neon light is trying to flicker on above the entrance. It reads 'Zarathustra's Drive Inn', although the 'Inn' part has fallen down and hangs at right angles to the rest of the sign. As I reach the door the sign flicks into life and I am surrounded by a lurid green glow. It only lasts a second though as it blinks off and resumes its struggle to provide another moment of illumination. I look back at the car park; enough spaces for about one hundred cars. There are only three, including my own, at the moment. I doubt if any more will turn up. It looks like a busy night.

The square building that houses the 'Inn' was destined to become a factory, and is built at the edge of an industrial estate just beyond suburbia. A great fuss was made when it was built, about three years ago. There were demonstrations from locals, but when the planning decisions were finally confirmed people returned to their homes and made ready for the articulated vehicles that they believed would be trundling past their homes through the day and night. This never happened, the developers had made a terrible mistake with the positioning of the site and few businesses were interested. The place has become quite a wasteland now, with weeds and grasses establishing themselves around fairly modern looking buildings. In fact I always find it quite eerie to see something so new decaying so rapidly.

It was the perfect site for 'Zarathustra's Drive Inn' because it was so cheap. The council had no problems granting a license to the owner, Joseph, because they didn't want to lose face over the whole ordeal. Now businesses come and go every few months, enjoying the hopes of their own autonomy for a while and then sliding into bankruptcy. I've often wondered whether it's the actual place that ruins them, or perhaps it is some precognition of their own downfall that draws them here. Still, at least Zarathustra's endures; though not for much longer if you listen to Joseph too much.

I stamp my feet on the 'welcome' coco matting in the entrance hall. A coat stand on my right has an old grey raincoat hanging on it. It has been here for about three months now. Someone must have left it but Joseph refuses to throw it away in case they return. I hang my coat beneath it and brush my feet again (Joseph cannot stand dirty shoes). I chuckle a little at the absurdity of this little bar. I'm standing in what appears to be the hallway of an ordinary house, checking to make sure my feet are clean, as though I was visiting my mother. I open the half-glass door that leads into the main bar area. It is entirely constructed from hardboard which has been used to create a vast bar area within a huge warehouse. I carefully pull the door shut behind me; the flimsy wall surrounding it shakes a little.

A shabby middle aged man in a suit sits on a bar stool, turning a glass of beer around and around on a mat, staring fixedly at it. Another younger man—also in a suit—is playing on a pinball machine at the other end of the bar in an area that Joseph had wanted to turn into a sort of fast food area with a 'drive-thru' facility. The drive-thru kiosks have been boarded over but the awful green and red plastic tables and chairs still remain. The area is hardly ever used now and only one fluorescent tube lights the place. The main bar area is the exact opposite, being homely and quite enticing. It reminds me of an old English pub, such as one would find in the heart of the countryside, with thick black beams from which hang a variety of strange mugs and utensils. The walls are tobacco stained and carry an array of old farming tools; the use of which an urbanite like myself can only guess at. Yet after this first initial glow of rural feeling one's attention is drawn swiftly back to how false the place is. The timbers are actually mouldings, the utensils plastic and the smoke stained walls have been quite crudely painted as such. I think it is this complete 'wrongness' about the place that draws me to it so much.

Perhaps it's 'wrongness' that drew me to Roberta Reid.

I've been friends with her since this place was built, I brought her once but she didn't seem to like it. Not that she said anything; you have to guess everything she thinks. Both this bar and Roberta have a funny way with them. They pull you in with some quirky charm and then you notice the details about them that don't fit in. Roberta works and lives in an urban environment yet she cannot seem to inhabit the place. She's always on the border of something primitive. It's as though she was never really present at any event. You could almost forget she existed; yet that's the hardest thing to do: the same with Zarathustra's. I don't even think of the place all day and yet most evenings I end up walking through the door as though I was driven here, half asleep. Maybe it isn't Zarathustra's that's bizarre—with its half-American deserted eating place and rustic little English bar—perhaps it's me, with my seven years loitering as an unpublished writer. And now, thinking of my own failings, I don't seem to want to judge any of us now.

I take my usual seat by the coal-effect fire and leaf through a few pages of my latest ideas; of course, I haven't finished the last novel that I began two years ago. Still, I don't suppose it hurts to have too many ideas, they'll all get used sometime. An abrupt bark awakens me from my thoughts.

'Good evening!' a voice calls, a harsh Germanic edge to it, mingling badly with the faked American accent. It is Joseph. 'Shall I get you a beer?'

'Yes please,' I absent-mindedly reply, but then remember what Joseph means by a beer, 'but I'll just start with a small one, okay.' Looking up I see him returning the three pint jug he was going to pour and selecting a pint glass. He is smiling like some deranged hirsute infant; a gummy grin poking through a straggly red beard. His bulbous red nose and cheeks are glowing—I'd guess he has been drinking most of the afternoon.

His son Georg must have the evening off because Joseph is wearing a large apron tied around his waist—Georg normally cooks and serves behind the bar (not that people order food that regularly). The apron bears a large colourful picture of Mickey Mouse (Joseph adores cartoons).

I can never get over how unreal Joseph looks. It's impossible to judge his age. His laugh is innocent and yet he can be cruel and vindictive. And if his manner is rather strange then his background is even more so, along with the events that enabled him to set up this bar.

I have heard his story so many times I almost feel it is my own history.

Joseph was born in Austria, in a village in the Tyrol. His parents were Croatian and devout Roman Catholics. He had four sisters and three brothers, Joseph being the eldest. His father was obsessed with religion and Joseph was rigorously instructed to live a Christian life. His father groomed him to become a priest, and the family worked hard to provide enough to save for when he would go to University. His adolescence is a little shady, he will not explain very much. At some point in his teens his mother died (I picked up that some responsibility lay with his father for this). Joseph finally made the journey to Vienna, where he started to study theology in preparation for entry to the priesthood. At some point during the first few months he met an American who introduced him to philosophy, which he appeared to have an affinity for. Without his father knowing he changed courses and began to study in earnest. Helped by this American friend he was soon making waves with rather radical ideas. One summer he even spent in New York, informing his father that trainee priests were required to complete some work abroad before they could be admitted to the clergy—I got the feeling that there was a little more to Joseph's relationship with his American friend than he has told me, but I haven't pressed the issue.

I wonder if Roberta Reid is gay.

Anyway, after he came back from America he continued his degree and was highly credited on graduation. His father and brothers made the long journey to see him graduate. His father had been sent a letter by Joseph confirming that he had obtained his degree and would soon be working, 'for the best of causes'. As his degree was awarded (in Philosophy, not Theology) his father leapt up in rage and promptly died of a heart attack. Apparently Joseph and his friend took the first plane back to New York and Joseph has never seen his family since. He tells the story as some triumphant and macabre joke. And when he tells it, his voice is quietly hateful. It seems he spent many years in America, circulating in a somewhat dilettante scene. His friend died and left him a fair sum of money with which he moved to England where he married a woman and had his son Georg. He does not speak of his wife much, all I have gathered is that she taught History at some University in the North. About five years ago she died—from cancer if I remember rightly—and Joseph could start to create the first of a chain of theme cafes, bars, clubs and restaurants all built around great philosophers of the past. This is where Joseph's enthusiasm for American culture becomes a little confused. He seems to have adored the glitz and glamour of the American dream—the plastic speed products, the false bonhomie and kitsch commodities. Yet he tried to introduce into it a loftier ideal. I have not read much philosophy but Joseph seems to have steeped his entire existence in it, everything he says is some hidden reference to some thinker that most have never heard of, let alone read.

So 'Zarathustra's Drive Inn' was meant to be the first in a chain. Joseph called it 'the prelude to the eating habits of the future, a solution to the nihilism of fast food'.

Well—I don't need to tell you—it never worked.

Joseph's grand idea for Zarathustra's was to combine the fast food drive-thru with an old English Inn and to show avant-garde European films on a large 'drive-in' cinema screen outside. The final part was never even attempted, but I admire the ambition. The restaurant and drive-thru kiosks were built, but never used.

The problem with Joseph is he is so lost in his little world, and he thinks other people are also lost there too. He still does a little food that he chalks up on boards around the bar area. These depend on what he has been reading most recently, last week the dream cuisine was 'Schopenhauer's Special': a bowl of garden peas, to be consumed using chopsticks. After explaining the dish to me (not what I would call a great culinary achievement) Joseph looked at me with an expectant grin waiting for my comment. It was lost on me and I returned to my seat to ponder the philosophical, and indeed the ethical, implications of 'Joseph's Menu for the New World Order'. One particular favourite of mine was a few months ago when he decided to do a week of cocktails, I embraced the idea with interest and quite enjoyed the 'Wagner Wallbanger': a peculiar mixture of cherry juice, schnapps and sugar syrup which floats on a double measure of tequila, so just as you are enjoying the sweet cherry blend suddenly a mouthful of bitter agave spirit surges down your throat leaving you choking.

I look through a few more sheets of ideas, not really concentrating. Then I notice Roberta's name on one of the pages and pull it out. Scribbled at the top of the sheet in purple ink is *Roberta's Dream*. I remember now, a few weeks ago I had met her for lunch in a cafe around the corner from the gargantuan office building where she works; it's some government department she told me. I'm not sure what her role is there, she never wants to talk about her work. She ordered a strawberry milk shake and I had a coffee. As I was rambling on about some idea I had come up with for a short story she suddenly spoke very seriously, with her usual calm, about her dream the night before.

'I had a dream last night, Jamie. I can't usually recall my dreams but this one comes back to me as easily as if I were still asleep.' She took a big slurp of milk shake. I was listening intently.

'I was in a large barren desert in the middle of the day. It must have been boiling hot, the air was shimmering, yet I didn't even feel warm. In front of me a naked man was walking towards a low stone building, he was naked but for some white cloth tied around his waist. He was covered in beads of sweat and his back was bent with tiredness. Across his shoulders were terrible burns from the sun, yet he still continued and I followed behind.

When we came to the stone building he began to descend some steps that opened into a chamber below. As I entered I turned and looked outside to see hundreds of people all dressed in white robes, and as I looked up at the sky it had changed to a dark golden colour. I followed the man down the short stairway into a tall underground room. There was a sort of wooden scaffold in the centre with some steps leading up to it. He ascended and I waited at the bottom. Everything was slow and ritualised, I felt as though I had done this before; a repetition of a long forgotten ceremony. He turned to face me on the scaffold and bent to pick up a thin curved knife that lay before him.

He was in his mid-twenties with a light growth of stubble and matted black hair that had been unevenly sheared. His eyes were filled with courage and conviction as he brought the knife to his face and slowly cut off his top lip.'

The last statement took some time to sink in. Roberta had spoken it so unemotionally. I felt my heart begin to pound, with fear or excitement. She reached into her pocket and took out a packet of cigarettes and offered me one. I shook my head slowly. She lit up and filled her lungs with smoke as the burning tobacco fizzed and crackled.

'He threw the lump of bloody flesh onto the stairs before me, and continued to his lower lip. I heard the flesh tear as he ripped it from his face leaving only a toothy grimace to mark his pain. The other lip landed before my feet. He took off both ears in swift downward strokes and began carving strips of skin from his stomach. Blood flowed from the wooden platform and it was difficult to see what parts of flesh he was removing because he was awash with blood. After some time the stairs were covered in fleshy lumps, and he began to sway. Just as he was about to faint he drew the knife deeply across his throat and collapsed. He died for me.

I turned and mounted the steps and looked out across green and fertile fields. The people were still there, shouting and cheering as I raised my arms to the deep blue skies.'

I hadn't been concentrating very well on the last few details. All I could think of was the gory corpse of a man mutilated by his own hand. I didn't know what to say to Roberta. I laughed awkwardly and muttered, 'I'm surprised he didn't cut off his own genitals as well, and do the complete job.'

She looked at me blankly and replied, 'Oh, that happened after the lips, but I didn't think you'd want to hear about that part.'

She took another drag on her cigarette.

'Well it's obviously some kind of sacrifice for a new season, for the crops to grow well. It probably means that you've got to give something up before you can move on to a new beginning,' I suggested feebly, still disturbed by the entire conversation.

She took a long slurp of her milk shake—draining it until the dregs stuttered loudly through the straw—and looked at me with her cold brown eyes; she seemed offended. 'That is not what it meant at all. That is not it, at all.'

The fallen branches and dry autumn leaves cracked and rustled beneath the slow tyres of a black car, winding its way ominously down a deserted track more suited to walkers than vehicles. The road led to a single cottage, at the edge of a forgotten wood. Birds broke from the trees at the approach of the noisy black object; out of place, threatening, a remarkable, shiny, black beast.

He heard the car approaching, and heard it grind to a halt outside the window, blocking the last rays of a stuttering sun. The clock on the mantelpiece stirred itself into action, seven strikes and then silence. The car door slammed, and moments later a confident knock was heard at the door. The visitor was on time, as always, unnervingly punctual. He rose from the battered armchair and opened the door.

'Good Evening,' the guest said, striding into the cottage without invitation. It was the voice of one who greets the prisoner before walking them to the scaffold.

The visitor stood in the low-beamed living room, dressed in a fine black suit and bowler hat, with a slim briefcase by his side. He was short and thin with a stern, wrinkled face that always carried an air of contempt and irritation; as though in preparation to depart for a more important engagement. Although in his early sixties his brown eyes flickered with childish malevolence—guiltless and selfish.

'Why don't you take your seat Mr Mortimer,' he said to the man who still stood by the open door. 'We have a lot to discuss, and I would not want you to tire your young legs from standing too long. You are, after all, an intellectual, and not a physical man.'

Mr Mortimer glanced up at his smirking guest from a face brittle with lack of sleep. He made his way over to the armchair on unsteady legs. His visitor had been right, they were young legs—Mr Mortimer being no more than thirty. He had neglected himself in the last year though, while the school was being built. It was to be his triumph: an archaic building built on unstable ground—already a ruin when the first stone was laid.

His sponsors had seemed keen, they had financed the place to become an orphanage. Edward Mortimer found this a great irony, and was pleased that he had managed to pull off such an outrageous mockery on such a group of old fools. As the plans had been drawn up and the work began uneasy feelings had begun to plague him, as his benefactor's motives became ever more sinister. Why did they want to alter his plans and add the extra turret? It was to be located at the top of a spiral staircase, with no entrance; the stairs were to suddenly cease. Edward Mortimer objected: it would spoil the appearance of his design. He had to give way though with the threat of the withdrawal of funds. He was confident that he could bring the old fools round though. If they wanted a blocked up turret then he would use one of the existing ones and keep intact his marvellous creation.

Edward Mortimer did not hate the world, or anyone in it, *particularly*. He had become too absorbed in abstract ideas, lost to thought and imagery far beyond his reach. His continual frustrations and pretentious plans might have consumed him with bitterness; as developers and planners ridiculed him and made light of his old fashioned designs. With each lost commission his anger built up and would have reached a crescendo had it not been for his bankruptcy. The sudden realisation of his financial collapse had dragged his thoughts from the fantasies of Gothic arches and large light-filled spaces back into practicality. He did not need much to survive, the queer decaying cottage had been a family home for years and both parents had died, his father in the war and mother a few years ago. Little linked him to what might have been called real, but his impending ruin seemed to force him to strive to find some funding to build the structure which would complete his dreams and theories.

It was his belief in his work, and assurance in his meagre abilities that brought him to the library at Overdon one morning. There he found a list of charitable institutions willing to fund a number of enterprises and worthy concerns. Within a couple of hours he had a list of addresses to write away to, but as he was about to close the thick book his eyes were drawn to a peculiar and particularly appropriate entry, 'Abraxas Lodge, c/o Mr A.M.Randall, 14 Beech Close, Hessington, Overdon. We invite applications for support, financial or otherwise, of unusual enterprises within all areas of artistic endeavour, particularly welcome this year will be completed plans for buildings in the more Classical, Gothic, or Renaissance styles. Please submit plans in writing to the above address.'

Filled with hope Edward Mortimer sent full details; blueprints, explanations, theories, other plans for places not yet constructed. It was quite a collection of material. He settled down to wait.

It had been in October two years ago that he had been awoken, mid-morning, by a persistent tapping at his door. It must be another lost walker, he thought, and rested his head on the pillow again. The knocking continued, louder and more urgent. He angrily pulled on some clothes and answered the door. He was astonished—there stood his cousin, Edith. He had not seen her since the Lord's funeral. He had only been seventeen and remembered Edith as a stern woman in her late thirties, ignorant and aloof from her family; she had only invited them from necessity, and they had certainly provided a contrast to the inbred aristocratic mixture of the Lotheringtons.

There she stood, in a long black dress, supporting herself on a delicate stick. A gleaming black Bentley had brought her to the cottage; the same car that his present visitor had arrived in. She had entered the cottage, in much the same manner as his present visitor had, and proceeded to tell him in bitter scornful tones of her involvement, or her late husband's involvement, with Abraxas Lodge. Most of the money that remained after his years of self-indulgence had been left in a trust fund for the lodge, it was to be managed by herself—'a cruel irony', she informed her cousin. She had been approached by members of the Lodge to help fund the project, and to make initial contact with the architect for the building. Reading the name of her own cousin, she decided to come and discuss the project immediately.

So it happened that the members of The Abraxas Lodge, by coincidence and the spiteful nature of Lady Lotherington's mind, decided to offer funding for the construction of a building—on unstable ground—that would serve as an orphanage for poor discarded boys. At the meeting in London, held in a dimly lit high room of a grand hotel, Edward Mortimer thought he had pulled a wonderful stunt on all the old fools in their black suits.

It was not—as is often the case in matters such as these—Mr Mortimer who had taken the advantage though. He knew that now, slumped in his battered armchair, watching Mr Randall taking documents from his slim briefcase and arranging them on the table, covering over the sketches Edward Mortimer had spent many hours producing; drawings of mad, impossible structures, constructed on tortuous mountainsides, towering cliffs, or vertiginous outcroppings of rock rising from tempestuous seas.

'We have been busy with our doodles Mr Mortimer,' Mr Randall said, turning to him with his executioner's grin. 'I would just trouble you for a moment to read these letters I have displayed on the table.'

Edward Mortimer's tired eyes looked up at him; a beaten dog about to be offered the bone that was used to break his back. 'What are they?' he enquired, raising his aching body from the armchair and moving to the table.

'They are some of the correspondence between yourself and Mr Wright,' Mr Randall explained. 'We have found them to be very interesting reading, and I have come here today to enquire as to the nature of our relationship. That is to say the relationship between *yourself*, Mr Mortimer, and *ourselves*, The Lodge.'

Edward Mortimer did not even bother reading the letters. He had written them and knew what they contained; his nervous speculations concerning The Lodge's intentions with the turret; what they wished to hide in there, why one of the existing towers could not be used, instructions to cancel the stone that Mr Wright was to supply for the additional turret, and a few personal remarks about Mr Randall who now stood before him—obviously knowing *everything*.

'Look here, I'm sick of you all trying to ruin the building,' Edward Mortimer said, preparing himself for one of the long drawn out battles he had had with his visitor before. 'You all agreed to the plans when they were proposed, I don't know why you want to change them.'

Mr Randall stared at him, as a child does with a trapped insect, deciding which wing or leg to pluck first. 'Why do we want to change the plans?' he mused, mocking his victim. 'Because we *can*, Mr Mortimer, and because we *will*.'

This was very characteristic of Mr Randall and his associates at The Abraxas Lodge; they had only ever done anything because they *could*, and if they didn't do it, what else would there be to do? This was not true in the case of Mr Mortimer's plans for the orphanage. They had very particular reasons for wanting this additional turret, and had Edward Mortimer been a little more astute he would have picked up an uneasiness about Mr Randall that clashed with his overwhelming cruelty and suggested that he was hiding something.

'We have been in touch with Mr Wright,' he continued, 'and requested that he continue with the preparations for the stone required for the final turret. We also have a team of builders on hand who are prepared to finish the construction work.'

'You don't understand,' Edward Mortimer objected, betraying his passionate love for his building. 'It will ruin my roof, it will look odd and out of keeping with the place.'

Mr Randall nodded slowly, 'I know, I know, Edward,' he said, as a father speaks to a wailing child. Then his voice turned to a vicious sneer of contempt, 'That is *precisely* why we want it to be there.'

'It will wreck the entire design, the whole plan will be wasted,' Edward Mortimer cried.

'Wasted?' Mr Randall replied, angrily. 'Why wasted? The whole damned place is sinking anyway. What does it matter that the place doesn't look right? It won't be there in a couple of decades.'

Edward Mortimer looked shocked. He did not realise that they knew about the ground that the building was being erected on. He had chosen the site himself and they were happy to accept his ideas.

'I can see, Mr Mortimer,' he said, collecting the letters from the table, 'from your expression, that you are surprised to learn that we are aware of the building having been erected on a swamp.'

It was true though, Edward Mortimer had no idea that his benefactors were aware of his aims for the building—his crowning achievement. This sent his mind worrying further about their motives. Who would be crazy enough to fund a doomed project such as this if they knew its fate? He felt threatened by their shady organisation, which had offered no explanation of its functions. He hadn't the courage to ask for such. He had been too concerned to conceal his overall aim for the building, it was meant to be his own private joke that the place was sinking into the fetid bog that surrounded it. His fears were overcome by curiosity, or necessity, and he stuttered a question from his lips, 'Why did you want to build it, if you knew it would collapse?'

'The same could be asked of you Mr Mortimer,' Mr Randall replied, looking at the clock on the mantelpiece and checking it against his own watch. 'But then again we would not ask such intrusive questions of you. Have you not found the entire process rather easy? Have we not offered you virtually unlimited resources and support? You have contacted us if the least detail has not been to your satisfaction, and now that we have stated what we wish from our arrangement, you object!'

Mr Randall had made it plain enough for even the confused Edward Mortimer to understand that their motive for the building lay in this additional turret.

'What are you doing here then, if you have already made the arrangements for the work to be completed?' he asked, feeling more confident in the face of Mr Randall's scornful manner.

'I came here to obtain your consent, out of a sense of decorum and procedure, and if unable to obtain that consent then to inform you that we shall finish it without you,' Mr Randall said, obviously growing tired of all conversation with him.

'What is it that you are planning to shut away in that turret? What secret do you want kept hidden that cannot be concealed inside one of the turrets I have already designed?' Edward Mortimer asked.

His bold visitor was not daunted by this show of defiance, he seemed to be amused by it, and his thin lips grimaced into his peculiar smirk of self-assurance and derision, 'There can be no harm in explaining a little of it to you,' he said, placing his briefcase on the table and reaching inside his jacket pocket for a cigarette case. '*Your* turrets are in keeping with *your* building Mr Mortimer, and we are certainly pleased to have helped create such a marvellous record of antiquated architecture.'

Edward shifted his feet uneasily, unsure whether this was a compliment or an insult.

'It is precisely the fact that the turrets are in keeping with the place that we require another to be built; entirely out of keeping with *your* building, so that *we* might draw attention to that turret and make of it an object of curiosity. So that one day, before the place sinks into the earth, someone might be taken by the urge to investigate that extra, odd, out of place turret that has no entrance.'

'What do you want them to find there, if they do investigate it?' Edward asked, already aware that there could be no dissuading The Lodge from adding this turret.

'Some texts, manuscripts, writings; things that have become a burden to our associates to store,' he replied, flatly.

'Why don't you burn them instead?' Edward asked, puzzled why one should wish to hide something that was no longer wanted. Destruction seemed the obvious solution.

Mr Randall scoffed, as though he were party to some ineffable secret that would shatter Edward Mortimer's mind if he ever understood it.

'Mr Mortimer, one might ask—again—why you wanted to design a building that was going to fall down. Surely you of all people should understand what is at stake here?' He looked over at Edward Mortimer questioningly.

'I'm afraid I am unable to grasp why you would want someone to discover these books, yet take such pains in hiding them, or why you will not burn them if they are not needed,' Edward confessed.

With the air of one who instructs a gifted algebra student in the most rudimentary arithmetic Mr Randall explained, 'That is precisely what they are made for: burning. We wish to destroy them and so are therefore under an obligation to preserve them. Their contents remained a mystery to us for a long time, and yet now that we have come to understand them we have found only that they are not meant to be understood. Therefore they must be passed on to those who will struggle with them as we have done. To burn them would be to complete them, to make of them everything that they instruct.'

Edward stared at him vacantly. He could understand his own theories concerning architecture. It was a joke on his part; to build that which was already crumbling, it seemed to accomplish (in its ruin) everything he had ever thought about. Mr Randall's remarks, however, did not enlighten him further as to their desire for the building, the turrets, or their mysterious texts. He knew only that he would not consent to the fifth turret, it would have to be done without him.

'I regret to inform you then, Mr Randall,' Edward Mortimer said, trying hard to remain defiant in the face of disappointment and loss, 'that you shall have to finish it without me. I shall have no part in the building of the fifth turret.'

Mr Randall stood there a moment, and looked about the room, before lighting a cigarette from his case. Each of his slow movements seemed to last an age and Edward Mortimer wondered how long he could stifle his anger and distress.

'That is a great shame, Mr Mortimer,' he said, pausing to take a long puff of his cigarette. 'We had hoped that you might see some sense in it all and agree to cooperate. I wish you every success in your future work.'

Mr Randall did not offer his hand, or even incline his head in some gesture of farewell. It was as though—at that moment—Mr Mortimer had vanished from his senses: out of his mind in a flash, as though he had never existed. Mr Randall departed from the cottage without drawing another breath, with the solemnity of one who leaves a graveside.

There remains little more to say on the matter, I have attempted to assemble the facts, as best as I have been able. Edward Mortimer disappeared some time during the following months, after the additional turret had been completed. Many rumours suggest that he changed his mind and helped to finish the turret. But that he fell whilst capping it and was lost to the marshy ground. Others suggest that he took it upon himself, one terrible night, to find out what was hidden inside and that he fell whilst breaking an opening into the roof. He may well have left his cottage, to hide himself in another town, another country, or to destroy himself completely. I shall not conjecture further, for why should I surrender to untruths when I have attempted to construct this account from the solid, stony facts of the matter? The school still stands, and that is enough to bear witness to the certainty that mysteries endure.

III: Ex Nihilo

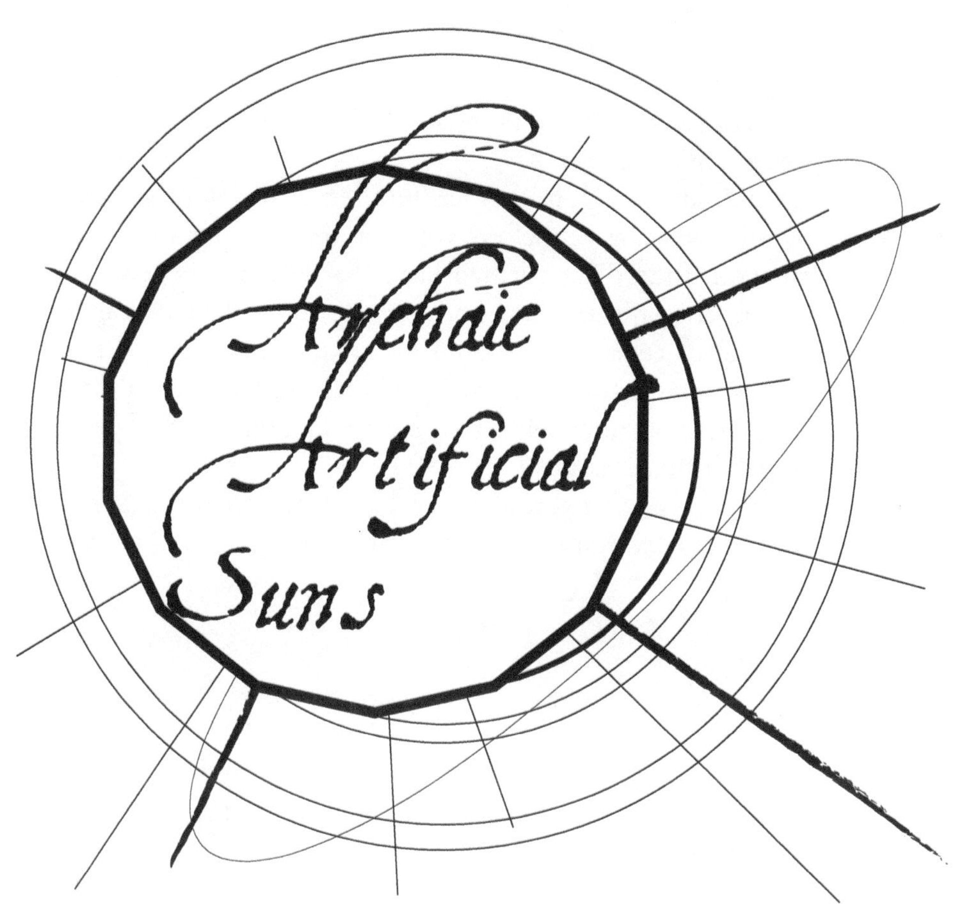

'The stage, you know, is only one third of the hall.'
Vladimir Mayakovsky, Prologue to *Mystery-Bouffe*

A few of us—sparks of nothing—will see shadows of the future; a moment of foreboding, a portentous dream, senses of the night. It is only a matter of record though with the great names in history; the artists, the warmongers, the proselytisers—all snivelling hunters after immortality. With Mikhail Afanasievich it was different. He had been a doctor back in the dawn of time and knew something of the meaning of his presentiments. He did not have a diagnosis but he knew that something had hold of him and would not relinquish its grasp. So it was in a spirit of acceptance, and nostalgia, that he eased the needle into his vein, which had been difficult to find. He felt the flush of a familiar calm.

After only an hour though he was feeling tired; it was not the same as it had been nearly twenty years before, when he took his last shot of that blessed pharmakon. Indeed then it had been that levelling nepenthe fog he most craved; a state of bliss where nothing rose above the frivolous and banal. Now he most needed release from his anxious rewriting of a play about the Leader; a man holding his own pen full of real strokes of torture and death. The draft was now being read by the Committee for the Arts and it had slipped from his control.

Yelena knew he was changed when he kissed her on the cheek and murmured that he needed some air; his eyes tiny black bullets of entropy.

∞

He wandered—numb, euphoric and slightly drowsy—down Kamergersky, to stare at the crowds. The Arts Theatre had been plagued again by that most wretched of inhibitors to artistry: success. The revival of Saltykov's *The Death of Pazuhin* had struck its bland chord with the blandness of the age and the crowds gathered nightly for the office to distribute its few remaining seats.

Mikhail stood a moment and wiped his brow clean of sticky summer sweat. He watched the gathering as it edged forward at a tedious pace. The crowd had assembled in an orderly fashion, assisted by a few security police stationed here and there, chatting and smoking with the joyous masses.

The line stretched around the street, into the distance as far as he could see. No doubt to the very gates of Hades. The unclean and the clean mingled merrily in the stagnant air, filing their way to the Promised Land: pianists, chauffeurs, blacksmiths, merchants, herdsmen, Christians, carpenters, schoolmasters, delegates, lamplighters, priests, directors, advocates, servants, actors, engineers, princes, students, papal legates, fishermen, Germans, miners, painters, soldiers, statisticians, cobblers, flautists, wireless operators, diplomats, laundry maids, and any number of other cardboard characters one may wish to add to swell the scene. Who knows, perhaps the devil himself stood in line awaiting his tickets.

How this theatre had troubled him, with its obsession with the director's craft. But now he returned with a coup. The deal was almost concluded and would at least be handled professionally by Nemirovich, and not some inexperienced assistant. Perhaps the crowds would be this vast for his new work.

For now though he must strive to put the theatre from his mind. He moved on, as purposeless as a fallen leaf stirred by a midnight breeze.

Slipping around the back of the building, and heading away from the throng he wandered by the stage entrance and scenedock. At the stage door were posed the most ridiculous group of characters. There stood, as in a tableau of sprinters after the starting gun, four actors in bizarre, yet familiar, costume. Two were dressed in the plain blue suits of the workers' theatre. Another was costumed as a plump Chinese with a vast pink robe and oversized straw hat. The last was equally padded with stuffing in his large waistcoat and baggy trousers. He had a dull brown peaked cap and sported a large, false, red beard and gripped two large bags, of what looked to be coins, in his hands.

It struck Mikhail suddenly where he had seen these characters before: in the costume drawings for Meyerhold's production of *Mystery-Bouffe*. That had been staged here nearly twenty years ago. Perhaps these buffoons had discovered them in a corner of the costume wardrobe and had decided to enact some absurd scene in the square.

As he pondered this question the group burst into existence from their still life.

They ran forward at a marked speed, more noticeable—no doubt—because of their previous stasis. They were exaggeratedly comical, pushing and shoving to gain advantage over each other.

Mikhail drifted after them slowly, amused by their antics. Despite their frantic energy they never seemed to progress much further from him though. After a few minutes, and just as his interest was waning, he saw them turn, as one, and gesture to him to come towards them.

He obliged. The one dressed as a Chinese seemed to be in charge.

'Might we interest you in a short performance of our own devising, on the instruction of our director?' he asked.

'Oh, no, though it looks quite fascinating,' Mikhail replied, 'I am taking a short walk to freshen myself before returning to my work.'

'But comrade, we could really do with the money,' the actor said, folding himself in half with staged, silent laughter. His three accomplices joined him in this silly spectacle, more unsettling in the oppressive heat which seemed already to absorb and deaden sound.

In that brief interstice hung the balance of revelation.

'Certainly, why not,' Mikhail replied flatly. 'I would welcome some entertainment.'

'Entertainment! That, comrade, is something we can always provide,' he affirmed, nodding his head frantically, making the straw hat slide ludicrously back and forth on his head.

'If you would care to follow us, we shall take you to our studio,' he said, whirling his robes in an affected curtsy.

With the servile demeanour of shop assistants the performers beckoned him on, through streets and parks, across busy roads and among crowds lethargic with the heavy heat. At every pause the players nodded, bowed and gestured keenly, as though entreating him to view some wondrous exhibit. Just as this ingratiating conduct was beginning to irritate Mikhail, and he was considering parting company with the fools, they stopped and stood rigidly to attention on a small grassy mound that inclined gently towards a tall building with a row of wide balconies on its lower floors. Mikhail recognised the place but after their absurd journey he could not recall how.

The group approached a balcony near the corner of the building. Mikhail followed dutifully again.

'Now let our soiree commence,' the 'Chinese' began. 'But first, a medley of the classics, before we move to the meat of the show.'

He knelt at the edge of the balcony, whilst the others watched excitedly. With an affected, youthful voice he began.

'But, soft! What light through yonder window breaks? It is the east, and Juliet is the sun. Arise, fair sun, and kill the envious moon, who is already sick and pale with grief that thou her maid art far more fair than she...'

He turned and placed his finger to his lips, calling everyone to be silent.

With one leap he was over the low wall and was at the doors to the apartment. His fellow actors followed. Mikhail still struggled with a vague sense of familiarity of this area, and most specifically this building, but he was more interested now in the purpose behind this performance.

Quietly the 'Romeo' opened the door from the balcony and beckoned the others to follow. They assumed crouched poses of stealth and ushered Mikhail along. He too stooped in a sympathetic attempt at quiet.

They entered a bright sitting room with yellow and gold walls and a large dining table in the centre of the room, made of Karelian birch; a light golden colour that complemented the walls. It was an unusually opulent room, with a beautiful chandelier and many framed photographs upon the walls. The balcony doors were framed by luxurious tapestry curtains that hung in thick folds.

Mikhail immediately remembered the place. He had been here only a couple of months ago. It was Meyerhold's apartment. He and a few others had been invited for drinks after the humiliating speech Meyerhold had given at the *Directors' Conference*. A few days later he had been arrested and God only knew what had become of him by now.

As Mikhail was contemplating this, a pair of double doors opened into the next room and a beautiful woman walked through dressed in a silk dressing gown, rubbing her dark curly hair with a cream towel. It was Zinaida, Meyerhold's wife.

She stopped still and lowered the towel. Her face flushed suddenly with anger.

'Are you back so soon?' she spat. 'I thought you had done with riffling our possessions.'

'She speaks,' the 'Romeo' said tenderly, sinking to his knees. 'O, speak again, bright angel, for thou art as glorious to this night, being o'er my head, as is a winged messenger of heaven unto the white-upturned wond'ring eyes of mortals that fall back to gaze upon him, when he bestrides the lazy-pacing clouds and sails upon the bosom of the air.'

She looked perplexed but her anger was not diminished.

'I demand to know the meaning of this idiocy,' she said. 'If you do not leave immediately I will call for assistance and report you to Beria directly—no, to Stalin himself!'

'I have night's cloak to hide me from their eyes; and but thou love me, let them find me here,' 'Romeo' implored, laying his arm across his brow in mock swoon. 'My life were better ended by their hate than death prolonged wanting of thy love.'

'I have had enough of this nonsense,' she said, moving towards the main apartment entrance. She caught Mikhail's eyes and stopped suddenly. 'But, Mikhail, what are you doing here with these NKVD dogs?

He did not have time to respond before the odd scene played on. 'Romeo' had risen from his knees and now puffed himself up menacingly.

'If you bethink yourself of any crime unreconcil'd as yet to heaven and grace, solicit for it straight,' he growled deeply, now playing 'The Moor'.

She still stared questioningly at Mikhail.

'Is it come to this?' she whispered. 'That we turn against ourselves like animals, seeking favour instead of food.'

Mikhail did not understand.

'It is too late,' 'The Moor' pronounced ominously, shaking his head sorrowfully. 'It is too late.'

With an unnatural speed the four actors pounced upon Zinaida and drew wicked stiletto blades from within their costumes.

They stabbed and stabbed, stabbed and stabbed.

They paused a moment to swap blades, though each appeared identical.

Then they stabbed and stabbed, and stabbed and stabbed again. The rabble of bodies struggled towards the open balcony doors as their victim attempted to flee.

Then Zinaida sank—disintegrating like a dynamited building—beneath the onslaught of brutality. The horror of the scene did not affect Mikhail. He was too deadened by the morphine. What he noticed most was the sound as the blades entered the woman's body—like paper, swiftly torn. He collapsed into a leather chair, mute witness to the terrible aftermath.

The four assassins ceased their attack and rose together slowly, reminiscent of actors rehearsing one of Meyerhold's own performance etudes. The 'Chinese' reached out to Zinaida's face, stroking her cheek gently.

'Sleep dwell upon thine eyes, peace in thy breast! Would I were sleep and peace, so sweet to rest!'

He looked up at Mikhail and smiled. His features were bizarrely altered. His skin had taken on a light brown hue and seemed unusually wrinkled. A beard seemed to have sprouted from his chin. There was something preternatural and uncanny about him.

'Death, that hath suck'd the honey of thy breath, hath no power yet upon thy beauty,' he whispered in Zinaida's ear. 'Thou art not conquer'd; beauty's ensign yet is crimson in thy lips and in thy cheeks, and death's pale flag is not advanced there.'

It was the crowning insult to their Shakespearean charade.

With a clap of his hands the show was over. The four 'actors' slipped swiftly out of their costumes to reveal the olive uniforms of NKVD officers. Yet there was something strange about them. Their faces seemed flecked with bristly stubble and Mikhail was sure that they were much shorter than they had seemed before. Indeed that was precisely the peculiarity of their uniforms; they hung limply from their bodies, looking like children dressed as soldiers.

The one that had played the speaking roles in the bloody performance pulled a grey cap from his pocket and perched it upon his head.

'I am Antonielich Vasielievich Nostradascov, or Popilovnovoskov to my friends,' he stated pompously. Here the other freaks giggled. 'You though shall call me Comrade Popi; on account of my senior rank.' He tapped an oval badge on his arm: a silver and gold insignia on a maroon background. The others nodded gravely and then bounced onto a chaise longue—serving as a trampoline—to each perform a Salchow before landing on their knees and waving their hands in the air as though performers in some travelling circus. Comrade Popi took a quick bow.

With the ineptitude of a troupe of clowns the other three then scrambled onto the table and arranged themselves into a ludicrous tableau again. This time mocking the pose of soldiers in socialist realist posters: in profile, their determined stances marching towards a happy, healthy, collective future. One winked and grinned at him, showing long sharp feline teeth.

Mikhail stared at them blankly.

'Not impressed, eh? What would you prefer, a trapeze of naked boyars?' Comrade Popi asked, his scrappy facial hair quivering as his lips contorted into a grotesque grin. 'We can do that if you want, can't we boys?'

His idiotic entourage stood suddenly to attention and nodded their heads with maniacal energy.

Mikhail was more disturbed by the quotation from his own writings, cruelly enough about the very man whose living room he now stood in and whose wife lay dying before him. He stared ahead as the bizarre creatures continued their charade, nodding for what may possibly have been an hour. They seemed to have shrunk further and appeared now to be no taller than a metre. Their facial hair seemed to get thicker and darker, now virtually covering their entire faces, even sprouting in awkward tufts from their oversized costumes.

They scattered and each attempted to impress their 'audience' with different tricks. One pretended to tame an invisible lion with a chair and poker from the fire. Another balanced along the arm of the chaise longue as though on a high wire. The other juggled oranges from a bowl on the table.

Comrade Popi, like a circus ringmaster, presented each in turn. His shoulders sinking as he looked disappointedly at Mikhail's bleak expression.

'God, you're a tough crowd tonight! Why not have a bit of fruit—*me old fruit*,' he said, with an absurdly exaggerated English accent. 'Might perk you up a bit!' He plucked an orange from the juggler performing beside him and threw it to Mikhail.

His reflexes were dull and it thumped against his chest, falling into his lap.

The juggler sympathetically dropped his remaining fruits to the ground with a thud.

'Oops, butterfingers!' Comrade Popi laughed, sending the juggler crashing to the floor with a horizontal punch to the jaw.

In a daze Mikhail began to peel the orange. Zinaida lay there before the thick curtains, the twilight breeze animating her torn dressing gown. The blood oozed in a thick pool around her. It seemed to well up from the floor, rather than from her wounds; as though the room itself were bleeding. She struggled to take in low breaths, her chest shuddering in obvious pain. Her eyes fluttered open and gazed at him, their pupils blank and uncomprehending—galaxies of emptiness.

Mikhail also watched events with glazed, dead eyes.

He could smell the peeled orange, reminding him of the evenings with Konstantin and the other boys, at the Solovtsov Theatre, where he would dissolve into the performance itself, becoming one with the dust and the footlights, whose heat would glow his face as the curtain raised itself on another world. For a moment he became a little boy again—as short as those malevolent spirits still cavorting around the room.

Zinaida struggled to raise herself, exhaling a breathy appeal to her absent husband, 'Vsevolod...'

'What voice is this?' Comrade Popi said, beginning again the theatrical mockery. 'Not dead? Not yet quite dead? I that am cruel am yet merciful; I would not have thee linger in thy pain.'

He crouched down, cradling Zinaida's head in one hand. Then, with sudden ferocity, he popped his blade swiftly into each of her eye sockets.

Again there was the sound of tearing paper. Mikhail felt it might be the brittle fabric of his own mind.

'Who are you?' was the best that he could muster as he looked on incredulously.

'We are the agents of endless abandon,' the beast said, very precisely. He stood, wiping the dagger on his uniform, which now looked huge upon him. He rolled his sleeves up meticulously and then collected a decanter of plum brandy from a cabinet beside the table and took a long draught. 'We are things rich and strange, I grant you that. But the great matriarch, authority, is only the vessel to birth us into the world.'

Here he tapped his military badge again, instructively.

'She is the ordered facade through which we burst to give to revelry its true force; the anonymity of lust. Without harmony where could we sow discord? It is, unfortunately as black and white as all that. We are the faceless perpetrators of every baseless desire. It was our blood that entered your veins this evening and fired your brain with joy. It was our seed that fed your pen with wit on every page you ever inked. We are, quite simply, the glint on every blade that ever pierced a sack of flesh.'

'What kind of game is this?' came the next inane question.

Comrade Popi took off his cap and sat on the arm of Mikhail's chair, shaking his head as though lecturing a child. His face seemed almost covered now with wiry brown hair.

'Ah, we're all players Miki,' he said, nudging his face up to Mikhail's; the bristles of his beard tougher than a stiff brush. 'It's all just dancing and frolicking in the end. That's what we're here for. You poor devils are just hourglasses, and you know it—dogs don't. I've never understood why you don't make more of yourselves. You know, put on some new clothes—pretend to be something else!'

He slurped another good fill of spirit. The other three were at the cabinet, draining bottle after bottle in what looked to be a competition.

'Now, can you ever imagine what it's like for us, eh?' he continued. 'We're only poor representatives of the eternal order of things; the "cycles of centuries" and all that razzmatazz. Do you have any idea what immortality does to the mind—what eons of ageless nothingness does for one's *joie de vivre*? *Would I were sleep and peace*, Miki. *So sweet to rest*!'

There came a quiet knocking at the door of the apartment and a soft voice calling, likely the maid.

'Oh, what a shame Miki, we'll have to go,' the abhorrent creature chuckled. 'But do try to imagine the millions of millennia of this earth in all its lush greenery, years before the primordial *creature* emerged from the salty soup to begin its slow crawl towards your sentience. Now imagine all the years after your lot have fought and fucked yourselves into oblivion, dancing arm and arm with us into the sunset. Imagine those countless centuries as this planet becomes dry and dusty and all record of its creatures and terrain are wiped away by dusty solar winds.'

The knocking came louder, and a shrill call for assistance.

'Knock, knock, knock! Who's there i' th' name of Beelzebub?' he shouted at the door. 'Sorry for the rude interruption Miki, where were we? Ah yes! Then imagine—kaboom!—the whole thing blown to bits by the last blast of the sun as it commits its final fission and casts all its broken atoms into the darkness again. That's just the prelude to the *first act* my boy, just the prelude! Imagine having to sit through all that. It doesn't even begin to capture what we will have to—and have already had to—endure.'

A more forceful knocking.

'Madame, are you in there? We heard voices?' a male voice enquired loudly.

A pause. Then, heavy thudding on the door.

'Exeunt, dear players. *Exeunt*!' Popi said, ushering his drunken accomplices into the night. Their transformation was complete: now so dark, stunted and hairy, that they resembled performing baby bears in a marketplace. Popi raised his cap in a gesture of farewell. 'See you at the end of time, Miki; be sure to wear something wonderful, it promises to be a very special evening!'

The hammering on the door continued. Mikhail stumbled onto the balcony and, as was to be expected, the creatures had vanished into the night. Dazed by drugs and revelation he too slipped into the darkness.

∞

It was this perpetual performance that he was destined to reveal. He must revisit the book. Now! Now! He must be read again; so that they should *know*. In years to come the lights would flare in civilisation's empty auditorium and the cast would play again beneath archaic, artificial suns—all supplicants to the mysterious miracle—including bankers, weavers, fantasists, Zionists, lovers, jesters, Tsars, revolutionaries, waiters, sopranos, jewellers, blasphemers, bailiffs, generals, narcissists, taxidermists, gravediggers, Futurists, butchers, bakers, candlestickmakers, murderers, vocationists, bloodletters, professors, pederasts, quiltmakers, homosexuals, blackmailers, dramaturges, eschatologists, cuckolds, satirists, pallbearers. Yes, particularly the pallbearers with their flair for fatalistic melodrama and their sad, sardonic smiles.

Verum, sine Mendacio, certum et verissimum:
Quod est Inferius est sicut quod est Superius,
et quod est Superius est sicut quod est Inferius,
ad perpetranda Miracula Rei Unius.
Et sicut res omnes fuerunt ab Uno,
meditatione unius,
sic Omnes Res natae ab hac una Re, adaptatione.

Naturally he would meet with Philomena first. His wife could wait. Indeed Mena had been an enduring thought throughout his brief imprisonment. Each night her face would peer down at him on his bare wooden bench and smile. He drifted in and out of sleep with her kind gaze watching over him.

Still stiff and weak in his left side he stumbled through the streets of the old town like some decrepit invalid, the officers and their whores giving him a wide berth. One particularly raucous party jeered and called after him, 'It's Meyer, the magician', 'It's Meyer, the thief'. But he was in no state for confrontation. His disputes with these idle military morons would be settled soon enough, but not in the manner he thought. There would be no triumphant encounter in the woods—sabres bared—nor would there be the resounding crack of the legal hammer declaring him right. No, within a couple of years he must leave Prague's dark streets of wonder. He will need to depart for a place more rooted in the world and its charades: Vienna, a city of majesty and might, where once again order might prevail in his mind and he would learn the mastery of words so necessary to resurrect the sorcery of worldly things. But all of that was far off for the broken pedlar in financial sureties and spiritualist claptrap as he hobbled his way across Charles Bridge to meet his beloved in Malá Strana that evening. And, as ever, I follow him.

∞

It all comes as a thick fog of faces. Memory I mean: the memory of these past weeks and the agonies of confinement. I will seek immediate recompense! I will see them all in the dock and then in the jail, undergoing the indignities I have endured.

But it is wonderful to breathe this early evening spring air again, without the rotten stink of bodies and the cries of the tormented. Here again at last the sound of birdsong and the scent of the river which, whilst pungent, is nonetheless the scent of freedom. After a coffee I am somewhat refreshed and must hurry to meet Mena at the 'Three Violins'. She will not have finished performing, certainly, but I can wait for her. The joy of our reunion will be sharpened by waiting. Perhaps Johannes and Milan will be there. We will drink to my freedom and curse the dogs of the regiment that put me there.

The moon is thin and what little light it casts is veiled by thick cloud. The lamps across the river are lit creating a thin tunnel of light gleaming across the river. The gentle waters ripple through it, casting strange flowing shadows. As I watch, these dark forms coagulate into a crowd of shambling figures—each stumbling forward and grasping helplessly towards me from the river below. These phantasms quickly disintegrate, replaced by a shimmering ladder of yellow light drawing me towards Kampa Island. Then, with a rustle of breeze across the trees on the riverbank the light dissolved into a shoal of golden fish swimming in eternal stasis. Something—some guide, or *Pilot*—drew me down the steps beneath the bridge into that warren of alleys that snaked towards the banks of the Vltava. I felt disoriented with cold and malnourishment and staggered through the looming streets with a sense of befuddled excitement and foreboding. I could hear the waters churning through the mill-race on Čertovka. But the sound seemed to come from all around me. It must be the damp river-mist distorting my senses, or else my weakened body craving some sustenance.

Out of the white swirls that crept around me I saw a dim luminescence. As I drew closer a low row of disheveled wooden houses appeared on the riverfront, little more than shacks. These used to house the barge hands taking the goods from Kampa. I thought they had been pulled down years ago, to make way for (or make safer) the fanciful merchant houses that now surrounded the mills. They formed an odd street, almost sinking into the river. The first house, facing into the street I now walked down, had a wide doorway leading into a cellar below. Tatty yellow curtains hung either side of the entrance and a large lantern hung behind them, shining its welcome light through their thin fabric. A shabby man sat on a stool outside adding to the misty vapours with long drags on a deep-bowled pipe. As I drew nearer he seemed to spring to life. I saw in his hands a thin stick, from which dangled an absurd cloth puppet. It was little more than a blue rag with a crude wooden head, but with each flick of his wrist he managed to make it cavort with a quality at once enchanting and repugnant.

'Come and enjoy some rest in the puppet theatre,' he mumbled through the thick pipe in his teeth. 'Let our performers relax you with their entertainments. Enjoy a drink and a bowl of soup. We have everything here, everything you could possibly want.'

I needed some food, certainly. Perhaps this was the place the ladder of light had beckoned me towards. In satisfying my curiosity I would also be able to enjoy the magic of a puppet show.

∞

He loved puppet theatre. Not for some atavistic or symbolic aspect. No, for their simple mockery of the human, both in form and in action. The puppet is allowed a freedom to ridicule and vulgarise that no actor or actress would ever be allowed, and in their clowning, clumsy movements he found solace in the fundamental absurdity of existence—and therein also its splendour.

So, carefully making his way down the worn stone steps into the dingy theatre, a childish grin could be seen on his face, broadening into a hopeful smile. He did not find what he expected though. Instead of a gaudy auditorium, with wooden scenery and marionettes strung along the walls, he found a bustling tavern room, with tables and stools set out with drink and food. The low ceiling forced one to hang one's head to move around the busy hall. Men were slumped across tables and on benches in varying states of drunken abandon. Clearly the puppet show, if indeed there was one, was not a focus of their evening. Young serving girls, no older than their mid-teens, moved between the tables bringing beer and steaming bowls of soup to their customers. Most wore tattered, but revealing, costumes that were reminiscent of a chorus of dancing girls from a Parisian revue bar. Many lay in the arms of the clientele, clearly indicating the true purpose of the establishment.

He was about to leave when he caught sight of a low stage at the farthest end of the hall. It was roughly formed from wooden crates with boards propped haphazardly on top. There was also a basic scenic backdrop, again fashioned from rough boards, which depicted the city from the castle to the old town, including Charles Bridge and the river. The perspective was much distorted, the castle appearing distant and minute, whilst the river itself seemed to take up most of the central panel, with the bridge floating ethereally above it. In each corner of this tawdry set a few puppets were strewn. He was struck by the sight of these small performing objects. They posed as though discarded and broken, yet seemed so heavy with a vital energy—ready to burst into movement.

The wretched cavern stank of sweat and stale tobacco smoke. And beneath that the faint smell of perfume and sex. The walls themselves were sticky and damp with lust. The girls moved back and forth between the 'audience', who exchanged furtive glances and took every opportunity to paw and grope them. A desperate mood was in the air, one that seemed at any moment on the verge of descending into full debauchery, but ever drawing itself back from the brink. There seemed to be no madam, or other director, presiding over the brothel. He took a seat at an empty table by the rickety stage and watched the frolic.

Events seemed to move to some preordained order, as though he were witness to some ancient fertility rite, corrupted through centuries into its present squalor. For beneath all the degradation there was a tangible pulse of order and obedience. And I mean that quite literally, for if you had been able to hear beneath the din of the revelry you would have heard a soft beat, as of a heart. And should you have touched those clammy walls you would have felt it too—a soft pounding—as though the earth were heaving lustily. But you were not really there, and nor—I must admit—was I. We too, my friend, crave that corporeal truth of sensation. We are no different to those desperate clients there clutching at adolescent bodies. We must try to piece it all together from our frantic imaginings.

∞

I watched the antics for about half an hour and was about to leave when three girls appeared from an entrance beside the poor stage. An air about them set them apart from the others. Two were dressed very similarly, in wide reds skirts with frilly torn bodices. One was quite short, with straight red hair; the other thin and tall, with short black hair which seemed to have been roughly, perhaps even aggressively, shorn. The third girl was very plain. She wore a simple grey tunic with an oily brown cloak. She had thick black hair which flowed freely about her shoulders. Her dark features and physiognomy clearly showed her as a Jewess. She looked peculiar and out of place, as though plucked from the kitchens of a nearby merchant's house. Her strangeness was further marked by her blank expression. Whilst the other two girls laughed and waved as the audience cheered their arrival this third girl did not react at all. She stared straight forward with bold green eyes that watched the red-head intently as she led the group toward the rudimentary set.

They took up their positions behind the flat boards of scenery, which they had angled in slightly more so that they could face each other. This blocked the audience's view somewhat. But it appeared to me that they played as much for each other as for the assembled rabble, who were, indeed, paying little attention. The red-haired girl seemed to be in command of the performance, as the other two watched her expectantly for the signal to commence.

Nothing happened for a few minutes. None of them gathered the puppets, to check or prepare their mechanisms. They just stared forward into space, each focused intently on some inner thought. I had the overwhelming sense of being present at a sacred rite.

Then the show began. One of the puppets, dressed as a bishop (complete with mitre and crosier) sprang from the heap. It was rapidly followed by a ragdoll (in a delicately fashioned basque and suspenders) and then by a cavalry officer (in an oversized double breasted jacket and plumed czako). These three then began an absurd chase around the stage, each evading and grasping for the others. They moved deftly, without the usual clunking awkwardness that is so endearing in the marionette.

I looked up to watch how these girls were controlling the things. They did not seem to be holding jigs, or even basic crossbars, in their hands. The strings must have been attached to their fingers, but how I could not perceive. The way they cast their hands back and forth I was reminded of the three witches from Macbeth. Their hands moved with such strangeness that it seemed the puppeteers themselves were puppets, driven in some fatal dance of death, or primitive ceremony—compelled to contort into forms arcane and alien to our common gestures. I was more captivated by them than their puppets.

I had, of course, expected the usual *Faust*, or perhaps a fairytale. This was an entirely different affair. As it continued other puppets joined in the romp: a Moorish character seemed to fence and duel with the officer before being eaten by what seemed to be a cloth puppet crocodile. Every now and then the new characters would join the officer, strumpet and bishop in their hilarious chase around the stage. There was no dialogue, purely the irreverent, and frequently obscene, gestures of the puppets themselves.

After a few minutes I noticed that the general din of the space had become focused on the performance, with gales of laughter and applause directed at the antics of these marvellous manikins.

The finale came with another chase, in which there must have been at least ten puppets. The bishop figure suddenly spread his arms wide and the others collapsed around him. He walked jauntily towards the front of the stage. In a single swirling movement he disrobed, revealing a polychrome harlequin marionette which turned and bared its wooden backside to the assembled crowd. The storm of cheers and thumping of tables was deafening.

I was amazed. Not simply at the audacity of this incredible show but principally at the skill with which they had achieved such control over the puppets. As this final puppet sank slowly to the floor the three girls seemed also to sink and exhale. Their frenzied concentration collapsed and they moved down into the crowd to great commotion. Each had gathered a puppet and carried it cradled in their arms, identifying their own proximity to childhood even more clearly.

I was left staring at the stage, to see if there was any other mechanism apparent for the movement of the figures. There was too little light for me to see clearly but there must have been a hidden gantry above, with further operators, I conjectured. Then I felt a hand on my shoulder. I turned to find the red-haired girl offering me her hand. I stood and took it, briefly introducing myself.

'I am Herr Meyer,' I said, bowing. 'I am most fascinated with your ingenious show. You must allow me to offer you a drink, and of course your fellow puppeteers.'

She laughed, holding the harlequin puppet in her left hand. Close-up it looked very rudely fashioned, each basic wooden limb jointed with fraying twine. But then I suppose that is the beauty of the theatre: that reality, with all its ugly baseness, is transformed into a magnificent facade, if only for a moment. The Jewess stood close behind her, being mauled by an amorous customer. She did not flinch. In her cradled arms she held the soldier puppet: a stuffed corn-doll. The other girl was using the rag-doll strumpet to tease a seated inebriate on the table beside me.

'Well, Herr Meyer,' she said. 'We are pleased to make your acquaintance. I am Rosina, and this is Miriam and Adéla.' She gestured to the Jewess and the short-haired girl respectively.

'Shall I order us something to...' I began. Rosina stopped me abruptly by holding her hand over my mouth. She tucked the puppet under her left arm and gripped my hand tightly pulling me up from my chair.

I do not understand why I followed her so freely. It was a strong, almost hypnotic, stare with which she held me.

She led me up the stairs at the back of the cavern. These emerged in a corridor along the side of the buildings on the river front and showed a row of curtained entrances to small wood shacks, the ones I had seen from the street. They were evidently the rooms where the girls brought their customers. Miriam and Adéla followed behind us, with their catches trailing drunkenly behind. We took the room furthest on the right. Within it there was a further partition, crudely fashioned from a blanket and piece of rope. On each side of this lay a grubby mattress on a floor of cold compacted earth, a small oil lamp, and a few personal possessions. Miriam took her man to the left one, casting her soldier puppet into the corner, and Rosina fell onto the right bed, with the harlequin, gesturing for me to join her.

Adéla stood in the doorway, tapping her rag-doll idly against the wall. Her companion, that had previously been fondling her as we departed the hall, had regained some soberness and stood in the corridor, somewhat sheepishly, waiting for her to take him to her quarters.

There was an awkward silence. This was soon filled by animal grunts coming from the curtained bay next to us. The lamp gave a dim impression of the events unfolding there, and it curiously resembled some ridiculous shadow-show; a parody of intercourse. It was clear that the brute was taking his pleasure from Miriam in as swift, and vicious, fashion as he was able.

Adéla and Rosina said nothing. I had to say something. I also had to satisfy my curiosity concerning the puppet show.

'The puppets,' I said, taking the harlequin from Rosina and examining its limbs. 'They have no wires, or rods. How do you operate them?'

Rosina looked at me sympathetically.

'These are not puppets,' she said. 'They are dolls.'

'We operate them with desire,' Adéla said, laughing. And turning to her companion she took him by the arm and led him away, pulling the curtain to our chamber closed behind her. Her laughter echoed down the wooden corridor with a hollow desperation.

Another long silence.

'We *operate* them—as you call it—through a yearning to become ourselves,' Rosina said cryptically. She eased me back onto the dirty mattress and we undressed each other. Settling into a comfortable harmony we lay there as the beast next to us ravaged Miriam. She did not make a sound.

I could not bring myself to enjoy Rosina, despite my body desperately craving the act after all these weeks of solitude. She also sensed my reluctance and fell asleep. I lay there with my mind alight with incredible imaginings.

∞

You probably infer that he was a moralist. How wrong. Such impudence! Morality is such a brittle little concept my friend. To have had her would have only been base copulation. It would have annihilated her exquisite otherness. He considered her a creature of the stars, as inscrutable and apocalyptic as Tzimtzum. She was an instant fulcrum to his tattered world. Do not demean him with your implacable hermeneutic hunger. I had not taken you for one who skulks behind the scenes to see God's entrance debased to pure mechanism.

∞

When I awoke I was not certain where I was. I turned and saw Rosina's face. She was awake and watching me, the harlequin marionette in her arms.

'I must go, I'm afraid,' I said, getting up off the mattress. 'I must meet some friends. I should have... I mean... I just wanted to ask...'

'Yes, please ask,' she said confidently.

'How, *did* you make the puppets move? It was miraculous. I mean, *truly* incredible. I have seen many things, and many people who have claimed supernatural gifts. But I have never seen such a feat as this.'

'I have already told you, *these* are not puppets,' she said. '*These* are dolls. *We* are puppets.'

I looked back at her uncomprehendingly.

'That these things are alive, as capable of movement and apparent autonomy as us, is no great revelation,' she said, jostling the harlequin doll into a comical jig. 'That is only workmanship, trade, mere mediocrity. The real miracle is how to give them essence—a soul—that is the true craftsmanship; a magical gift. A master of such transformation has finally discovered the extension of their own being: an immortal. Death will be drawn into life and everything will appear as it truly is.'

She reached into the corner of the room, behind her mattress. She gathered a handful of dust and dirt and held it out on the flat of her hand before my eyes. She touched her forefinger on her other hand to her tongue and lightly touched the heap of dirt. I did not catch the single word she whispered, but it was brief.

Gradually, as though awakening, the pile gathered shape and formed itself into a bizarre figure with two solid 'legs' and spindly arms that waved like tentacles. A blob that might be called a 'head' had fashioned itself from where one might say shoulders should have been. The object made a couple of faltering steps across her hand before the entire thing collapsed again into the dust it had been formed from.

'It comes as much from the dirt that surrounds us as the glorious spheres above,' she said, opening my hand and sprinkling the dirt into it. 'There are many ways to give life to what seems dead, not least is through the word itself. The word is a gift. Now go, seek, find.'

She nestled back into her torn blankets, clasped the doll to her breast, and closed her eyes. She had the look of one who has never been fully born into the world. By that I mean there seemed to be an aura around her of discomfort, but also mockery—as though the thin fabric of reality were a little more frayed in her presence. She saw beyond the ordinary to some spectral dimension, comprehending truths which would shatter sanity. In her presence I felt everything was at once incredible and worthless. She made the world into a jewelled crown from a child's toybox—a wooden plaything transubstantiated by imagination.

All sense of time had gone down there in the dark. Days may have passed, or only hours. I do not know. But as I finished dressing and awkwardly pulled on my filthy trousers I saw Miriam watching from above the curtain dividing the room. She stared blankly at me. Her guest was groaning and snoring and woke briefly to paw at her. Still she stared at me until I broke away to pull on my jacket and head for the grey curtain at the doorway.

I turned to say something to her, perhaps to apologise. She was no longer looking at me though. She was gazing down at Rosina sleeping. That was true love: that gaze. But there was nothing human about it. It was awful: a total abnegation of selfhood. I stood looking at a hollow being. There was nothing left of Miriam. She existed solely for Rosina.

I made my way down the stairs and into the main drinking hall. There were a few bodies curled in corners, obviously too drunk to make the journey home. One of the girls awoke and laughed at me, beckoning me to her with a limp gesture before collapsing back onto the floor.

I regained the steps to the street and was greeted by a cool gust of wind coming up from the river. It revived me violently, almost knocking me off my feet. I checked in my pocket for the handful of dirt that Rosina had so strangely animated. It was still there, passing slowly through my fingers, formless. Had it all been some elaborate trick? I had seen many prestidigitators, mostly working with lacy ectoplasm, but I had never seen any as gifted as Rosina.

Casting a glance back I caught Miriam standing just behind the curtains of the entrance to the bawdy puppet house. The dark blue light of the encroaching evening filtered through the yellow fabric, casting a greenish light across her face which—as stony and terrible as ever—made certain of my departure. I imagine her there still, guarding the essential purity of her continually defiled beloved.

I quickened my pace, as though urged on by some unseen force. I felt eyes upon me everywhere. Not the eyes of some fretful bourgeois who might be surmising my business in the house at the corner of the street. No, I felt watched by eyes that eternally stared and never judged—eyes that viewed me with some languid disinterest—a gaze of indifference and horrendous fatalism.

This uncanny city could kill a man solely with its atmosphere.

As the lamps from upstairs rooms flickered their yellow glow onto the street below I had a feeling that, as Rosina had said, we all cavorted like puppets through the streets of that dreaming city. Dancing not to the hand of some celestial divinity but by the dark will of the buildings themselves;

buildings that would as soon vanish into the air than give up their infernal secrets. The place overwhelmed me with a perverse and scintillating horror; the kind of fascination I imagine a man must feel in the last moments of being hanged and drawn, seeing his entrails—the incredible secrets of his inner workings—displayed before him as he sinks into eternal night.

I must leave this place before it consumes me.

∞

There he is, crossing the square before the Church of St Nicholas (with its perfect dome thrust into the air like a great eager prick—ritual penetration of the empty sky). He feels guilty, no doubt, for the previous night. He feels sorrow for neglecting Mena. But no matter—what secrets he has learnt, what gifts he has received; better than those years of clairvoyant humbug with the dilettantes and the charlatans. A workaday whore had more mystery than all the alchemists of Europe.

He checks his pocket again for the handful of dirt. A treasury of brothel sweepings.

I am behind him as he enters the 'Three Violins'. You are welcome to join us. Come, we'll linger by this table of his cronies. Yes, some of the other drinkers have noticed something is not quite right in the space where we stand, but they will see nothing. They will leave only with a faint impression that they were being watched, nothing more sinister than that. It is an everyday feeling. A common event.

See how they all cheer his return. What a triumph of failure!

But where is Philomena? Do you want to see her? She is the short one with the beautiful curls and childish face: a doll.

They embrace. How touching. Almost like love.

∞

Finally I found my way to the 'Three Violins' where Mena would be found, by this hour, with our friends. There were many of them, and the welcome was uproarious. In my frail condition the room spun with faces and glasses, cheers and shouts for drinks. They had gathered around me like some joyful crowd around a clown. And then from the haze a delicate smile emerged, and deep lush brown eyes framed with curls of luxuriant dark hair. It was Mena. She embraced me with a strength I had not expected and, cupping my face in her hands, covered me with kisses. More cheers from our friends. She held me there for what seemed like minutes gazing deep into my eyes. It felt like making love, as she seemed to strip my soul down into its component hues. I gazed back into her and the cacophonous world fell away. I began to perceive in her features the ghostly residue of Rosina, as in a superimposed photograph. But beyond that face I saw another, blank and envious: Miriam. Her dark green eyes washed into my very being, never to leave.

∞

But, my friend, they are—in simple fact—*your* eyes, *your* stare, *your* desire.

> Let us get up early to the vineyards; let us see if the vine flourish,
> whether the tender grape appear, and the pomegranates bud forth:
> there will I give thee my loves.
>
> Song of Solomon 7:12

This is the story of my son. You must remember this.

This is the place.

It is a rural village where the colours are brighter than in your cities; spring is a ferocious green and the red of its dawn will blind you with hope; the purple of our autumn twilight will bruise your soul and the dark brown of late fallen leaves will crumble to black soil in your cracked hands as though your pulsing blood had quickened their decomposition. Everything is becoming itself—a passionate degeneration and a violent resurrection.

Here, our throats are always dry, calling for the relief of earthy liquor—ice cold and yet aflame!—to slake a thirst that reaches into our hearts: hearts hollow with toil and brimming with unfathomable lusts. And when such desperate yearnings are not contained by the dark comforts of the plough and the wanton sorrow of the bottle we reach for other bodies—as though flesh could satiate the call that comes from a deeper inside than the void of the hungriest stomach in the darkest of winters! Our night skies echo with the lusty cries of bodies frantically searching for union, collapsing into the inevitable with one lost sigh. And then, after the months evaporate and the passion bears fruit, it begins again.

The land slides to the interminable horizon where the clouds—pale proliferating tumours—fold it away into oblivion. The furrows of the fields beckon everyone into eternity. It was in such a place—a landscape interrupted occasionally by low farm buildings, stacked against the heavy snows that enfold us most of the cruel year—that our lives were played.

So, that is the place.

And the time? The time is as it has always been, somewhere in the middle of forever.

But what of the people? We are not even memories, merely a sepia dust upon a windowsill that glimmers briefly in the growing morning light. You too will be such embers.

There is my wife, Maria. I married her when we were very young and I was romping around the world in search of something, with a gun and a uniform, toying at being a man. She tolerated my ways. We loved. From her homeland she bought the trinkets and baubles of a stern religion, which in my youthful eagerness I had all but forgotten.

There is my son, Alfred. He is at that brittle age where all the enchantment of childhood dissolves into the fever of adolescence and the world passes from fantasy into feral sensuality. His mother wished him christened Alfredo, after her father. That, I said, could never be. So he was Alfred and this, I remind you, is his story.

And then, there is me. I am long gone, if ever I were truly present. I vanished in the happy months after one horror had ceased—the guns cooled briefly—and the aching years of suspicion and denunciation began. A new horror uncoiled, for there is never a shortage of violent men with their *ideals*, *vision*, and a taste for tyranny. Some of us recently released from the camps were taken to new ones. These were far away in countries where the snows last longer and bite deeper even than in our homeland. It was there that I was released into the ether with a simple bullet. And from that moment I was able to see again: to see everything with the delight and terror of an infant.

But oh, that I had flesh again!

I. *Katabasis, or, A Quiet Apprentice*

It was not the church that dominated the humble skyline of our village. It was instead the schoolhouse. Once an aristocratic residence of some reputation its family had long since left for more urban pleasures. It was now a place all of us had passed through; its sprawling rooms having been divided into wings to accommodate the two sexes separately, as was only proper. Its mysterious masters maintained an air of privacy and metropolitan arrogance that subdued even the adult population. They were maintained by a local tithe which further sealed their superiority over us. They strutted the streets like great exotic animals escaped from some travelling circus, each with his, or her, own absurd eccentricity that only confirmed their spectacular nature.

It was in the classroom of one of these chimerical beings, a Dr Borowski, my son Alfred discovered the true magic of existence—not through the banal iteration of tables and formulae, the slavish recitation of the classics or the hollow exegesis of The Book, but rather in the simple grain and ancient graffiti of a schooldesk.

Dr Borowski—inconsequential archetype—crawled around the front of the classroom, a great ant, his fragile arms like ridiculous antenna, scratching out equations with the squealing chalk that itched its tedium into the brain as erratically as its smooth white dust fell incessantly, smothering the room—and all within—in eternity. He had become—through cold years of self-characterisation—a poorly strung marionette with the over-puffed black garments of a celibate, dancing his anachronistic jig to the lowly applause of us peasants: his eager and awestruck audience.

Of an evening, in his childless home (severe with books and silent as dust), he must surely have collapsed back into an expressionless rigidity, as the mice raced around the cobbles of his hearth and nibbled at the soles of his shoes, until the dawn animated him once more.

But there was one delight sure to bring a flush of red to Dr Borowski's cardboard cheeks and a flicker of a smile to his pencil mouth: the casual lash of the cane. He used it with vigour and any slight infringement of the constantly proliferating regulations might incur his keen wrath and a good few strikes.

Alfred had only a further year until he would be able to leave this provincial enclave, already his skills in drawing marked him for higher things; an architect perhaps. But he was not a studious boy. His mind wandered along the monotonous tones of Dr Borowski's voice and would skip as easily into dreamy self-absorption as another might walk through a door.

Alfred had sat at his schooldesk these last seven years thinking little more of it. It functioned as all such desks did. There was an inkwell, filled each morning and emptied each evening. There was a metal ridge beside this that held the thin pens that crackled like static across the rough paper exercise books each child was issued with. The desk slanted towards the student at a steep angle. This enabled a good storage area within, for books and papers and other paraphernalia associated—obliquely—with learning. When Alfred had first arrived he had struggled to see beyond it to the blackboard and had to sit propped upon three stout volumes of 'The Encyclopaedia'. The wooden bench that served as a seat was bolted to the main frame of the desk and did not enable any further movement (no doubt intended to reduce the propensity to fidget instinctual in young boys).

As his years here had edged by—in that everlasting manner that time crafts specifically for young minds—he thought very little about his desk. It merely *served* him, as all such objects might be thought to do.

One early Spring day, during one of Dr Borowski's frequent digressions into the more impenetrable realms of trigonometry, Alfred found himself examining some details on the surface of his desk that had previously been of little note.

Decades of grime, ink, scratches and abrasions had weathered the surface of the desks. Each child knew, through years of experience, the pitfalls of their surface; where the nib of the pen might burst the paper (with a resultant punitive crack of Dr Borowski's cane) or the remnants of another's bored carving might drag a compass point astray.

Alfred had, until now, never considered this particular relationship each boy had to their desk.

Today he thought differently though. Boys had carved their names upon it. Why not, it seemed only natural. Those names were the most obvious, and often deepest, scars. There was Piotr, Tomasz, Michał, Tadeusz, Ernst and Viktor. These were arranged in a list, one beneath the other, Piotr being the most faded and difficult to discern. Across the top of Viktor's name another boy, more recently, had left his mark: Otto (with the 't' of Viktor forming the first 't' of Otto). As he examined the surface of the desk more closely he found more faded names, gradually filled in with dirt and ink—a filthy palimpsest of existence.

Alfred had seen these names repeatedly over the years. Yet now they seemed to connect to each other in ways he struggled to comprehend. These were the steadily fading memories of the procession of boys that had filed through this place (before the village had consumed them with its own demands), each coming to know this desk (thinking for a few years, at least, that it was *theirs*) and each struggling to answer questions and solve equations upon its gradually degenerating surface. There were Andrzej, Stanisław, Oskar, Jacek and Mariusz (this, Alfred was sure, was Mariusz the village baker—he was right).

There was one unusual name though, scrawled hastily in the bottom left edge: Natalia. Had a girl crept in here late one evening to mark herself upon a desk in the boys' quarters of the school? She had risked a lot to do this, not least the severity of Dr Borowski's retribution, which would have been as fierce for her as it would have been for any of the boys in his charge.

She had been in love, Alfred thought. She had been in love with Piotr, the boy who had marked his presence at the other corner of the desk. Alfred saw them now living together in some far-away province, where the sun always shone and they could prove themselves through honour and kindness. They had become a generous Lord and Lady with land and...

The crack of the cane came across the back of his neck, luckily somewhat protected by the collar of his short coat.

PAY ATTENTION!

Alfred paid *some* attention, but only briefly.

His mind was already racing with all the possible friendships, the rivalries, the lives cut short, the heroic scenes. Ideas enough to fill a thousand books of folk tales flourished within an instant.

As stealthily as he could, timing Dr Borowski's pacing through the classroom to evade another beating, Alfred noted down as many names in the back of his exercise book as he could find upon the desk. He even explored the inside of the lid, where suddenly an even wilder world emerged. There were not only names here but also curious symbols. These were things that had been carved in great danger (one was not meant to open the lid unless permission had been granted). There were concentric circles that dizzied the eyes with their labyrinthine structure; vaguely human forms; oddly leaning houses, and animal-like creatures so hastily impressed upon the wood that it was difficult to make out if they were real or the trick of blemishes within the grain.

Alfred returned early to the classroom after that day's lunch. Dr Borowski was not yet back at his own desk. Within a few minutes Alfred had made swift rubbings of the images both within and upon the desk. He even found some etched upon the legs: what looked to be a map of vast standing stones; a detailed ziggurat and a flight of birds—no more than elongated Vs in a formation—rooks, surely!. He was flushed with euphoria as his imagination multiplied the context and history of these things, conjuring realms and peoples from the faintest of scratches.

One final image brought him back to the chill reality—even, perhaps, the deeper design—of the classroom. It was a crude skull, with wide, deep eye sockets, gouged somewhat frantically on the inside of the desk, beneath the hole for the inkwell. And then, as though on some theatrical cue, he heard Dr Borowski's shoes upon the ancient wooden floor of the corridor. Alfred's body prickled with fear as he frantically rubbed his stick of charcoal to obtain an impression of this carving. The deep eyes broke the paper where he pressed too hard and the resulting rubbing was truly horrific; a negative of death.

Alfred was sat upright on his bench, in attentive pose, before Dr Borowski had made it to the doorway.

Dr Borowski was suspicious of Alfred's early return to the classroom—but then suspicion was as innate in him as cruelty in a cat. But without at least some little evidence of wrongdoing he would not be able to administer any form of punishment. A frustrating few minutes of silence passed as they awaited the return of the other boys.

Alfred was hardly able to contain his joy that afternoon and Dr Borowski sensed in him some form of insurgency (the detection of the undercurrent of rebellion being another of his supernatural gifts). To stem the insurrection Dr Borowski tasked Alfred with cleaning the inkwells after the bell had sounded for the others to depart. This was usually considered a chore but Alfred didn't mind. It would give him some time in the classroom without Dr Borowski and enable a more careful examination of the rest of his desk which had now, within the space of a few hours, become an obsession.

He completed the cleaning of the inkwells in record time allowing him to make some further rubbings of the desk. The last one had been crafted quite well, perhaps over a number of years. It was a tree in full leaf. It was to be found on the underside of the desk, and took up almost a full quarter of its surface. Alfred surmised that it had been fashioned blind, the child-craftsman having felt his way around the branches with his fingertips, using a compass, or small pocketknife to gradually bring it to life.

As he was making ready to leave he noticed a small strip of wood that had fallen away a little from the underside of the desk, just above where the tree was. There were a number of scuffs and dents towards the back of the desk and Alfred assumed that one pupil must have repeatedly kicked at it during his tenancy. This angered Alfred in a fashion he found quite remarkable. He tried to repair it, but could manage little more than holding the strip back up and hoping that by force of will it might remain. It did not. In fact Alfred's tampering had now loosened it further. He was getting a little worried that Dr Borowski might return at any moment and find him there and then administer a good beating for defacing school property.

He tore it off with one determined pull.

That petty act of defiance gave him fresh enthusiasm, but a sense of shame. The desk had given him something fascinating and he had repaid it with violence. From then on, he decided, the strip of wood was to be held as a special object that, like some rudimentary magician's wand, could transmogrify the everyday into the marvellous. He placed it inside his exercise book where it would mark the end of his schoolwork and the beginning of the incredible aspirations of his imagination.

On his way home his thoughts were already busy with the people and places of his imaginary kingdom. A voice called his name from what seemed a great distance.

Alfred slipped back into reality momentarily and saw Agnieszka, the daughter of Artur and Ewa, our neighbours. She was a couple of years older than Alfred was and had left the school some three years earlier to help her mother run the house. With three daughters and only one son Artur struggled to run the few acres of land they owned.

Alfred trusted Agnieszka and he ran to her excitedly, burbling out the day's events in detail, telling her of the fantastic world that teemed within his desk if only one were patient enough to unravel the intricate lines of its signification.

She listened patiently to the embryonic story of King Piotr and Queen Natalia (they had, in only these short hours, become royalty); the generals, Otto, Ernst and Viktor, and the skilful emissary Michał who spied on other kingdoms. He showed her the fiendish axe of the executioner, Jacek. He traced a path for her through the countryside of this land; the standing stones with the great magical menhir that came to life on Christmas Eve, the labyrinth designed (and haunted!) by the mad monk, Stanisław the foul. There were flora and fauna too: the great tree whose vast branches were shaped at night by the loving hands of dryads; the flight of rooks, presaging a death in the royal household. Everything coalesced into an abundance of meaning that his agitated lips could barely keep pace with the telling of.

Alfred saw Agnieszka's face alight with the same passion that fermented within him and he swore her to secrecy.

A week of late afternoons on the grassy hillsides with Agnieszka, and later nights alone in his room, gave life to this other kingdom—reached through only a sideways glance away from this black and white reality.

And through all that feverish excitement I watched him.

In those sketchbooks my son began to come alive. With each redrawn rubbing, diagram, or dreamy vignette, Alfred's blood flowed deeper and more vigorously, drawing upon those infinite wells of being that enliven us all, crafting a young mind with the drug of imagination. But as each evening opened to unbounded wonder so too the dark shadow of isolation crept upon him. From this, not even Agnieszka's complicit enthusiasm could retrieve him. The world became tinged with incredible golds and silvers and every sound exploded into a potential symphony as steadily he became mesmerised by the power of his own mind. Each ordinary thing transubstantiated into the addictive fog of the fantastical.

I understood that he had become an ardent student of the universe. He stared into the void and in the mirrors of his dark eyes I watched the world tumble in dissolution, transformed by the joy and marvel of an eager initiate.

II. *Epopteia, or, Pain is Truth*

The passions of the keen student will always lead to error; failure illuminates the path to knowledge (would that the path to truth was so straightforward).

Alfred's book is soon discovered, that is inevitable.

Fittingly enough the event occurs during a grammar lesson, as Alfred devises new languages for his other realm. Dr Borowski catches sight of a page of script in letters and runes he cannot read. He tears the book from the boy's hands and flicks through its pages, finding Alfred's weird drawings, the rubbings (another mystery) and energetic creative ramblings. This is insolent self-indulgence—during grammar!

The strip of wood too seems somehow deviant, a secret boundary between learning and creativity. Dr Borowski waves the wood before Alfred's face amidst the usual admonishments.

Alfred is told to stand and hold his hands out flat: the old ritual.

The cane is retrieved from the front desk. Dr Borowski's walk is purposefully slow: further embellishment to the ceremony.

This thin cane has served Dr Borowski for many years. In a little corner of his mind (a special secluded place) he has even given it a name—Genghis! Every man that now walks our little village has felt its sting.

Its wooden blade rips the air apart with a sharp whoop of delight, until it strikes home across Alfred's palms with an uncanny *plop!* that sends a sympathetic shiver through the flesh of every boy in the room. The first stroke flares Dr Borowksi's and Alfred's eyes wide, the former in barely concealed delight, and the latter with the rapture of agony. And more strikes come, some swiftly, some with more delay—everything calculated to make the experience more unnerving, more shamefully debilitating.

But these blows have not reduced Alfred to the tearful penitent that Dr Borowski expects. No tear is shed, no words of apology burble from trembling lips (such as the role usually requires). Alfred stands there, recalcitrant, ready for the final blow.

It does not come.

Dr Borowski devises a different denouement for this brutal scene.

He slides the strip of wood from the exercise book.

He runs his fingers along its splintered edge in front of Alfred's eyes. It is rough and sharp; it snags the skin.

The final strike must be delivered by this symbol of mischief—this is, after all, justice; it is only right that there should be irony.

This weapon does not emit the satisfying whistle of the cane though as it cleaves the air. Instead its rough surface roars like a great fire that swallows the oxygen from the room. It bursts against Alfred's hands and splinters into a shower of fragments, its form relinquished as the force of Dr Borowski's vengeance meets the stubborn resolution of Alfred's will.

One of the shards—a thick, rounded splinter—has penetrated Alfred's palm. The blood wells and drips upon the desk.

Time ceases. The boys stare, forever frozen in horror. Alfred stands for eternity, contemplating the deep wound.

A breeze, as light as life, animates our little players.

Alfred flees the schoolroom, clutching his wounded hand.

Dr Borowski does not even watch him leave, staring into space like some grim executioner—Borowski the foul!

He turns on his heels and picks up 'Genghis' and returns, slowly, to his desk. There is an empty seat in the classroom—the boys will remember this for some time.

This is how order is upheld—such is the work of the torturer.

∞

Alfred is racing through the lanes where the simple dwellings seem to hunch towards him in an effort to soothe and cradle, as they have done generations of our children before. But he is seeking a wild space, anywhere that rejects the relentless progress of humanity. His body is tingling, as though alive with swarming creatures. In his left hand he crushes the splinter deeper into his palm. The blood flows and the tingling increases—it feels as though his entire skin is crawling away from itself.

Agnieszka, who is in her kitchen with her mother salting milk for oscypek, sees him and—sensing something momentous—runs to help.

Alfred makes for the woods—a place where beasts, such as himself, should dwell.

It is a wood of legends, with its tall firs forcing an umbrella of foliage upwards to obliterate the sky and hide its microcosm of ferns and insects from the eyes of God—who, in his lust for evolution, abhors his primordial designs. Where gentle knolls disperse the trunks a little, enabling a glimpse of brightness to penetrate, it seems as though the light holds one motionless as the trees whirl about, animating everything as though the world is merely a sequence of children's' drawings in a zoetrope.

I remember the joyful canters through those woods in my own youth.

But we are here with my son, and this is not a joyful canter. This is his story, I reiterate. He must not suffer the futile nostalgia of his wretched progenitor; his anger and terror are enough to fill one hundred stories such as this.

Agnieszka keeps him in sight, catching flickers of him through the trees, like a hunted animal. She, being older, taller, and stronger, gains gradually on him. Her heart pounds as fast as her mind races, imagining all the things that might have happened to cause his strange flight.

Finally Alfred sinks to his knees, exhausted, in a wide clearing ringed with trees. There is a plush carpet of needles, forming a soft mulch that never fully decomposes—each year gathering another thin layer. It is a place that oozes time, having been used—by our people—as a trysting place for generations. Before this, through the tides of civilisations it must have been venerated and cherished, or perhaps shunned—a site of worship, or sacrifice. It secretes its magical history—blessing and curse—into Alfred and Agnieszka.

Agnieszka reaches down and opens Alfred's clenched fists. Thick blisters already bubble upon the skin, and long red lines trail across his palms. In his left palm she finds a stiff splinter rising from a wound already crusted with dark dried blood.

She gasps and half closes his fist again, as though the injury might vanish purely by the wishing of it.

She looks up into Alfred's face with her brilliant, rich eyes and nods. It is a moment of understanding—senseless brutality, the fragility of skin, the joy of another's soothing touch; millennia of youthful mysteries.

He stares back at her with eyes that seem already ancient. There is no sadness, no anger, merely two dark circles opening into pain.

She kisses his open right palm and gently moves it aside so that she may tend to his left hand.

Her lips feel strange on his skin. They are slightly cracked, like the brittle bark from a tree branch, but in their centre is a moist warmth that makes him feel both elated and upset.

As she opens his left hand again he sobs a little, not in pain but from yearning.

There is another long pause. He does not speak. She slowly uncurls his fingers and examines the wound as best she can.

She reaches down and pulls a wide leaf from a nearby plant. She folds it in half and gently crushes it, before dabbing away the dry blood.

The leaf feels cool. Alfred feels the greenness of it pass into him with a sharp tingling sensation. It is nothing like the tingling he felt when running away though, as he pushed the wooden splinter deeper into himself. This is merely the everyday chatter of the body. The other sensation was altogether different.

Then, as he attempts to understand this further, the rush of pain is back. Agnieszka is attempting to pull the splinter out. Fresh blood wells in his hand and a flap of skin hangs loosely from the broken end of the chunk of wood.

They stare at it for a moment. She had not realised it had gone so deep; had not realised indeed how large a fragment it had been. Their hands are now covered in sticky blood but still she holds the splinter between them as they gaze at it—some sacred object.

Then Alfred takes it from her, still handling it with reverence. He then grips it between the thumb and forefinger of his injured hand as if it were a great needle.

He holds it before Agnieszka's face, as though about to perform some magic trick. She is still kneeling beside him in the blanket of tree needles. He smiles at her. She smiles back at him, clearly confused.

He places his open right hand on his knee and slowly brings the wooden shard down to the centre of his palm. With a flick of his finger he slides the splinter under the skin a few millimetres.

Agnieszka gasps but watches, captivated, as Alfred continues to push the foreign object further under until it is entirely inside him. He flexes his fingers a moment and the dark wood dances beneath the skin of his palm, as though an inky stain has burst from his veins.

Angieszka's lips tremble. Everything is still again as though the world might finally have rid itself of its evil shadow, time. The terrible beauty of this stasis drags the sky asunder and blasts the earth to ashes—all is elemental.

The grinder soon cranks the handle and we turn again.

The sun breaks through the low trees, night is approaching. With this portent they rise, their souls rampant with dark possibilities. The unfathomable romance of Alfred and Agnieszka begins.

III. *Anabasis, or, The Suture*

Alfred's collapse will be swift. In the days following his beating he will become morose and withdrawn. This is entirely natural, of course. But his malaise will deepen until Maria becomes particularly concerned for him. He will be even more withdrawn at school, eyeing Dr Borowski with a contempt that even that strict disciplinarian will find hard to endure.

Alfred will devise ways to remain in the schoolhouse during hours when the other children are at play. His fascination with his desk will become morbid, absorbing his every thought. He will begin to break small splinters from it—in hidden places at first, until his urges will make him forget to mask his vandalism.

On his journeys home from school he will see Agnieszka and they will share some pleasantries. She will notice too, as his Mother has, that his mood is grim. He will not tell her his fantastic visions anymore, merely idle chatter as he toys in his pocket with the broken wooden fragments he has stolen that day. As her lips move with excited talk of fields and flowers he will hear nothing, his thoughts only conjuring the mechanics of his other worlds.

But what does his little collection of wooden souvenirs mean? That too will become as apparent as the storm—heralding the first showers of autumn—gathering in the distance as Agnieszka and Alfred share the last words they will ever speak to each other.

Yes, from then on he will not address her again. Indeed during the next week he will speak to fewer and fewer people until, by that Sunday, he does not even speak to his own mother. People will comment upon this. They will also note the odd limp he develops. During the course of those final days walking appears to be a terrible discomfort, and then an agonising struggle. Maria will ask him repeatedly, 'What is wrong, my dearest Alfred?' 'Nothing mother,' he will reply, sharply. 'There is nothing *wrong* at all.'

You will have guessed by now, I am sure, that he will have filled all the pages of his school exercise book with drawings, scribblings and plans. He will not sleep during this last weekend. When Agnieszka calls, because she has not even seen him return from school that week (he will follow a different path home—a back route, out by the woods, where few would wish to follow him), Maria will send her away. 'Alfred does not wish to see anyone. He is working on his project,' she will say, sadly.

The next day he will be due to go to school. Maria will attempt to wake him but find him feverish and drowsy. She will keep him at home to sleep off whatever malady afflicts him.

Early that evening Agnieszka will call again. She will have heard that Alfred was not in school that day.

Maria will break down on the doorstep and after sharing a pot of strong black tea, during which they will discuss Alfred and his odd behaviour, they will both venture to his room to tend to him.

They will find him in the height of fever, dreaming madly and writhing as though battling nightmarish foes. His bed linen will be sodden with sweat; a sticky halo has formed upon his pillow—my little mortal angel. His eyes will be clamped shut—all is inward and aflame.

In his delirium he will scream for the world of his dreams and cry for the servants that attend him there. Little will my beloved Maria know that only some feet from her lie the etchings and crude rubbings that give some guidance to these realms of mystery which she will hear only as the mutterings of an agitated mind. Agnieszka will recall something of them though. She had listened to him rambling about these other places in the dawn of their creation. She had watched his eyes dart like little tortured birds, battering against their tiny cage, attempting to escape into the shimmering blue of the skies and into the breathless blacks of space. But she will not dare to break her promise, although she will hover at Alfred's bedside like a tormented moth around a guttering candle.

That night they will discover the extent of his imaginings.

By midnight nothing will have calmed his ravings, yet the doctor is still not called—he is a village away and besides there would be his fee. The women will feel redundant. The least they can do is bathe his body, until the nightmares subside. They will gather towels and warm water. Agnieszka will run home for a bar of rose soap that she has treasured for many months. She will hope that this simple, loving gift might somehow guide him back from oblivion.

Uncovering his legs they will discover the cause of his sudden deterioration. His shins and knees dark blue and purple with bruises, dotted here and there with thin dark lines as though a vine had crept beneath his skin and wound its way towards his torso. They will find his calves swollen with great red weals, also interspersed with solid dark patches.

Maria will lift his nightgown still further and reveal the chaos of his thighs amidst a miasma of rot that will leave them retching. Here long striations of black will be paralleled by lengthy yellow and red pustules which burst the flesh, seeping across his skin in sticky rivulets.

Broken bodies draw the gaze as much as they deflect it—twisted mirrors beguile the grotesque fascination.

The two women, horrified, appalled, traumatised, will avert their eyes and wail—the fervent passion of mothers and lovers at a deathbed. But slowly the cold dark of their being will overcome them and they will look again—tentatively, curiously—upon the ruination of Alfred's legs. The skin will fester in great mounds within which, like erupting volcanoes, puffs of pink matter broil and sputter, flecked here and there with great clots that seem to cling like beetles to the gaping lesions. Cracked flesh, surely days old, will have blackened into hardened craters that break the fetid corpulence of his bloated limbs like bullet holes. In contrast his withered ankles will appear to writhe with throbbing veins heavy with poisoned blood that pumps his body with agonising bursts of putrefaction.

Agnieszka, looking beyond the horror of these wounds, will notice the points of thin wooden strips poking from them. Some will have been forced into the flesh at almost right angles and others slid under the skin to create these dark blemishes. The more she looks beyond the rot of infection and the bruised flushes of blood the more she will be able to read these black stains. Like some crude tattooist Alfred has etched the marks of his schooldesk into his body using thin splinters of wood.

There on his shin, just at it appeared in his exercise book, will be the great swirl of The Labyrinth and the great menhir; on the left thigh the arrival of the rooks and the wide-eyed skull. There also, etched in tiny splinters across the knees, will be written the names of Alfred's imagined court; King Piotr and his Queen Natalia; Prince Tomasz and his Generals Otto, Ernst and Viktor; the spy Michał.

Maria will watch the understanding dawn on Agnieszka's sad face and a smile will appear, even a little laugh. And then she too, although not fully comprehending the black sigils etched upon the fading flesh of her son, will begin the work of reading.

They will pull up his soaking nightgown further. They will witness the gruesome blossoming of his sex, torn by thick shards of splintered wood. It will seem as a dying pink lily, its fleshy petals curling into decay. Agneiszka's heart will pound with the ecstasy of repulsion and her soul will soar with appalled adoration. This moment will be the revelation of his purpose. They will know this to be the work of a precocious genius.

His body will become a radical canvas, as richly detailed as the nightmares of Bosch; as magnificent and instructive as Raphael, as terrible and apocalyptic as Goya, as playful and abusive as Wojkiewicz. Maria and Agnieszka will tremble before the magnificence of its malign affront to God himself. Even in its nascent form it promises all the wonderful colours of creation and all the traumatic signs of disaster; auguring the entirety of existence and its exultant collapse.

There will be a brief interval in which everything—bodies, bedclothes, black sky—is weightless and yet resplendent, like the vast possibility of the dreamer upon wakening, before the rosy clouds of intimate vision are rendered servile to description. The entire world will flare white—only limitless effulgence. Maria and Agnieszska will feel the warmth of a fiery sun, even though the night will be so cold.

Then the screaming carousel of disintegration will begin its exigent call.

Alfred will open his eyes momentarily and lay his palms upon their cheeks. He will smile. Their bodies will fight back sobs and cries. Nothing can prepare them for the myriad dancing forms they will glimpse within his glittering dark pupils; flames will roar and waves surge; mountains will rise and crumble; a kaleidoscope of creatures—human, bird and beast—fold into each other in an instant; buildings form and dissolve again until finally a great tree rises against a stormy sky before being engulfed by a burst of apocalypse from its roots—all Pandora's mad things loosed at once. And then his eyelids will flick shut upon the Armageddon unleashed within his mind.

The smile will remain upon his lips, even as their gentle red fades rapidly to frozen blue. The morning chill will have a sharper bite.

Maria and Agnieszka will shed delicate pink tears and in each of these gentle drops of humanity a foetal coil will swirl, ready to enrich the world with fresh flesh. Agnieszka will weep there by Alfred's bedside until the sun rises and warms the room with bright yellow light; a light as yellow as the rivulets of disease that crawled across Alfred's legs, or as yellow as the yolk of the eggs that Maria will collect later that morning for the hearty breakfast that will fortify their lean, aching bodies. They will need to eat well, in preparation for the dark years of toil ahead of them.

'One day, perhaps, we will write, think, and act collectively.'
Novalis

You will have heard, no doubt, of Tullis' work. He (I am guessing Tullis is a *he*—I have no way of knowing of course) is ever the topic of late-night arts shows and the name on the lips of every literati, and no doubt the subject of a dozen doctoral theses by now. His writings are frequently read on the radio. I believe work has begun on a number of films and shorter adaptations for the small screen.

Perhaps you have already read some of his work, few now haven't. Last month Tullis published four novels, fifteen short stories in different collections, three other collections of short fiction (never previously published) and two non-fiction titles; one on the ritual practices of the Mayan ballgame, the other a biography of the Austrian artist and puppeteer Richard Teschner. Besides these major works there were a myriad of articles in academic journals, newspapers and magazines, on topics as varied as Franklin's attempt on the Northwest Passage, politics, horticulture, property investment; let alone the book and theatre reviews. S. D. Tullis has become the great writer of our century; and all this in just the last few years.

After the publication of his first collection of short stories, *Dreams of the Masses*, three years ago, his popularity and critical acclaim has increased as exponentially as his output.

The truth is: I am S. D. Tullis. Well, that is not the full truth. I am only a fragment of S. D. Tullis; a splinter of that monolithic mystery.

Let me explain. One morning, nearly four years ago, I received a letter. I had been prowling about the house doing odd jobs, in a useless attempt to conquer an impasse I had reached in the novel I had been writing. This block had been plaguing me for weeks. So, sitting with my fourth cup of coffee of the morning, I leafed through the post in the hope of finding something that might enliven my tired mind.

One letter held quite a surprise. It had obviously been typed carefully on an old typewriter, with that particular black blur of a new ribbon:

> Dear Potentiality,
>
> I was very pleased to notice some of your work in a collected edition of short stories I acquired some weeks ago. Your writing struck me as innovative and engaging. You have an eloquent style I find particularly appealing.
>
> I hope you will not find my direct approach off-putting, but I thought you would appreciate plain speaking. I am currently beginning a project that I think you may find of interest.
>
> You, as much as anyone, will appreciate the difficulty of the writer's task; the search through the dusty labyrinths of imagination for an original approach. The struggle to transform thought into words. Often the work accumulates over time from the momentary jottings of the mind allowed between the wretched everyday responsibilities.
>
> You will also have had the suspicion that there is more at work here than the words themselves. Try as you may you will be subject to

the whims of the publishing industry. Those you court, in whatever fashion, may return favours and recommend you to their own carefully cultivated networks. But it is all a brittle construct of bluff and flattery, as likely to fail as succeed.

And, what then, if you should succeed?

You have achieved your cherished ambition: to see your masterly words set into the confines of the printed page, and bound in flimsy cardboard (to cut costs and achieve maximum sales at an affordable price).

So, what next?

The doubt deepens that the fine reviews of your treasured volume are themselves the products of the sycophancy of a further coterie of bribed lackeys; only another layer of stooges, residing in pale towers just beyond those you have already made yourself subject to.

What if your work were assessed dispassionately, without the fog of your fame, or obscurity?

Imagine, if you will, a sort of organising body that would enable the presentation of material entirely without prejudice, and without the labour of construction and assembly. Consider a sort of supreme editorial enterprise that would enable all the great discarded moments of our writing energies to be brought together into one ultimate personality that erased identity itself.

That is my proposition to you! Let us unite in anonymity and enable the true merit of literature to rise again. Each work sent to me will appear as a perfect fragment. However, it will exist in relation to the other works submitted and we will assemble a true collective mind; emerging from the isolation of your thoughts the work will engender new connections and dimensions impossible for the individual writer to accomplish alone.

Please send your contribution, however lengthy, or brief, to me at:

S. D. Tullis
PO Box _____
Edinburgh

I look forward to you joining our fraternity.

Yours faithfully,

S. D. Tullis

The signature suggested an elderly hand troubled by arthritis. The content of the letter reminded me of a number of hoaxes, and I thought that a literary friend had perhaps sent it as a joke. But something in its tone spoke of fidelity to a deeper belief, as idealistic as the work of the Schlegels and Novalis in *The Athenaeum*, or the similar attempts in French journals of the 1960s. Surely it was worth a try. It was, no doubt, as equally doomed to fail but without trying I might miss a genuinely creative opportunity. Perhaps now, in the age of global cultural exchange—for good or ill—it would be possible to bring together a disparate group of writers who could then speak, collectively, through one place; through one constructed persona—if I had understood the enterprise correctly.

And so, with a passion not a little mischievous, I penned a short paragraph:

> It was there, up on the dusty high road, that I heard the Lamia singing. I listened a while and soon in thrall—to beauty delicate and fine and melodies unheard by any human ear—I sought to woo her; though I knew that by such reckless deed my soul was damned.

I thought it might prove somewhat testing to include alongside any contributions that may have been received from others. I looked forward to seeing if this S. D. Tullis' work ever appeared and indeed if my brief passage might be included in the publication.

It was a year later that *Dreams of the Masses* appeared. It was with a small press somewhere near Oxford: Quintessential Press I believe they were called. I didn't hear about it for a good few months after it was released and missed out on purchasing a copy of its limited run. But I managed to borrow a copy from a friend of mine. I searched through its 300-odd pages, getting the feel for the work (comprising 14 stories). Naturally I was eager to see if my work appeared within.

No, there wasn't a single line of my writing.

Over the following weeks I read it carefully, to the exclusion of all else—even my own proofs that had come in from my publisher. It was an impressive piece of work. The stories were twined together in subtle ways, with characters overflowing from one to the other and taking on the speech of others in previous tales. If it had been composed from a number of different contributors, and each had sent in as little as I had, then it was a masterful piece of editorial construction. Tullis must have been quite a writer to have blended these stories from such disparate voices.

But then, surely few people would have sent him so short a contribution. Most, of course, would have sent in whole stories, perhaps even novels. It was probable that Tullis had merely tidied up an entire collection that some naive, but gifted, writer had sent him in desperation. That had to be the answer.

No doubt he thought my contribution flippant, maybe even insulting. He had discarded it as useless to his con-trick. He merely played on the insecurities and hopes of those who had been unable to get their work accepted for publication elsewhere. Certainly he had discovered the hidden gem amidst the dirt, but it was no more than that; an elaborate confidence trick. Yes, that *had* to be the answer. I was certain of it.

Over the following months I managed to get my proofs corrected, although I was more concerned to obtain, and thoroughly digest, the two novels and three collections that appeared from Tullis over that period.

Again, there was nothing of mine within them.

I gradually got back to my own work. A few short stories emerged and the beginnings of a new crime novel.

Then, with the publication of *The Temptation of Grief*, his ninth novel (within eighteen months of his letter to me), I found this, in chapter six: 'He was found, pale and broken, up on the dusty high road where I once kissed Daisy one fine summer's evening, just as dusk disintegrated into night'.

That was it: *up on the dusty high road.* Could I even be sure that this had been taken from what I had sent him though? In many ways discovering these few words was more frustrating than finding nothing. It was not a common phrase, certainly, but surely it was uncommon enough to suggest it had been taken from what I had written.

Wouldn't you agree? Those were my words, not those of another.

∞

My doubts deepened. I re-read the letter. There he had written: 'Each work sent to me will appear as a perfect fragment'. That had to imply that the passage would be reproduced in its entirety, or not at all. I recalled a line from Friedrich Schlegel, 'A fragment should be like a little work of art, complete in itself from the rest of the world like a hedgehog'. Tullis would not be ignorant of this, indeed it epitomised the entire project that his work suggested.

I would have to wait to see my work appear complete, with all the aphoristic fervour of a quotation; and when it did, I would be able to laugh again.

But, after three years, and having read every book and story he has written (over seventy novels, five hundred short stories, and literally thousands of articles) I have found only those few words: 'up on the dusty high road'. I cannot write anything now. I have enough of a schedule keeping up with all of his writings in my search for myself.

I even traced the Edinburgh PO Box to a residential home in Clermiston. My enquiries brought forth nothing but deeper mysteries. The staff there had never heard of an S.D. Tullis, and had never had any resident with either an obsessive literary interest or a large volume of correspondence. And here again my doubts surfaced.

I asked them if there had been any other enquiries here for an individual named Tullis (for the press must, by now, have a copy of his letter, listing the Post Office Box). They would have tried to trace him before I had, surely.

But no, there had never been an enquiry at the home for a Mr Tullis, S.D. Tullis, or any other form of Tullis.

A nurse escorted me out of the building before I was able to ask any further questions. I thought I caught a wry smile on her face though as the door closed.

I am beginning to think that everyone I see is Tullis now, and that we are all complicit in the great deception. You can see the mixture of guilt and pride in every eye, as we watch each other thinking: 'Do they know?' And this proud treachery festers in each of our hearts: 'Could they have discovered the truth: that I am Tullis?'

Tullis is a microbe, a great disease spreading across the defenceless globe—exponentially; a prolific epidemic of words. No, no, he is a chimera, a beast: the great beast—an amalgam of parts; a beast whose great wizened tits suckle replicas of itself from teats that dribble sweat, blood and tears!

Tullis is the vortex into which everything is now falling.

But really, Tullis is a mirror.

Tull*is* is.

I cannot even say *is* now without thinking of Tullis.

Tull is. Lis ull tu, li listu ull.

Tullis. As complete from the rest of the world as a hedgehog, or rolling along and gathering the entire world, like moss, upon him—I have no mind left, only correlation.

What do they call the spines of a hedgehog? They must have a scientific name, not simply 'spines'. They should be Tullae.

Do you see now how Tullis becomes everything? Every thought, and conversation whispered on the street corner, becomes his. Everywhere people must be recording everything and sending it to him. All of us Tullises, or should that also be Tullae?

Yes, yes! We, Tullae.

Tull is. Lis ull tu, li listu ull. Ull is Tullae. Tullis ul tu—tul is Tullae.

Might all language (ul lis) soon be transformed?

I am waiting for the rest of my words to be included. It is only a matter of time. I will find them there one day; the Lamia, the beauty, the singing, the reckless deed, the damned soul. Not just the words. The words alone are not enough. They have to be gathered together close enough to what I sent him to suggest the entire theme of my short passage; a perfect fragment, complete in itself from the rest of the world. It is not enough to have the tantalisingly brief 'up on the dusty high road'. Given the number of potential contributors—possibly every one of us—these words could have come from anywhere. Only with the full inclusion of all of my work can I be sure that I have been accepted.

Then, I will have achieved something; the *only* achievement I care for now.

And only then, when I am fully Tullis, will I be everywhere and nowhere, perpetual motion in stasis—truly, and finally, myself; fractured, immortal.

Tullis is a brotherhood of nothing; faceless, blank, null. Tullis ul tu—tul is Tullae.

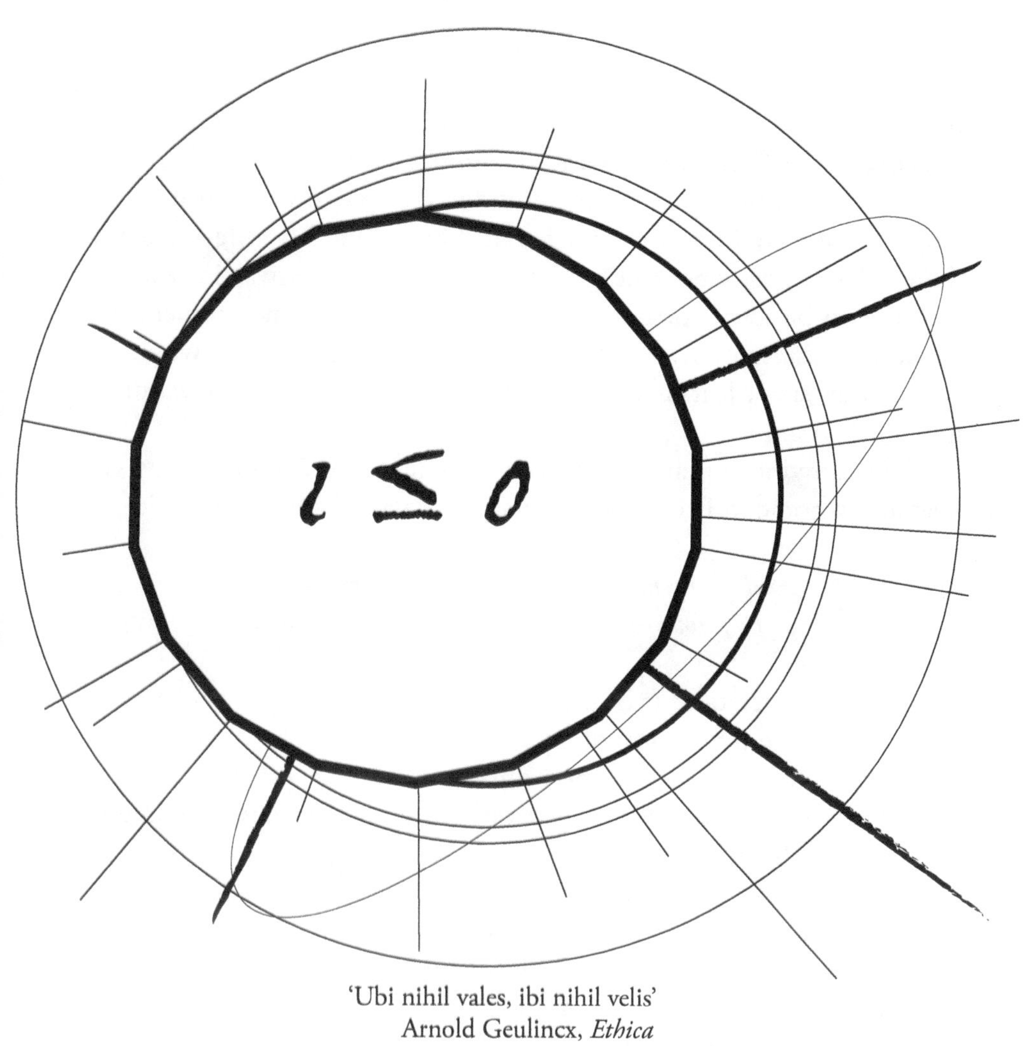

'Ubi nihil vales, ibi nihil velis'
Arnold Geulincx, *Ethica*

I am here, on Christmas Eve, at my church. I have watched my shadow, cast across the door, gradually fading as the winter sunlight dwindles. I should be taking Midnight Mass this evening. I will, of course, be there. I will scream into the packed nave where the rosy cheeked celebrants will be struggling to sober up. I will cry my throat dry with obscenities, with blasphemies. I will strike out at the choirboys and kick at the altar. But will happen, no one will notice me. Not a sound will be heard, not a candle will flicker. There will, as there has been for the last week, some commotion. People will go hither and thither through the village in search of me. Perhaps the bishop will have organised a replacement, if not then the curate, Dr Pleasance, will lead the service.

My faithful parishioners are perplexed. Supposedly I went missing last Sunday. They say I never arrived for morning mass. My wife and son were there. Mrs Davis, who kindly plays the organ for us, was in tears. I was nowhere to be seen, apparently. And that is precisely the problem. I have become as transparent as the wind. No, I am less than the wind, which can at least stir a leaf or chill an exposed cheek. No, I have *no* presence remaining. I am nothing.

I am convinced that it began last New Year's Eve, at a party my cousin held at his home in Inverness. At least that's what I think started it.

And if any man think that he knoweth any thing,
he knoweth nothing yet as he ought to know.

As you will understand it is difficult to be a vicar in a provincial parish. I had studied, and lived, most of my life in London and I was used to a more active social life. Not everything I did there focused—as it does here—on the church fete and the harvest festival. I attended theological conferences and enjoyed the opera and theatre. Since taking up my position in Lesser Gollington, some twelve years ago, my life has shrunk to the orbit of the parish newsletter and has thus placed a pressure on my family that seems to me the origin of my strange state. Please don't get me wrong, I'm not one of those men that seek appreciation of his work. I am, after all, a clergyman. We are every watchful for the sin of pride. I mean to say that nothing in my experience had prepared me, my wife Cathy, or our son, Thomas (then ten years old), for the strangely invasive solitude of village life. By that I mean that nothing is private, yet one is never able to indulge one's own interests, leading to a condition of almost abject servitude. And, yes, service is my vocation. But there is nothing to do here but focus on the parish and its community. No doubt some would say that is a good thing. But it becomes a burden over time. It becomes a terrible responsibility.

So that evening, almost a year ago, I had rather let myself go. I was drunk. It was a relief to leave the parish with the curate and have a week away to be myself again. To my family I mean. Thomas was in his first year at Cambridge. He had gone there to study philosophy. We had always clashed over spiritual matters. I remember he would argue with me even as young as six. I thought he resented the long hours I worked and the continual procession of visitors to the house. This situation worsened when we moved here. People call for a tea and a chat. It all takes time. It takes endless amounts of time. You can't turn them away. So his bright city world was stolen from him just as he had begun to appreciate it and the resentment accumulated with the years of village life. I thought he would seize his first opportunity to return to London, but he didn't. He skulked around the village for a few years after school, working in the pub and on a nearby farm. Then he decided to study philosophy, particularly modern continental philosophy, which is more than a little dubious. It was not a spiteful decision on his part, at least I hope not. He had become interested, in his early teens, in Existentialism as an alternative to the explanations I offered him from a Christian perspective. I had tried to explain to him the strong thread of Christian Existentialists; Kierkegaard, Jaspers and the like. He was not interested. The Parisian cafe culture of Sartre and Camus, with its black-clothed artistic fug of Gitanes and red wine appealed to his adolescent angst. I should have understood. But as the years passed so the gap between us widened. We had argued every weekend that he had visited home since he started university.

I should have been more controlled at the party. I shouldn't have drunk so much. I shouldn't have started an argument with him. It was minutes before midnight. There were about thirty people there, mostly friends of my cousin. There were few family members there, which is why I relaxed so much, no doubt.

Thomas seemed to be engaged in a debate with a few other students, who had probably also been dragged here by their parents. I made my way over and listened to his conversation for a while. He was discussing Zarathustra's revelation to the masses that 'God is dead!' It was banal enough; a tiresome, rehearsed speech that I had discussed with him on a number of occasions, always ending in bitterness. Something about his audience's rapt attention frustrated me. I struggled every weekend to deliver positive messages of hope to a steadily ageing and dwindling congregation, and here was my own son preaching nihilism to young minds that seemed eager to lap up a madman's ravings.

I leaned over and mentioned that they might profit from recalling the warning of worshipping false idols illustrated by Isaiah Chapter 41:

Behold, they are all vanity; their works are nothing: their molten images are wind and confusion.

They all laughed, apart from Thomas. I do not recall whether they laughed at me, or with me. But either way I laughed too. I believe now that he thought I was laughing at him. That was far from the case. I laughed at the frailties of our human intellect in the face of God's supreme knowledge. At least that's what I thought I laughed at. Perhaps now, if only I could hear my laughter I would hear simply the empty sound of the bell that brings us all home. For, ultimately, isn't all laughter only the echo of an original revolt against the almighty: a never-ending scream against the absurdity of our exile from him?

'Well, *Father*,' he said, emphasising the clerical nature of the 'Father' with a hostility I had not expected. 'Our works may be as nothing but at least we *know* it. Rather than deferring to the bible, I prefer the phrase from Geulincx, "where one is worth nothing, one should want nothing."'

He stood then and leaned closer to me. I heard the bells of Big Ben begin to announce the New Year from the television in the next room. The party crowd gave a cheer.

'Did you hear me, *Father*?' Thomas sneered. 'Where one is worth nothing, one should want nothing.'

I have always found the turning of the year a peculiar time: an instant infused with the joys and disappointments of the whole previous year, and ripe with the hopes of the coming one. It is always a magical moment, or a cursed one. Here, with Thomas' hate-filled face close to my own, it took on a fateful aspect.

Cathy had found us. She always loved New Year. She held us both together in an awkward embrace as she sang *Auld Lang Syne*.

The following couple of days were also uncomfortable. Thomas wouldn't speak to me. Cathy, once I'd told her, was annoyed. She thought I had been unfair. She always thought that engaging in discussion with Thomas was pointless. 'It's just a phase,' she always said. He was twenty-two. Just a phase?

A few days after our return to the village Thomas decided he'd go back to Cambridge early. Thinking of that day now I realise it was the first indication I had of my changing nature.

Behold, ye are of nothing, and your work of nought.

I had come down a little late and had to prepare for a funeral that afternoon. I went through to the kitchen to make a pot of coffee. Cathy and Thomas were there. Three bags were piled beside the backdoor. I knew they were discussing me: Cathy looked upset, Thomas angry and determined. The kitchen is not large. I stood by the door expecting them to awkwardly change the subject as had happened so many times before when I had interrupted one of their 'chats'.

They continued though. Cathy was pleading with him to stay for the next four days and she would drive him back herself. He refused, claiming it would be best for all of us if he went back by train now. There was a taxi coming to take him to the station in half an hour.

I cleared my throat, confused by how they couldn't have noticed me there, only a few feet from them. Both turned quickly and muttered nervous 'Good mornings'. Cathy started wiping the kitchen table, clearly distressed.

'Thomas is going back to halls today,' she said, obviously irritated with me. 'Perhaps you could give him a lift to the station.'

'There's no need, Mum,' Thomas said. 'I've told you, there's a taxi coming. I don't want to disturb you both anymore.'

She looked up at me from the table, having sunk into a chair, head in hands.

Maybe at that moment I could have changed everything. Yes, I could have spent some time with him. We could have talked it over. I couldn't have undone the years of distance between us but I might have healed this wound.

Instead, I gave up.

'If he wants to go today then it's his choice. He probably has university work to prepare,' I said limply. I held out a ten pound note. 'At least let us pay for your taxi.'

A typical student, he was not too proud to accept some money.

'Thanks,' he said, with the monumental tone of a conclusion.

The taxi arrived later and some blank goodbyes were exchanged.

Over the following months the distance grew between me and Cathy. She clearly resented me for that ineffectual parenting. She went to see him on a couple of occasions, staying overnight with her sister in Luton. She did not discuss these visits with me very much.

Further odd moments began to accumulate. Frequently I would find Cathy on the phone, in either the lounge or kitchen. She would be talking to her sister, or mother, about the problems between us. I stood quite nearby but she didn't seem to register that I was there. We started to argue about the fact that I was 'creeping up on her'. On one occasion she walked straight into me with a mug of tea. She screamed.

'What's wrong with you? Why do you keep skulking around like this? You're scaring me.'

What indeed was wrong with me? Nothing. What was wrong with her? I thought she was deliberately ignoring me to try to provoke an argument.

The problem worsened when Thomas returned at Easter. He too started knocking into me and claiming that he hadn't heard me on occasions when I called him down for dinner.

What seemed to be a cruel, but infantile, family conspiracy soon became more distressing though. Whilst working in the village I would encounter similar moments of surprise as parishioners would bump into me with exclamations of 'Oh, sorry vicar, I didn't see you there.'

In the early stages of any degenerative illness you seek other explanations for the disturbing events and pains one is experiencing. I realise that I too was trying to explain this gradual vanishing by reasoned means.

That was until the day, in mid-August, that Cathy looked right through me at the back door, calling to Thomas, who was reading in the garden.

'Thomas, could you find your Father, I have Mrs Galen on the phone asking about the availability of the church hall this Thursday,' she said, not two feet from my face.

I walked into the lounge, still unnoticed. Cathy and Thomas were now calling for me all around the house. I stood in the hallway. They both passed me on a number of occasions. In the full-length mirror I saw the horror of my emerging reality.

There was little there really, just a shimmering translucent outline. I saw no more than a heat haze, a disruption of natural laws.

For if a man think himself to be something,
when he is nothing, he deceiveth himself.

This new state did not endure for long. However, the regularity of these 'disappearances' increased and their duration became much longer. I also seemed to become more incorporeal, occasionally objects would slip through my grasp as one of these 'episodes' came on.

Thus I find myself here now, with a red sky descending on Christmas Eve; an evening of celebration and hope. Over the last week I have not felt the need to eat, or service any other bodily functions. I have returned home every evening to find Cathy distraught and Thomas there attempting to comfort her. I am not a ghost. I am not lucky enough to have died. I am outside of everything, looking in. How many others are there like me? All those people who are supposed to disappear each year; how many of them do so quite literally? Did I once live surrounded by those such as I am now, ever watched and overheard?

And what of God, the three in that I had placed all my faith in? I do not know. Certainly I am forsaken. There can be no ultimate justice, no absolute judgment. Instead there is only the senseless condemnation of the innocent to a life of immortal witness. I realise now the hopelessness of a world in which is equal to nothing, perhaps even less than nothing.

For now ye are nothing; ye see my casting down, and are afraid.

'I must confess to you that I was not a journalist. In truth, I was a thief.'

The antiquities and curious objects that had been gathered by Mr Umbroldi, over 50 years, had become legendary; more so because of his eccentricity and reluctance to catalogue his collection. There were collectors across the world that suspected Umbroldi of having secured the last few items that would make their own collections complete. He never replied to their letters, personal visits, or other modes of communication.

I was surprised, therefore, when he accepted my first application for an interview. No doubt you were also shocked at the ease with which you gained an audience, or perhaps you have plied him with gifts and pestered him with requests for many years. Well, either way, you are here and have to listen to my story before you are able to begin your own. If you will allow me a few moments of your precious time I feel obliged to entertain you with a short tale; perhaps you could even call it a fable.

I had heard something of Carl Umbroldi many years before. You see I was interested in Japanese antiquities, principally inro boxes, netsuke and ojime. But I also dabbled in militaria and had heard that Umbroldi had a collection of yari heads and items of samurai armour, including some kabuto and rare examples of mempo. These items fetch good prices these days. Everything I had heard of Umbroldi's collection reminded me of the eccentric, Charles Paget Wade, and the collection he had gathered at Snowshill Manor. Umbroldi's collection though sounded vaster, and just as idiosyncratic; an emblem of himself, as every true collection should be. I came across the name again in an auction catalogue. Incredibly he was parting with a fine Harbrecht armillary sphere, from the 1570s. Perhaps he was beginning to run out of finances—it often happens later in the collector's career—and was attempting to consolidate his collection around some specific themes that he no longer had the resources to achieve. I resolved therefore to see him, and the collection, at the first opportunity; to investigate the potential for a burglary with rich rewards. You see, often a collector is little interested in the simple banalities of existence and by the time they begin to think of security I have done my work. It was a thrilling life. I wouldn't have changed it for anything.

As I mentioned, it had been my first attempt to gain access to the man, a notorious recluse. I had expected it to fail. But he had accepted, in a charming letter that suggested a date and time only a couple of weeks from my first communication. Then, I believed that he had succumbed to what I call the "Collector's Curse". I suggest that this *illness* troubles most collectors in their latter years. As the urge to accumulate subsides, and most prized objects have been acquired, with only a few elusive articles remaining, the collector realises that their project—that had kept them so energised over all the years—is futile. They have, no doubt, sacrificed friends and a family life, perhaps even the joys of children, to amass their great treasure trove. But it exists only as a private language; a history of connections and conquests that they alone understand. To others it is a bizarre assemblage of useless *stuff*, antique or otherwise. It is then that the collector remembers the world and strives to immortalise not themselves but the meaning of the collection. They aim to secure its future. They try to justify its structure and integrity in current form. The juxtaposition of one object alongside another must be maintained, another curatorial hand could destroy the years of careful construction. They frequently court the press to make of their eccentricity a local legend, at least to secure some protection from the merciless predation of family or friends who might inherit what—to them—is merely a wonderful gift, only one quick deal from liquid cash. Yet, as ever—when courting the devil—one must be guarded against those keen to take advantage; those such as myself. So, although hopeful, I had not expected Mr Umbroldi to be so readily prepared to meet with me.

But before I detail our encounter let me tell you something of myself. All good collectors want to know the history of the objects they encounter. My fascination with antiques had begun straightforwardly enough. Idling, in my many days of truancy, around the boisterous Bermondsey market and dodging boots from the ragmen on Portobello Road I discovered a grimy sub-culture of subsistence trading; the fermenting corpulent bowels of civilisation. There, amidst the dead-men's clothes and broken domestic paraphernalia, one could find gold.

One morning, just as day broke, I found a tray of what looked like wooden buttons covered by a box of rusted carpentry tools. The trader was busy offloading furniture from his cart and so I huddled beneath the groaning table of his wares and dragged the box out to check its contents. Much of it seemed to be discarded wooden blocks, mostly spherical, the purpose of which was indiscernible. However there were a number of small carved items that seemed blackened by fire. Thinking back I believe they may have been Victorian bogwood brooches. I was a child, their dull etchings of churches and gravestones did not interest me.

Then I found something so different that a magical awe descended to mark a moment in which my life shifted course. It was a grotesque round face with a piggish snout and grimacing mouth exposing sharp teeth. Two embryonic horns marked its unusual demonic nature, as did the hollow eyes, which bore into my soul and etched my fate instantly. I did not know it then but it was a boxwood netsuke by the carver Sanshō. I stared at it for some time, rubbing my dirty fingers across its smooth surface, worn down for centuries by other hands, no doubt filthier than mine. A bizarre urge came over me. Not simply to steal the thing—that was certain—but to conceal it in my mouth like some foraging rodent. And so, I did.

That is the mark of the collector's descent into fixation: the fusion of tactile pleasure with cerebral curiosity. I adored the wooden ones the most. They always seemed warm, as though having been passed on from their previous owners only moments before. The ivory ones were cold and lifeless, but they certainly showed me the lucrative aspects of my work. For one day I discovered an intricate example in a tray of broken pottery. It was of an octopus hiding in a hole. This work was doubly intriguing as it was inscribed with what I later learned was a haiku: *Takotsubo ya / Hakanaki yume wo / Natsu no tsuki*. It was marked with the signature of two great carvers, Mitsuhiro and Masatsugu, who had both worked on the piece. I had discovered this item only a few months after my first one. I swiftly pocketed it and took it back to my stash, now numbering over a dozen other specimens. I took it to a dealer, one who would not ask questions; he offered me ten pounds. Ten pounds! Of course I took it. In the 1950s, to a child, ten pounds was more money than I'd known my entire life. No doubt the dealer sold it on for five times that, and I still regret parting with it. But it inaugurated my passage into the darker criminality of exchange.

So I became fascinated with these Japanese trinkets. Though still a criminal I stole for the love of the object. Something in them captivated me and beckoned me into imaginary realms where their previous owners laughed and fought beneath empty blue skies. It was not simply their Orientalism—I was used to the many races of London's ghettoes—I did not fetishise the foreign. It was their obvious functionality mixed with their comical beauty that captivated me. They seemed to speak of genuine histories.

It seemed I was also a collector, then.

My father had died of tuberculosis in his mid-thirties, shortly after I was born. He had been a miner before the war, somewhere in Wales my mother said. They met when he was on leave, in the midlands, and they had settled in London shortly before his death. Mother was a strict woman, although I believe she had not always been so. After the death of my father she was stricken with fear that I should become a 'bad boy' without the stern supervision of a male parent. So she assumed both roles; the nurturing one gradually becoming effaced by the authoritarian.

You can imagine her reaction upon finding some of my treasures, and a fair amount of money from the sales of those I thought were valuable. I had no opportunity to explain. What, indeed, could I have said? I was a thief—and my damnation was certain. Salvation, mother raged, was to be found in the riding crop that hung on the pantry door. With each beat of the crop—and there were many—the sin in me was *not* driven out. Rather, it blossomed. Evil rose like a blooming of fetid yeasts breaking the skin of bruised fruits. Mother unearthed in me that day all the hate, perversity and crime a soul could disgorge and from then on I was lost to whatever god might have once been able to save me.

So I continued to thieve, in fact I increased my deviousness and learnt more artful ways to deceive and lie. I prayed mostly on the vanities and secrets of those I courted. Soon I had a network of those indebted to me in various ways, and a willing chain of fences and collectors eager to acquire the trophies of my crimes.

So, Mr Umbroldi was marked down as another victim of my cunning, albeit a prestigious one. His home was not what I had expected though, located in the suburbs and suggesting little in the way of privilege. Most of these people are of fairly noble birth and live in crumbling heaps befitting such station. Umbroldi's home, though relatively large, was by no means stately, or indeed of any great age. It had most likely been chosen for its functionality. There were perhaps six or seven bedrooms, and a sizeable extension had been added to the place recently, as could be seen from the short walk up the road, a cul-de-sac, in which his was the last residence.

He answered the door himself, another great advantage I thought: there were no servants. If he lived alone it would be fairly simple to almost clear the place with some thoughtful planning. I had discovered that he had fled his native Italy with the rise of the fascists and so must be in his late eighties by now. Indeed, the man I had imagined was the one that greeted me. He would have been tall and well built, in his youth. Now though he leant heavily on a cane and stooped low. He wore a brown suit, including waistcoat, with a gold watch chain peeping from his pocket. He was, despite what I had heard, relatively genial.

He invited me in, and we talked in his dining room as he served dark tea with lemon. In the couple of downstairs rooms I had seen there was little of noticeable value. It appeared to be the home of an elderly bachelor that had made a comfortable living and was enjoying a secluded retirement. I maintained the deception over tea, asking questions about his life and his collection, explaining that my paper was interested in profiling local people that may have been neglected by the usual stories of minor political misdemeanour and charity fun runs. He was very forthcoming with biographical details of his early years, his move to Britain and his interest in antiquities. Whilst this background discussion was a necessary part of my disguise I was keen to get to see the collection as soon as I could. He detected my eagerness and offered to show me to the display rooms.

We climbed the stairs, he with surprising agility, to another realm. He must have made his living space entirely on the ground floor for upstairs was decorated as an opulent boudoir; at every window hung thick velvet curtains, tied with silk cords. The walls were a deep maroon, and the mahogany display cases that lined every wall seemed to melt into them. It was not a gloomy space, as you know by now. Instead the surroundings were designed to retreat from the objects they framed. This succeeded very well, as each case was lit with rows of gentle bulbs that picked out each piece delicately.

We passed through each room in silence. I searched the cabinets, revelling in the quality of each collection, and privately estimating the value of each. He watched me closely and I attempted not to give away my own knowledge; I was, after all, meant to be a local hack. I asked questions calculated to show my ignorance. He answered them patiently.

In the third room, which had been knocked into the fourth to make a long gallery I found the Oriental collection. Fine prints hung on available spaces between cabinets and at the end of the room three full suits of samurai armour were displayed beside an entire wall given over to the helmets and face-masks I had come here to inspect. I calmly proceeded towards them, again feigning ignorance. But just as I entered the furthest space of this double room I saw a large, lighter coloured, wooden case, bolted to the wall. Within there was the largest collection of inro, netsuke and ojime I have ever seen. And I have seen many.

Scanning the case I saw familiar examples from the great carvers and a number of works that would have been a real pleasure to have handled and discussed with him. I was conscious though not to give the game away. But I had not expected to encounter that same octopus piece that had been so magically unearthed, and rashly sold, in my youth. There it was, on the middle shelf, along with a collection of common themes, such as the fisherman, ratcatcher and a selection of ivory erotica. I gasped, astonished to discover it here. Certainly, to any observer, I had betrayed myself as rather more than a journalist after an interesting character story.

"Yes, it is rather beautiful isn't it," Mr Umbroldi said over my shoulder, startling me further. "'*Takotsubo ya / Hakanaki yume wo / Natsu no tsuki*' or '*In an octopus trap / Dreaming useless dreams / The summer moon!*' "

I had never known what the words on the octopus netsuke had meant, although I had learnt the text by heart, as though the sense of it might be revealed by subconscious processes. I must be grateful to Umbroldi for that translation, at least; and for the joy of seeing the thing again.

I tried to regain my previous control.

"I was rather surprised by the explicit pieces here," I said, already realising how feeble an explanation this was.

"I did not think journalism a profession that tolerated much prudishness," Umbroldi said, leading me back out into the hallway and towards the extended area of the house. "I had another here, quite some time ago now, a Mr Joseph Tress. He was interested in the Japanese artefacts too. I must confess I found him rather vulgar. Of course, those of us who collect—obsessively you might say—are prone to be possessive and covetous of other's collections. But with him it was almost hateful. He certainly had some tales to tell though, and showed me many of my own failings. It was a joy to listen to him."

He chuckled and I felt, for the first time during our meeting, that I no longer had the upper hand.

"I have seen many phases to my collecting over the years. Indeed the different parts of my collection mark all the different people I have been," he continued. "Initially I was fascinated by the *studioli* and cabinets of curiosity: those gathered by Vincent, Cospi, the Corrteris, Besler, Settala, the mighty Rudolf and others. Then, I had very specific interests, or more precisely periods of interest; antique books, wooden toys, Oriental art, automata, icons, Meissen porcelains, the list is long. But I returned, in a fashion to my original passion, or close to it.

I had amassed many fossils, coral sculptures, stuffed animals, anatomical deformities and other natural exhibits. And what is it that binds all of these together my good fellow: existence. These things were all trophies of past lives, in one form of another. As I reassembled the collection, plundering my previously carefully constructed cabinets and display cases, I found a new direction to my work: the artistry of death. The more I looked through what had been amassed under the guise of other phases of the collection, the more of the work I found concerned with death; an illustrated first edition of *Ars Moriendi*, the crossed bones of St Nicholas, some fine specimens of carved Whitby jet, including a ring with a lock of Sir Richard Fairbrace's hair. And what was to be the finest part of this new curation of my existing artefacts? It was my own history."

We had come to a doorway, and I stood there listening to him as though he were some venerable grandmaster instructing an initiate. In so many ways this was the truth.

"I come from an ancient Italian family," he told me. "My move to Britain was made many years ago in the tumult of the century as my country struggled to etch its mark in history; a tiresome arrogance. I brought with me a case containing family relics: the index finger of every male heir in twelve generations. Each had been carefully removed, prepared to bone and etched with the name and the date of each death. I had kept this heirloom separate to my collection, thinking it too personal. With the realisation of the new direction the collection had taken it seemed the perfect centrepiece.

But over the years it became clear how little even these bones represented, mere marks of life: bland souvenirs. I wanted more. Something more in the spirit of the great marvels of de Vaucanson and Théroude. I wanted beautiful artefacts that could give us back all the lost moments; things that could recall every detail of existence. I wanted true 'phenomenon machines' not the dull comforts of historical anecdote."

It is here that he was overcome with fanaticism. His eyes flared with a passion far beyond the ordinary collector's. These 'phenomenon machines', as he called them repeatedly, would furnish us with an intimate, and potentially infinite, record of life. He joked that one could spend an entire lifetime listening to one of them and never exhaust its supply of stories, hinting that he had already begun work on such marvels. He did not seem like an engineer or designer and so I was sceptical of such promises, but intrigued. Still desperate to cover my carelessness with the netsuke I enquired whether I might be able to see one of these prototypes. Thus I sprung the trap.

Leading me through the door and along another hallway, to the newer part of the house, he revealed a room in partial disarray with cases in various stages of display preparation. By the window on the far side of the room—where no doubt you now stand—there was a tall cupboard of dark black wood. It was not antique, I guessed, but its proportions (tall, thin and shallow) made it fitting for the task that was to be revealed to me.

With not a little theatricality he opened the case and there was arrayed—each on a thin black cushion—rows of human skulls. There were probably thirty in total, each bearing a trace of gold upon their forehead:

a name, and a date. He took one out and offered it to me. I took it—as no doubt you have done—appalled and enthralled by the impropriety of this act; ridiculous, given *my* motives for being in his home. And then the thing began to unravel its past, its words arising around and within me at once. He left me there as it poured out its tale. I may have listened to it for hours, I do not recall. I merely remember the marvel, and terror, of standing there like some naive Hamlet, skull in hand, awaiting his return.

And return he did, with the air of a distant relative bearing sad tidings.

"Isn't it the saddest thing that all of life, which can only ever be our experience, is lost at the moment of death?" he said, his worn face folded around the rapture of his eyes. "Every beautiful landscape, every heartbreaking moment and every instant of elation dissolves into time. For me it is not enough to imagine what Neanderthal man thought as he witnessed lightning for the first time. I want a record of this world, a whispering testimony of life and all of its journeys. I believe it is what God created man for: a listening device that he might understand the vastness of his own creation. Time will only be completed—it is an ancient belief, I'm sure you know—when all of the distant elements of that gargantuan mechanism are reunited with that great universal archivist. I do not want that. So little by little I am stealing that back from him. And you, my little shard of godliness, will be another eternal jewel in my store of truth."

And so, my mortal glory faded.

Thus you find yourself here too, with my skull cradled to your ear. Perhaps you thought it an ingenious device, with a hidden reel of tape, or some other broadcast trickery. No, I speak inside your mind: your audience enacts me.

I do not know what has brought you here—useless dreams of summer moons? Maybe you are, as I was once, a trickster and a fool. You may be simply, and more unfortunately, an interested collector, a historian, an academic. I believe all the endings are the same. For now you too, having patiently followed this confession of mine, will find yourself subject to that cruel fate delivered by this strange collector of curiosities.

Hark, I hear him approach.'

I have no aversion to hospitals. They have become places to which I have grown accustomed, having been present at the deaths of all of the members of a large and insular family of which I am now the only remaining one. The sweet bleach that washes the floors carries with it the delicate scent of final moments and the air is filled with whispered words of forgiveness and embittered memories. I have even absorbed the sounds of a busy ward into my night consciousness, so much so that I find it difficult to sleep at home—it lacks the gentle pacing of nurses outside a sickroom and the metrical chiming of ventilation units, heart monitors and other clinical paraphernalia which have become a dark symphony that beckons me to sleep.

This may explain why I was sleeping whilst my father died. Well, that is not strictly true. I had not awoken until the very end, despite almost two weeks of vigil by his bedside. I had not been awake during his confessional, and there was much to confess. Nor, apparently, was I able to be woken when he became delirious and hallucinatory. I was told later, by the doctor, that he had called my name, and that of my mother (but perhaps all doctors say that to grieving relatives), before screaming at the approach of two gentleman that he had seen waiting by the door. The doctor assured me that this was quite usual in cases of the disease that my father had; diseases that force one to linger as every credible faculty of reason and perception is gradually eroded and the mind slides into some memory of pre-rational fear and isolation where every movement, every flicker of light, each distant sound, threatens and excites with equal measure. So, without waking me, the assembled nurses and the doctor had left, no doubt to acquire sedatives, clean the bedpans or to attend to other patients at the threshold. So I was alone with father as he too clawed his way from this world.

It was not his yelling that awoke me; I had become quite used to that. I recall awaking with a sense of excitement, of expectation and wonder. Of what this urgent awe concerned I had no idea. My father was sat upright in the bed—a pose he had been unable to sustain, unaided, for a number of weeks—and with a fevered agitation was tearing at his left forearm, scratching and gouging with such ferocity that the sheets were already soaked with blood. As I rose to restrain him he began beating himself all over screaming: 'keep 'em under, keep 'em under'. I noticed that there seemed to be ripples of strange movement across his skin, like a lake where fish rise to its surface. Within these ripples something erupted—a little like a boil I would say—rapidly, and in many places at once, but as each of the pustules arose it blackened and became an oily swelling which he struck with his fists. I was quite frozen, unable to move at all, watching my father's body become a corpulent mass of bubbling black boils which rose and receded with each of his frenzied strikes. I watched my father beat himself to death, and a saner man—one who has not been introduced to the mystery of which I shall tell you all too soon—would have concluded that these dark tumours were actually bruises from his own hands. But I saw those things which writhed beneath his skin and heard his final words, which were addressed to me, with wild, imploring eyes.

'Keep 'em under!' he pleaded, and then died.

There was some confusion, as one might expect, when the staff found my father's battered and broken corpse, which they had left only minutes before without any such scarring, and me standing beside it with an expression that must have revealed both shock and fascination.

However the doctor assured me that he had seen a similar event before and whilst the medical incidence of it was rare—and as yet unexplained—he had coined a term to describe it and was confident that research on its occurrence would soon take place. He called it, with some hesitancy—even embarrassment: 'Immediate Metastatic Outbreak'.

I had no interest in his medical distinctions: that crazed obsession with a nomenclature of death. I had observed my father pass away in the most gruesome and bizarre agony and every part of my body seemed taut with anger and frustration at the pathetic half-measures of this feeble society. It seemed to me then that, for all of our media-world of high technology and fast this-and-that, we had not advanced one step in our ability to deal with the dead. In fact, despite all of our wretched taxonomy of illness we had retreated from the real issues: the ritual, the significance of a human death. No doubt my mind was as volatile as my body was exhausted and these two conflicting urges had made me unusually aggressive.

It was then that he told me of my father calling my name and my mother's, and of the two gentlemen he claimed were standing by the door. I must have become annoyed at this devious consolation, at his underhand attempt to soothe a pain that cannot be assuaged. I heard his voice drifting into the distance and I nodded some kind of response here and there as he may have explained his theories on 'Immediate Metastatic Outbreak', or perhaps he was discussing the passing of his own father, mother, brother or sister. I do not know. His voice had become a whirring background to my thoughts which tumbled in violent contemplation of destroying the entire structure of the hospital. It seemed to me that it would be as simple as tearing up a postcard; as though with one gigantic hand I might rip the building from the ground and crumple it into old wastepaper.

I came to my senses then, catching the last words of the doctor as he led me to the door, '…and it is imperative that you get some rest. You'll see things clearer then. You have my sympathies.'

I turned to him with what must have been a terrible expression, given his own terrified face.

'I have no need of your sympathies,' I spat. 'Your little toy hospital is nothing but a charade. I should have dragged him into the forest to be devoured by wolves rather than probed by your needles and gadgets.'

I really wanted to hurt him at that moment. A euphoric wave of antagonism rose in me and I leaned toward him threateningly. I wanted to smash the fool into his filing cabinet, spill his blood among the papers and the prescriptions. Instead I settled for kicking over the bin by the door and a sneer of contempt as I slammed the door. It may not seem much but my entire life had, up until that point, been a hazy repetition of what had been asked of me, by parents and teachers, bosses and lovers. Everything had passed away in a dull mist of acceptance and drudgery, but now—in that very moment—walking away from the scene of my father's death, I felt an urgent, insistent, call to live. But at that time I had no idea at all, not even the vaguest inkling, what *living* really meant.

∞

In the days that followed I continued my routine. I attended work and made the necessary calls that would ensure my father was buried, although I did not go to the funeral. I paid the bill when it arrived, but I was expecting something else. It may have been the knowledge that all those I had known, and in my way had loved, were gone and therefore I was next.

No it was not that. I have always had a heightened sense of mortality. That was not what burdened me now.

I now know what I was expecting: a call. Indeed I lingered often by the door or the telephone. I even began to peer from the curtains into the street below watching the passers-by for any that might be familiar, for any that might be my awaited visitor. But they were all strangers, although there was something familiar in each one that I was unable to identify. Perhaps merely their difference had become apparent.

One Sunday morning I seemed to jolt from some kind of reverie and found myself standing by the front door. I must have been there hours, dressed in my suit and tie. I opened the door then and was unsurprised—a reaction that surprised me—to see two gentlemen advancing up the path towards my house.

One was tall and lean, with a pronounced limp in his right leg. His face seemed stretched tightly across the ridges of his high cheekbones and his eyes seemed dull and tired. The second was in many ways his opposite, being of almost comically diminutive stature and quite portly. His face was full and beads of sweat glistened across his balding forehead. His eyes were small and deep yet they too seemed weary and dead. Something about them gave me the impression that they were related, their mannerisms seemed somehow complementary. They were dressed in suits almost identical to mine and carried with them wide black suitcases bearing golden initialling which read, respectively: A.F. and Dr C. I was certainly intrigued as they silently entered the hallway and proceeded through to the lounge, where the taller man took a seat on an uncomfortable stool by the window. The other took his bag, and placed it with his own beside the stool, before standing behind him in a pose which gave me the impression that he was some minder or bodyguard for the taller man.

'I am Aloysius Fremm and this is my associate Dr Craput,' the tall man said, unbuttoning his jacket and positioning himself as comfortably as the stool would allow. 'I gather that you have been expecting us.'

'Well, I have been expecting somebody,' I said. 'Not necessarily yourselves.'

'We are here in connection with the incident you were fortunate enough to witness at the hospital,' Fremm said. 'Dr Craput and I would like to extend to you every opportunity that was offered to your debauched father.'

I had been about to take a seat opposite them in my favourite reading chair. But this insult seemed to relight that anger that had smouldered since my father's death.

'Who are you people?' I started, advancing across the room. I half expected Craput to advance upon me in return but instead he stared blankly at the wall beyond me with an idiotic smirk on his fat face. 'I'll not have you talk of my father like that. Whatever his ways may have been he still deserves respect.'

'You misunderstand me, doesn't he Dr Craput,' Fremm said, turning slightly to his companion, who nodded his head in a fashion that reminded me of those dogs that sit in the back windows of cars. 'I have nothing but respect for your father. It was entirely due to his indulgence that he was offered the gift that you witnessed.'

'Are you saying that this is some kind of judgement?' I demanded. 'Some moral code he breached made him deserve that death?'

'Oh no, I hope we haven't given you that impression. We wouldn't want to give that impression would we Dr Craput?' Fremm began, looking up again at the curious doctor, whose lips curved into a senseless grin. 'I mean to say that all beings, whether at one end of your *moral code* or the other, are capable of engaging with our—shall we say—organisation. It is a case of extremes, where the most virtuous and the most dissolute are joined in revelation concerning the undercurrent of this space we all inhabit. I meant in no way to suggest that there would be any question of judicial structure, even of a *celestial nature*. Let us say instead that the more intensely one lives the more likely one is to experience *the truth*.'

I could not help focusing on the peculiar manner in which he pronounced *moral code*, *celestial nature* and *the truth*. He seemed contemptuous and celebratory, exultant and derisory. The words were layered into meanings that enticed me to demand an explanation. I was made to feel both intrigued and repulsed, a situation that Fremm seemed entirely content with—a situation he had, no doubt, come to expect.

'I'm somewhat lost at the moment,' I confessed. 'Your arrival seems so intrusive, so vulgar and improper, but…'

Fremm nodded knowingly and implored me to continue with a wave of his bony hand.

'But I also sense that I have been expecting you,' I said, with satisfied nods from both of my guests. 'And I also sense that you have been waiting for the opportunity to visit.'

'Oh, yes, you understand our position entirely,' Fremm said, evidently very satisfied with my response. 'We represent a certain party that would be most pleased to have you as one of its members.'

Recalling my earlier frustrations at the hospital and the growing social dissatisfaction that had played on my mind recently I must have misunderstood him. He seemed to imply some kind of organisation: a political party, some fanatical religious group perhaps. I was in no mood for any surreptitious attempt to enrol me in some crackpot faction of social misfits.

'Look, I may seem a little agitated at the moment,' I said. 'But kicking a bin over at the hospital hardly makes me a revolutionary.'

'Quite so, quite so, social revolution is the first mistake. Your revolt is of an entirely different order,' Fremm said. 'We are here, as representatives of certain academies that specialise in educational projects. We only offer you the time to learn, a window of opportunity—so to speak.'

'And what might this teaching consist of?' I asked, humouring them a little.

'It would illuminate the elements within you that are the broken residues of a being that has torn itself asunder to relieve the burden of an insane and lonely desperation. It has, quite literally, divided itself into separate consciousnesses for the sake of its own pleasure.' Fremm said, without the least suggestion of a joke. 'You are a constituent component of that entity and we offer you the chance to learn those ways most suited to its, and your, continued entertainment.'

I looked at them both in amazement, but could see from their blank stares that these words were meant most seriously.

'You are suggesting that I might be reunited with some onanist deity, that has somehow separated me from it merely to enjoy my struggle to return,' I said, confident now that these freaks were recruiting for some outlandish cult.

'Again you are mistaken,' Fremm said, with his usual patience. 'But, as I say, we are here to offer you insight, so allow me to oblige.' He leaned across to the wall of my sparse lounge and gently peeled away the wallpaper, or at least that's what I thought he was doing. It seemed that he had taken a whole section of the wall away. I could see the plaster and brickwork clinging to part of the wall, which he now draped over his arm like some piece of cloth. I could see a dark undulating mass which writhed delicately beyond the area that Fremm had peeled away. Dr Craput gazed at it longingly, even lovingly, and I will admit that I was immediately captivated by the sense of witnessing a powerful presence to which I was, in some way, joined. I sensed a familiarity, as though greeting a friend one has not seen in years, but also there arose a desire to flee and leave that repugnant being alone. But there was nowhere to flee to. Fremm had shown me the pulse that ripples beneath everything and I understood how much I needed to learn. For if I refused their offer, every moment in this world would be a maddening attempt to conceal, or disbelieve, the awful reality that softly moves in all things. So with the choice between two paths of lunacy I accepted the one that might most reward me sensuously: the decadent course, complicit in my own destruction.

∞

In the weeks they stayed with me Aloysius Fremm and Dr Craput showed me things. Rather than 'keep 'em under' as my father had urged me to it was revealed how best to 'let 'em out'. Using the instruments they had brought with them and from the charts written in extraordinary books—whose pages opened inwards in a manner that only now I begin to fathom—these guests unlocked the secrets of my bones and skin. They made my body a parchment for the writing of ineffable verses, my blood the ink of idiotic scriptures and my voice the host of alien choirs, whose exultant wails echoed inside me towards a void I had not dreamed could exist in any being.

I was tutored in the cruellest elements of existence, the labyrinthine threads of life were unravelled in me and I was rethreaded so that my maniac limbs might dance to prehistoric melodies. My revolt was indeed of a different order! I know that now and so much more. I cannot tell you how much more I know, after the visit of my comrades.

Aloysius Fremm demonstrated how to lack completely and Dr Craput made my mind a cage for philosophies and theologies so foreign to the human brain that their thoughts ached and strained inside me with infernal desire to escape my form. I struggled and groaned, screamed and laughed, under the teaching of my associates. They sought to correct my mistakes, and they have done an excellent job. I had assumed that this world is governed by an entity, or some such divinity, with the knowledge and concern to distinguish between good and evil. It is now clear to me that such a moral quest, our foolish ethical preoccupation, has been humanity's greatest folly. For the teachings of Aloysius Fremm and Dr Craput have shown me that the world is sui generis, innocent, ignorant and mad and we—its lost and lonely toys—must perform those macabre waltzes that so fascinate and divert its shattered, deviant intelligence.

There can be no doubt: you will be the tyrant!

You rose to the top, congealed scum in the frothy tumult of bureaus and institutions. Whilst petty battles—mostly laughable ethical irrelevancies—laid waste your contemporaries, you endured. Who could doubt your constancy? Your mind was nurtured in those empty halls of administration until you could burst out, revealing that womb to be a tomb, gestating death—your double.

Those years of dull toil have given you a crookedness you try to correct, but overcompensating you appear pompous and strange. Your impatience has become a feral desperation that sits uneasily in polite company. Your humour has degenerated into an edgy pre-emptive laugh that echoes with the silence of space. It has a trace of sad childishness that your superiors always found endearing, for a while. But what will it matter—your bland attire and the nothingness of your hair and face—everyone shall adhere to your codes. There will be no 'polite company' left. There will be only 'The Truth'. There will be no hierarchy on your dusty plateau of obligation, where you will make a mountain of your image.

There is no great plan, beyond the achievement of such ground. That is the fundamental misunderstanding of every subversive; that mere error and chance, elsewhere called opportunity, are the only things that will raise you up. But with calculation you can minimise the accident and load the dice.

Let us calculate the madness!

Your sister, or brother, adored you. That kept you fettered to the world for a while. But their loving gaze also bred in you the lust for power and possession, and taught you the mean politics of guilt and retribution, at which you are adept. They died in the spring, just as all the blossoms appeared. The April winds blew the petals like blood-flushed snow as you marched to the cemetery to return their body to the emptiness you glimpsed in all things. You had cried then, on approaching the coffin, seeing their pale hands around the pink hyacinths your mother had requested. You wanted to see their eyes, to prove they were not sleeping—but were not allowed. Since then you imagine those eyes in every nightmare; great hollows of dark decay.

The last shackles are broken now. Your father and mother dead, within months of each other; they knew how to love—something you did not consider a failing, then. And as you saw the last of your lineage eased into the cold ground you felt the freeze of prehistoric winters fill the vacuum of your heart. Devious inner mechanisms transfused your blood for oil and you toiled like a piston pounding in an abandoned factory—all for the 'great work' that you would impose upon the weak, until they finally believed they had chosen it. So there you remain, in a cell of emptiness, weaving history from yarn of hair and hatred, on a loom of bones that chatters against the cold stone floor in the cellar of your impenetrable citadel. The blood runs in rivers to the sewers. The blood runs in rivers, but the cloth is fine—so fine you can barely see the thread. It will make a terrible robe, of bile and bitterness—worshipped by your entourage of sycophants.

But who shall crown you? There are no more crowns, we are all equal—as you so obsessively inculcate. You shall crown yourself in a private ceremony, somewhere deep within you.

Let us divine your future!

The 'great work' must, in the early stages, appear honourable—for a greater good. It must appeal to idealists and pragmatists alike. It should be clothed in the golden garments of integrity, community and progress. As the time passes it will be revealed for the rotten corruption, vanity and nepotism it is. Indeed it *must* be revealed to provide the opportunity to unmask the dissenters. Without such crafted obsession the rebels will skulk and hide within the apparatus of bureaucracy, apparently content with their labour. They are to be exposed by others, like themselves, whose yearning for power is only a baser version of your own. They will not stay silent—creeping the corridors in darkness until the opportunity to strike presents itself. Instead they will denounce, in public and in private, their colleagues and friends—all for your approval.

Your intellect reaches no further than opposition—this is not a disadvantage. All values are to be inverted, not overturned. Cowardice must triumph over courage and idiocy over wisdom. Whilst everywhere you sow discord you must proclaim advancement and industry, visiting the workers who are weary with smiles. You must kiss the children that dare not cry. Your vision must seem to be justice, in reality it is a binary perversion fed by vengeance.

Your omnipresent image must penetrate every thought, not simply the posters, the adverts, the billboards. Your words should resound across every newspaper, book, and broadcast—they should replace communication itself. In time every gesture will become your own. People will hold their cigarettes as you do, and laugh with your nervous suspicion. Their favourite drink will be yours: Sauternes and soda water, or something similarly vulgar. Their step will be in time with yours and will, over glacial years, assume your gait and stride. Your penchant for yellow roses, not red, will be noted in the florists and in the homes of the aspirant classes—and gradually all colours will fade from the plants, even in the provinces, giving the land a sickly pallor. Nothing will taste right unless it is seasoned with that Szegedi paprika you adore: all food will gradually become red—ironic, if you consider the flowers. There will even be talk that people aspire to affect that soft animal whine you make at climax; you know the one, when you have the gutter boys and girls gathered around to watch, before you pop their eyes into darkness with a crack of your thumbs—everyone knows it, none dare speak!

Those who are not complicit in your reforms; the open-minded, the diligent, the confused—have them disposed of, it is the only way. Let rumours of their departure—by whatever means—leak out to your confidants, it will find its way into general knowledge, much improved by the telling.

If you are female then indulge your fellow women as though they are sisters, although they are not. If you are male then taunt your fellow men as though they are enemies, although they are not. Either way you will find a willing harem. Give your inner circle barely distinguishable responsibilities; they will fight like dogs for your blessing. Let shame do its corrosive work. Foment envy and distrust, reward success with ostentatious gifts and hollow promotion, punish failure brutally. Those close to you must fear for their family and friends, if such remain.

There must be a rigorous code of conduct: traditionalist control masked as innovative development. You must cultivate a fanatic zeal for decency, whilst everywhere morality is beset by the cancer of mistrust. It matters little what the penalties are: flogging, torture, imprisonment, banishment, the key is to keep the perpetrators alive. The real effect on your subjects happens within; a gradual withering of selfhood into a kernel of embittered impotence. That is the true mark of a great tyrant; not heads upon poles or broken bodies gibbeted against the skyline across an empire of immortal sun. Instead, their gradual descent into abject servitude should be your lofty aspiration. Every deed and utterance you make should be crafted to effect the erasure of all autonomy, whilst appearing to grant freedom and empowerment. Any censorious condemnation should be equally—and randomly—as likely to result in magnanimous absolution. It is thus that you nurture fear and doubt: your judiciary a synonym for duplicity and your police only retributive thugs.

This is not a bleak vision: the hordes of faceless imperators, such as yourself, queuing to be born—each with a seed of terror and subjugation in their hearts. Some might even think it a consolation: those lines of tyrants, like mendicants on a street of riches. The masses will survive you, and your despotic brethren—it is only the misery that endures.

But, picture your soul: a solid black box whose surfaces all face inwards, an impossible facade of yourself where everything outside is absorbed into the depths and becomes you.

You, who are most feared; deserving only bloody death. You, who are most frightened; deserving only tender love.

Yes, you. You are the tyrant.

You. Unbounded, endless you.

First Editions: An Afterword

Peter Holman

I

It was a shame I was out of the office when Paul Lythgoe rang, for I'd not spoken with him for several months. As he'd called at three in the morning though, he couldn't have been very surprised to have missed me. 'I'm making good progress,' Paul said, 'but there's something I need to talk to you about.' A day or so later I got a postcard from the Imperial War Museum, a photograph of Joseph Goebbels officiating at a book burning.

'Dear Agent Orange,' Paul began, his handwriting even more hieroglyphic than it used to be:

> I've done 4 chaps of conspiracy but it isn't working out. Anyway, I think all conspiracy theories are made up by a little man in a room somewhere. I've got something more interesting on the go. Lunch?

Wonderful. The advance I'd screwed out of Simon and Schuster (or 'Shuman and Shyster', as Paul insisted on calling them, among other names) was not substantial, but my client had signed the contract, agreed the manuscript delivery date and, most importantly, taken the money. I couldn't afford to fall out with anyone; the agency might have been doing reasonably well, but it doesn't take long for word to get round. Nevertheless, I was curious about Paul's plans. He'd always been reliable up to now; his little scissors-and-paste book on the Hawker Hurricane, rushed out for the Battle of Britain 60th anniversary had done rather well. He had his manic moments, but most of us have them occasionally. I wasn't overly concerned.

II

Paul lived out at the end of the Northern Line. The train clanked and swayed its way under London, before emerging into the light and clanking and swaying its way across the dismal hinterlands towards Colindale, its route lined with oppressively elaborate graffiti and 'To Let' signs. Looking over a book proposal, I paid little attention to my fellow passengers, but two stops before I was due to get off, someone bustled into the carriage and sat down opposite me. He was a squat little man in his mid fifties, dressed in a Chairman Mao-style grey tunic, a camouflage forage cap and a pair of blue nylon 'slacks', flared and obviously too short for him. His dark glasses were so opaque that I wondered for a moment if he was blind. He crossed one leg over the other, revealing remarkable yellow vinyl boots with Cuban heels. 'Don't suppose you know, do you, Chief?' he said, perhaps to me, perhaps to someone only he could hear. I stared at my papers. 'You look the sort of chap who would know,' he continued. 'Literary gent like you.' When I didn't reply, he began to rummage in a black plastic carrier bag. I moved away and stood by the doors, ready to make a quick exit. Paul had promised to meet me, but there was no sign of him on the shabby station concourse. Drizzle fell on a ragged bank of willow-herb which partially screened the sodden remains of a fly-tipped sofa. A streetlight flickered. The only other person to alight was the man in the yellow shoes, but thankfully he seemed lost in his private and un-navigable neurosis and scuttled away, rustling his black bag.

Having finished the book proposal on the train, I had nothing to read, and pacing up and down outside the station for half an hour, I was tempted to give up and catch the train back into town. I couldn't get a phone signal and was about to abandon my visit when Paul came at last into view, waving to me from an old fashioned black bicycle. A tall, angular figure in his early forties, he wore a brown tweed suit, a crumpled shirt of plum corduroy, and a brown fedora, hardly the traditional uniform of the London cyclist. 'There you are,' he said. 'Looks like I timed that pretty well. Brought you some lunch.' He thrust a paper bag into my hand. Inside was half a sausage roll. 'We got a bit peckish. Still, should tide you over. Good to see you. Follow me.'

He began to pedal away up the hill into a maze of red-brick terraces.

I must have walked the best part of a mile, feeling like one of the chasing pack in a long distance race, before he dismounted outside a featureless house. 'Home is the sailor, home from the sea,' he sang, somehow lugging his boneshaker into the hall and disappearing into a tiny galley kitchen. It was clear that Paul's life had undergone a marked change since his divorce. Unopened letters, most of them in ominously official envelopes, congregated at the bottom of the stairs like hopeless petitioners outside a Victorian prison, while the hall was crammed with shelves improvised from bricks and planks; the steep staircase had four or five volumes on each bare step. I opened a door into the front room to find that it contained two folding picnic chairs, a single-bar electric fire and hundreds of paperbacks arranged according to a classificatory system I couldn't appreciate. Books and photograph albums were stacked higgledy-piggledy in mounds on the floor, along with orange cardboard wallets covered in scribbles. *Archaic Artificial Suns* it said on one of them. Another bore the word BUTCHER in thick black felt tip. A light-bulb hung from a plaited skein of flex in the centre of the ceiling. The net curtains were grey, the window sill covered in dead bluebottles.

I made myself uncomfortable on one of the chairs and was scanning the shelves when Paul returned with a packet of smoky bacon crisps, a bottle of Bell's and a chipped tooth-mug. He poured me several fingers of scotch with all the solemnity of a priest administering the sacraments, and then sat down opposite, cradling the crisps in his nicotine-stained hands. He fumbled in his suit and brought out a tarnished silver cigarette case. 'I do love a bit of snout,' he said. 'I find the psychological benefits of nicotine inhalation far outweigh their physical consequences.' He couldn't settle, and was soon walking to and fro, the bottle in one hand and his cigarette in the other. 'Working notes,' he said, prodding the mound of files with his foot. 'They're like an exterior brain, those folders. Everything I've found out about him is in there.'

'About who?'

'The man who wrote *Emporium*,' Paul said. He looked round the room in conspiratorial fashion. 'I know more about him than anyone else alive, I think. It's like *The Quest for Corvo*.'

'What's *Emporium*?'

Paul burrowed into his archive and produced the torn remains of an auctioneer's catalogue. 'This may be the only copy in private hands,' he told me. 'It's from September 1985.' The catalogue began with a brief biographical sketch, which Paul read to me.

> Little is known of the quiet and retiring D. P. Watt. Born in 1931 in the Northamptonshire village of Chumble Marzal, he was educated privately and at Sidney Sussex, where his tutor was that redoubtable antiquarian, F. S. Grimsdyke. Following a short period of national service curtailed by serious illness, Watt studied archaeology though he did not complete his degree. He worked for several years as a wine merchant in south west England, during which time he published his first collection, *Damocles and Other Wonders* (Jonathan Cape, 1958. Signed Copies Lots 14-19). The same year he became briefly notorious for what the *Manchester Evening News* termed a 'tasteless and grotesque charade' involving a séance to contact the victims of the Munich air disaster. Following complaints from the families of the deceased, his pamphlet about the crash and its aftermath was withdrawn from sale (Lot 32).
>
> A legacy allowed Watt to become a professional writer in 1960, though he spent much of his time engaging in archaeological and topographical research and amassing materials for a history of puppetry which he worked on intermittently for some years though never completed. In 1964 he published a second collection of short stories, *They Dwell in Ystumtuen* (Cape. Signed Copies Lots 24-28), the title story of which appeared in the January edition of Michael Moorcock's *New Worlds* magazine, alongside fiction by J. G. Ballard, Langdon Jones and Cassandra Stewart (copy of this issue, Lot 45). In 1968, Watt moved to the East Midlands, where he was involved in the partial restoration of the Grace Dieu priory near Ashby-de-la-Zouch, work which inspired his novel, *High-Vaulted Heaven* (Cape 1970. Signed Copy Lot 60).
>
> Shortly after the publication of this work, Watt became an intimate of the occultist and self-styled 'King of the Witches' Alexander Sanders, apparently participating in a number of

rituals and magical experiments in northern England. In 1971 he was listed as one of the 'head consultants' on *We Put Our Magick On You*, an LP by the saxophonist and organist, Graham Bond. Watt helped to design the set for Bond's proposed British tour in 1972, although this never progressed beyond a few sketches because of Bond's financial and psychological instabilities, and the project was abandoned in the wake of his suicide in 1974 (for Bond-related memorabilia, see Lots 101-117).

Watt's interests were now largely in book collecting, *avant garde* European theatre, folklore, philosophy, puppetry and the occult. Following a mysterious accident in June 1975, he became increasingly reclusive. In 1979, a third volume of short stories, *Pieces for Puppets* appeared, again with Cape (Lot 63), and one story from the collection, 'Strategies', was read on Radio 4's *After Midnight* by Tom Baker. Although the collection was well received by aficionados of supernatural fiction, Watt published nothing else before his disappearance in October 1980. He was last seen late on the afternoon of 31st October, dancing along a breakwater at Cromer in the company of an unidentified man in dark glasses.

Although there has been a great deal of speculation in recent years that Watt was either murdered by the members of an occult society to which he belonged, or, less sensationally, that he was inspired to follow in the footsteps of errant M. P. John Stonehouse and fake his death to avoid near-crippling debts, the truth concerning his disappearance has yet to be told. The author's sole surviving relative, his sister, Magdalene, has been forced to sell her brother's effects in order to finance urgent medical treatment.

'I've never heard of him,' I said. 'Should I have?' I was beginning to feel I'd made a mistake in coming over to Hendon and an even bigger one crossing the threshold of Chateau Paul 'freely and of my own will'. There was a time, not that long ago, when Paul had been a refreshingly unpretentious and hard-working commercial writer: he'd ghosted a jockey's autobiography, knocked up a very readable book on maritime disasters and some splendidly ghoulish true crime stuff. His wife, Susan, taught history at a sixth form college. They had a daughter called Helen or Helena, or was it Jenny? I couldn't remember, but Paul had always seemed thoroughly, for want of a better word, *normal.* I began to wonder if it was simply the divorce that was affecting him. He certainly drank too much, and had lost weight since I'd last seen him. His sandy hair was flecked with silver, and his eyes were feverish; they flitted restlessly around the room and avoided contact with mine. Not that I was in any hurry to meet his gaze, and turned to the tattered paperbacks behind him: *The Morning of the Magicians, The Black Arts, The Spear of Destiny.* The complete works of Carlos Casteneda and Doris Stokes rubbed up against Northrop Frye's *Anatomy of Criticism.* Stacked alongside were bound volumes of *The Listener* and *Man, Myth, and Magic* from the 1960s, old Penguin Classics of Balzac and Gautier, and a leaning tower of audio cassettes with Paul's hieroglyphs on their spines proclaiming 'John Peel 28/10/86', 'R4 HPL Docu' or 'Dapp Intvs. 1-3'. As the room filled with the smoke from Paul's cigarette, it became increasingly claustrophobic without getting any warmer. Despite the December chill he made no attempt to switch on the fire.

'You can see why I've stalled on the conspiracy book, can't you? Watt's much more interesting. A biog of him that solves the mystery of ...'

'Of what happened to a minor writer of horror stories who nobody remembers,' I said harshly. 'Can't see that on the three-for-two table, somehow. Didn't he just fall in the sea?'

Paul gave me a superior look but didn't argue. He took a long drag on his cigarette and breathed out so much smoke that he might have signalled the election of a new pontiff. 'The book's in the bag,' he said, casually. 'Just got to write it up. But it's all here'—he tapped his head—'it's all in here.' He took another swig from the bottle and I put my whisky, untouched, to one side. 'Changed a lot, of course, as I've got into it, but that's the nature of these things. Never know what you'll get till you put your clay on the wheel. You just never know.' He stubbed out his cigarette and lit another. 'Can' tell you how good it is to see you, Chief,' he said, after a pause that might have done Pinter credit. 'Don't get many visitors apart from the doctor. Do you want that sausage roll, by the way?'

'I wouldn't mind some lunch,' I replied. 'And I wouldn't mind knowing what you're up to, either.'

III

Ten minutes or so later, I found myself safely ensconced in an altogether more congenial world, nursing a pint of excellent bitter and a cheese and onion cob. Snug beside the fire, I began to make allowances for Paul's behaviour. Even hacks were contractually obliged to have their eccentricities, while the squalor of the house was easily explained by his having the same priorities as Chaucer's Clerk – books before bread. Perhaps even his fascination with D. P. Watt had possibilities, but first things first.

'I may as well be blunt,' I began, aware I had another meeting that afternoon. 'Are we going to make the deadline?'

'Oh don't *worry*,' said Paul. 'Simon Schama'll get his book alright. It won't be a problem.'

'So am I going to have to renegotiate the submission date? If I am, just be honest with me.'

'I've told you, don't worry. I don't wish to seem unduly *Panglossian*, but all will be for the best.' He looked around cautiously, but apart from an old man sharing a bag of mini cheddars with his border terrier, we were the only people in the lounge. 'The project has moved on though, I don't mind telling you that. I really do want to do a book about Watt. I think I know what happened to him.'

'Does it fit with conspiracy theories? Let me guess: the Masons,' I said, imagining the conversation I'd soon be having with our commissioning editor.

'Oh, balls to conspiracy theories. Balls to the Elders of Zion and the lizards in the pyramids. Balls to the Holocaust deniers and the fake moon landing and the Man in the Iron Mask. I don't want to write some crappy little book that ends up in the three for a fiver pile. I've spent my life recycling other people's stuff. I'm sick of living on Grub Street. Either you're going to back me on this or I'm off.'

'It might be a bit easier if you had something you could show me. A chapter or two. Just an outline would help.' I didn't want to lose him; he might not have been J. K. Rowling, but he was productive and, until now at least, reliable. 'As it is . . .'

He clutched my arm. 'I have got something,' he whispered. 'A book no one, and I mean no one, knows about. Watt's last work: *An Emporium of Automata*. Dapertutto gave it to me. It's a sort of riddle, I think.'

'Who's Dapertutto?'

'He knew Watt; Watt wrote about him. Or a version of him. Now I meet with him. I saw him just before I met you this morning. He asks me some things and tells me other things. He's a doctor, a remarkable man. Remarkable. *He doesn't have a shadow*. We are incubating a monstrous egg,' he said, looking suspiciously at the man with the dog.

'Well, when it looks like hatching, you get in touch. I'm a busy man and I must be going.' I swallowed a last mouthful of beer and stood up. 'If you want my advice, finish the book you're supposed to be doing and then get started on this Watt character, if that's what you want to do. Just let me know where I stand and then I can do something about the publisher. That's all I ask.'

'If that's how you want to play it, Chief, you suit yourself. I'm going for a smoke.'

I left.

IV

Just before Christmas, Carrie from Simon & Schuster called me. There'd been what she called 'an incident' at the publisher's offices, when Paul had turned up with a couple of stout linen sacks containing his advance in 20p pieces. He had emptied these in the foyer and set fire to his contract, before getting into a contretemps with members of the security staff. He had been aided in this by a curiously dressed 'little man in dark glasses' who had 'egged him on' during the 'ugly scene' that followed, an imbroglio that had led to fire alarms going off, the police being called and Paul being taken away for questioning. His accomplice had apparently escaped in the confusion. 'We're not going to press charges,' said Carrie, 'but obviously, in view of what's happened . . .'

I tried phoning Paul but just got static and beeps. I emailed him but the message bounced. Finally I wrote explaining the situation: three weeks later my letter came back covered in coffee stains with 'Gone Away' scrawled on the envelope. That, I thought, was that. I had bigger fish to fry than Paul Lythgoe.

V

Six months went by. Then, one morning, my in-tray contained, in addition to the usual utility bills, take-away menus and optimistic but dismal synopses of first novels, a large padded envelope with a printed label. Inside was a package, swathed in bubble-wrap, stiff cardboard and old newspaper (*The Sun*'s Page Three girl was Samantha Fox). Must be from a book-dealer, I thought, cutting through the many layers that protected the precious contents. I couldn't remember ordering such a thing, but then, the internet often induces amnesia. The credit card statement has replaced the diary as something sensational to read on the train.

When I finally managed to hack my way in to my new treasure, I found a beautifully calligraphed card on which was written:

With the Compliments of Dr Dapertutto

I was right: it was a book, though it would be more accurate to say that it was something that had the appearance of a book without quite being one. It had an exquisite dust-jacket and carried with it that smell, somewhere between incense and stale cakes, always associated with antiquarian volumes. Yet it looked new; its jacket crisp and fresh, with no sign of shelf marks, spinal tears or rubbing. Out of it protruded a bookmark made from what seemed to be brown tweed, which ended in a plum-coloured velvet tassle. I turned the book over and over in my hands, breathing in the smell of it. As a material object, it was wholly delightful, from its elegantly-lettered spine to the handmade paper of its pages. *An Emporium of Automata*, it said. *D. P. Watt.* It couldn't be new, I told myself, not if Watt had died in 1980. Paul must have sent it to me in lieu of sample material for the biography, I decided, wishing he had included a note of his current whereabouts.

It was then I found that I couldn't open the book. It was tightly shut, not because its pages were stuck together or uncut, as I at first suspected, but because there were no pages. The whole thing was simply a solid undifferentiated block, out of which grew the tweed bookmark. I pulled at this cautiously, but it was stuck fast, as if the book had once been liquid and had somehow set round it like wax or metal.

There was nothing else in the package, and no sign of where it had come from. It was, I mused over my coffee, an odd volume, and my initial online research about it could offer little in the way of enlightenment. There was no reference to it in the British Library catalogue or the Library of Congress: Watt seemed *pictor ignotus* as far as America was concerned. All I could find about him was that copies of his first book changed hands for £70-80 and that no one knew his current whereabouts or even whether he was still alive. *Damocles and Other Wonders* apparently featured a story called 'Dr Dapertutto's Saturnalia' but I wasn't going to pay seventy quid to read it, and I didn't have time to order it from the BL, even assuming I could get a seat there. Besides, from what Paul had told me, I didn't think *Emporium* had ever been published. Maybe this was a dummy copy Watt had made for himself? I wondered if it had some hidden catch that would open and reveal a stash of secret papers or access to the pains and pleasures of the Cenobites, but half an hour of messing with it left me none the wiser. It made for an interesting curio, but it did leave me a little discomposed. Perhaps it was simply turning it over in my hands, but it felt warm somehow.

VI

From that day forward, I began to experience an uncomfortable sensation of being watched and followed. The occasional touch of paranoia is a vital element of one's defence against the all-invasive metropolis, but I could feel that mine was worsening, or indeed, becoming more justifiable, with each passing hour. I stopped travelling on the underground except at peak times and started to take ever more circuitous routes to the office or to my preferred watering holes. I was relieved that *Emporium* had not been delivered to my home address, but No. 225 hardly felt like a sanctuary. Friends remarked that I seemed anxious and preoccupied, several noting that I was behaving like someone in the throes of nicotine withdrawal. I was sure I saw a man observing the office with binoculars from the roof of a neighbouring building, but I couldn't begin to guess why anyone would wish to do such a thing. It was strange though, not least because spy was such a squat little fellow. I struggled to imagine him scrabbling up a fire escape.

He was obviously playing on my mind, because after I thought I'd seen him for the second time, he turned up in a horrible dream I had. I came out of The Swan and hailed what I thought was a taxi, but when it pulled up beside me it had become one of those black Citroens driven by Alain Delon and Lino Ventura in French crime films of the 1960s. Although I knew I should not get into the car, I could not help myself as the door opened and a man with a black peaked cap pulled down over his eyes said 'Where to, Chief?' I blurted out my address, only for him to swing the car round in a sickening arc and speed off in precisely the opposite direction. In the car was one of those archaic cartridge players, out of which issued a singularly unappealing melange of Hammond organ and mystical incantation. The driver was wearing black leather gloves with chequered flags on the backs, and he weaved his way through the traffic with nerveless skill. At last, we pulled off the main road into an industrial complex of some sort, where the man's insincere and oily voice told me that I was to be *remaindered*. I woke up with a shout, my fists clenched.

A day or two later there was another mysterious incident. I was caught up in a crowd crossing the road in Piccadilly Circus and, jostled, fell over, hurting my wrist. 'Whoops! Sorry Chief,' someone had said, but there were so many people milling about that I couldn't see who it was. Then, the following week, my taxi was stuck in a traffic jam near Battersea Bridge. The driver had some oldies station playing, and started singing along to 'Ghost Town' by The Specials. I looked out of the window to take my mind off the ever-rising toll on the meter and saw a stocky middle-aged man wearing a Chairman Mao-style tunic, a camouflage forage cap and some half-mast blue nylon flares sitting on the wall making notes in a ledger of some sort. Beside him was a black bin-bag. He looked up and stared across at me, and if he had not been wearing very dark glasses, our eyes would have met. His gaze seemed to hold me in some form of suspension, and despite the taxi's throbbing I felt perfectly still, frozen almost. Thankfully, after a minute or so of this unpleasant inertia, the lights changed and we pulled slowly away. At this, the man on the wall gave me a salute, just as the DJ said, 'The Specials and their very dapper two tone there.' The taxi-driver took this as a cue to go off down Memory Lane and tell me about the all-night parties he'd been to in Brixton in the 1980s, but I listened with only half an ear. The salute was insolent somehow as well as threatening, but now I was moving again, I could rationalise my encounter. The man was obviously a tramp of some sort, the unfortunate result of a misfiring community care initiative, an eccentric, nothing more.

That night, I had another unpleasant dream in which I found myself in a suburban garden centre. As if this was not bad enough in itself, I was looking at a tray of Venus Fly-Traps, thinking that I should buy one for my children. As I inspected one particularly impressive specimen, I saw that inside its 'flowers', which should have been the colour of sunburned skin, were tiny pages, covered in what looked very much like Paul Lythgoe's distinctive handwriting. I watched in appalled fascination as these jaws closed on a too inquisitive bluebottle, which buzzed and struggled in vain. 'Nature red in tooth and claw,' said one of the centre's staff, a stumpy, middle-aged man in a cap and overalls. 'Are you a keen horticulturalist, sir?' he wheedled. 'Would you like to see what's in the greenhouse, sir?'

By this stage, I was becoming ever more jumpy, but those friends in whom I confided had little more to say than that I was working too hard or should 'lay off the vino'. It was another fortnight before the affair reached what must be considered its climax. I'd just had a very very good lunch with Nigel Hughes from Harpercollins, dining both wisely and too well on lobster and a couple of bottles of Pinot Grigio. Things were certainly looking up, I told myself, as I wandered home from the tube. Why hadn't I hooked up with a historian before? Put a swastika on the cover and Robert's your father's brother. Won't sell too many copies in the Fatherland, of course, but with the sort of advance Rupert Murdoch could offer, the sensitivities of a few cabbage-eaters didn't bother me overmuch. Everything in the garden was rosy.

'Want to see what's in my bag?'

Wrenched from my boozy reverie, I spun round in shock to see a man standing in a skip beside me. He wore what looked like a tight fitting collarless tunic and some sort of peaked cap. 'Got something for you,' he shouted. His breath smelled of whelks. He waved a black carrier bag with manic enthusiasm, as if signalling the end of a Grand Prix. 'Want to see? Want to see who I've got?' He brandished the bag at me again, bouncing up and down on an abandoned mattress like some demented jack-in-the-box. 'Nice and smooth, ain't you?', he said to something in the bag. His voice segued into a growl and whatever was in the bag thrashed and wriggled. I quickened my pace and turned off down a side-street. Before he could leap out of the skip, I was running blindly along the avenue without looking back. My lunch-time bonhomie was swept away by a panic fear that intensified as the voice seemed to come from the privet hedges all around me. The wind in their leaves sounded like the rustling of polythene. 'I loves a good book I can get stuck into,' came the voice again, 'just loves it. Have a heart, Mr Ten Per Cent.' I jumped on the first bus I saw and hid at the back of it as best I could.

When I at last got home, I took *An Emporium* into the garden and set it alight. It burned with a curious green flame, and as the fire consumed it, the binding whistled and popped, seeming almost to sob until at last, it was only ashes scattered by the wind.

Acknowledgements

Special thanks to James Scott, Robert Brocklehurst and Jennifer Jones for their wisdom and patience. Particular thanks to Nick Freeman for his astute advice, Peter Holman for his excellent afterword, Daniel Corrick for his wonderful introduction, David Rix and Douglas Thompson for making possible this reprint edition, and to Dan Ghetu for his interest in the work and for first publishing this collection in 2010.

Hannah Taggart, Neil Cocks, Michelle Greet, Bill Overton, Carolyn Scott-Jeffs, Jennifer Cooke, Kerry Featherstone, Catherine Rees, Dan Sage, Mary Brewer, Neal Swettenham, Eluned Owen, Brian Jarvis, Julian Wolfreys, Anne-Marie Beller, Gabriel Egan, Gillian Spraggs, Elaine Hobby, Mark Simpson, Dave Hill, Dan Salahuddin-Clifton, Simon King, Jonathan Taylor, Mike Wilson, James Ferguson, Brian R. Banks, Daniel Gerould, Andrzej and Teresa Welminksi, Krzyzstof Pleśniarowicz, Tomasz Tomaszewski, Jarosław Fret, Grzegorz Ziołkowski, Magdalena Mądra, Michal Kobialka, Freddie Rokem, Martin Hainz, Daniel Meyer-Dinkgrafë, Fred Dalmasso, Hannah Nicklin, Virginie Ganivet, Laura Cull, Steve Barfield, Richard Gough, Esa Kirkkopelto, Nenagh Watson, Sean Myatt, Giselle Leeb, Deborah Maurice, Mike and Pat Charlton, Dave Mumford, Steve Evans, Ruth Lane, Diana Hayes, Rich Davies, Mario Vendredi, Victoria Nelson, Jean-Marie Avril, Nick and Amanda Mazonowicz, Jodie Bray, Rachel Rogers, Marcie Hopkins, Cathy Piquemal, Antony Pickthall, and of course my family, have all provided advice, inspiration or support over the years, my sincere thanks to them all.

Recent friends and colleagues whose comments, observations and general discussion have been helpful, include Samantha Beckett, Mark Beech, Quentin S. Crisp, Nicola Harvey, Malcolm Hendersen, Eve Katsouraki, Claus Laufenburg, Daniel Lower, Al Lester, Des Lewis, Tom Newport, Clive Nolan, Reggie Oliver, Charles Schneider, Brian Showers, John Smith, Ben Stanley, Simon Strantzas, Mark Valentine, and Scott Wetherby.

∞

'Dr Dapertutto's Saturnalia', 'Of Those Who Follow Emile Bilonche', 'Room 89' and 'The Comrade' were first published in *Pieces for Puppets and Other Cadavers*, InkerMen Press (2006). 'They Dwell in Ystumtuen', 'Erbach's Emporium of Automata', 'The Condition' and 'One is Less than or Equal to Nothing' were published in the InkerMen Press collections *Green and Unpleasant Land* (2007), *Lands End* (2008), *Loss* (2009) and *Cold Turkey* (2009). 'Apotheosis' was first published in *Null Immortalis* (2010), 'All His Worldly Goods' in *The Horror Anthology of Horror Anthologies* (2011) both by Megazanthus Press. 'Pulvis Lunaris, or, The Coagulation of Wood', 'Archaic Artificial Suns', and 'The Subjugation of Eros' appeared in *Cinnabar's Gnosis* (2009), *The Master in Cafe Morphine* (2010), and *This Hermetic Legislature* (2012), Ex Occidente Press collections in homage to Gustav Meyrink, Mikhail Bulgakov and Bruno Schulz respectively.

'D. P. Watt's *An Emporium of Automata* is a marvel. A strange concoction that is equal parts Borges, Millhauser, Kafka, and Ligotti, all viewed through a distorted lens; the book is not one so easily definable, and yet is instantly unforgettable. These stories will affect forever the way you view the world, as all great weird fiction must.'

Simon Strantzas, author of *Cold to the Touch* and *Nightingale Songs*

'This particular text is full of great stories that stand on their own – Jamesian, Samuelsian, Ligottian, Meyrinkian, but above all Wattian... This book, by retrocausality of night's fidgeting words, now takes on a new vantage point, where aeon swallows moment, and vice versa.'

D. F. Lewis, author of *The Last Balcony* and *Real Time Reviewer*

'Watt has real talent. His work is not easily defined, but his stories, like Aickman's, may be categorised as 'strange'. They deal with questions of identity, illusion and reality, shifting perspectives and moral structures. This may sound daunting, but the quality of the writing engages the reader. Watt writes in a neo-decadent style: elegant, euphonious, with an observant eye and ear... Watt is a writer who offers us a consistent vision. It touches on and reflects the world we know, but as in a glass darkly. Performance and puppets play a role in many of these stories because they both examine and defy what we imagine to be reality...'

Reggie Oliver, *Wormwood 17*, November 2011

www.ingramcontent.com/pod-product-compliance
Lightning Source LLC
Chambersburg PA
CBHW030546310726
48979CB00010B/2048/J

* 9 7 8 1 9 0 8 1 2 5 1 7 0 *